SHOULD HAVE RUN

LAKE SPARK INN

BOOK 2

EVEY LYON

HOLDEN

I'm doomed.

If one more thing goes wrong with my schedule, then I'm absolutely unlucky. My eyes slide past my laptop on my desk and land on the photo of my two little devils—my kids. They are such joyous creatures, causing chaos in my life. Okay, I do love them. A lot, actually. I'll always have a soft spot reserved for them. Lori, my twelve-year-old, and Harry, my ten-year-old. I want to believe they make me a better person. That's fatherhood, right?

But holy fuck, they are challenging me in a game I'm not sure I know how to play. I'm good at games. I played professional hockey for twelve years. I win, always. Except with them… I don't.

I huff out a deep exhale and decide to look out the window of my office to find some tranquility in the scene of Lake Spark on this spring day. The blue sky and the bright sun would be perfect, except Illinois in March can be unkind on the temperature front, and it's a solid high 40s with a breeze.

The Dizzy Duck Inn is my post-pro-athlete life. It was

something different and fun. There are so many professional athletes in this town and people escaping Chicago for a weekend away. It's a prime business opportunity that I snatched up when the old owners wanted to retire, then I packed up and moved my family here a year ago. I have two investors, but it's me running the show. Lake Spark is a calm little town with an excellent private school nearby that was an extra draw for parenting my kids. After all, my ex-wife decided to exit the picture long ago, leaving me to do it all.

I can be Superman.

Just not lately.

I think I'm on nanny number six in the last year alone.

I sigh as I lean back in my chair and interlace my hands behind my head."To be fair, I ignored all their attempts to flirt," I say to myself. Well… that might be a tiny lie. There was one a few years ago who seemed like a good one-night kind of drunken Christmas party thing, my bad. But I've been a perfect boss since then. My little angels? Not so much.

I shake my head, knowing that I need to focus on some numbers before the interior designer shows up to start the project of freshening up the look of this hotel. It's not that it's in bad condition, I just want to rejuvenate the atmosphere. With the spa and wedding venue here, I want to step it up to ensure guests have to book well in advance. We already have an award-winning chef.

My attention is drawn to the door when I see my friend and business partner Stone Madden peek in. We're from similar hockey circles, though we never played on the same team. We just hit it off at some charity fundraiser way back and have been friends since.We have one other smaller investor, but he takes zero part in almost everything, as it's purely the old owner's wish that his son kept a stake.

"Hey, Holden, you alive?"

I chuckle. "Today, yes. What brings you by, considering you firmly said that you would invest in this place, but I quote, 'don't want to do one fucking single thing in regards to management, nor do I want to hear about it.' End quote."

He quickly holds his palm up. "I won't deny that, but I also said I would invest so that one day if I needed to impress someone, then I could slide in this little fact to gain me points."

My expression flattens. "And?"

"I'm using my part-ownership card. Harlow and I are taking a room for a week or two while the contractors redo our house."

"This place is getting a makeover too."

He shrugs. "Yeah, but this place has charm."

"We do our best." I grin cheekily.

"By the way, your old coach's daughter, Lexi, starts today, right? Met her a few times at various sponsor gigs long ago."

"Something like that."

I have examined her portfolio, and it's what I need. Apparently, she had grandparents that lived around here when she was younger, and she has a best friend, Summer, that lives here in town who I see around. Summer also recommended Lexi. I've met Lexi a few times. After all, her dad was my coach up in Michigan. Let's just hope she's changed since I saw her last, which was a few years ago after she graduated college. I remember running into her once during her college years. A true sorority girl who valued social life just as much as academia. I'm hoping she's a calm adult now, with baggy jeans and an oversized t-shirt. It's what I need to keep me concentrating on the task at hand. I can't afford distractions.

Besides, once you leave hockey, the team rules still apply; stay away from the coach's daughter.

"Good luck, or rather, keep it locked in. See ya, buddy." He waves his fingers in the air.

I tip my nose up in acknowledgment, and the moment the door shuts, I'm back concentrating on my task. I must lose time though, because as I'm busy typing away and clicking my mouse, I hear a soft knock on my door.

The door cracks open. "Hi, Holden." Lexi's voice sounds chipper, or excited at least. I'm sure she wants to do an excellent job on this massive project ahead.

"Hey, Lexi," I say as I glance up from my laptop while I press save on my screen. But the moment my eyes hit the image at the door, I instantly do a double-take.

Oh no.

No. No. Nope. Fuck no.

I'm cursing to myself inside my head as I attempt to keep my face neutral.

Well, wish one is a massive failure. Lexi's in jeans, except they're tight, which isn't ideal. Wish two, a total miss too. She's in a sweater, even a turtleneck, but unfortunately for my dick that suddenly twitched, it's not a baggy shirt. Instead, it highlights her tits and taut body. I didn't even predict her long dark blonde locks that frame her face. Confidence oozes all around her.

She is what I recall, yet with less makeup, which makes her hotter… and now she's older, too.

Bad. This is bad.

She's supposed to be that college kid that I remember when I was in the height of my career and way past the early-twenties stage. It seems that she's turned into a woman that turns heads even when dressed perfectly respectably.

I swallow and throw on a polite smile. "Good to see you again."

"Yeah, I guess it's been a while. I ran into Stone in the

lobby. It's like déjà vu seeing everyone from the hockey world again." She doesn't even wait for me to invite her in. Lexi strides straight in with poise and heads to the chair in front of my desk to sit down.

Oh yeah, we're supposed to have a meeting. Not me staring at her and studying the shade of gloss on her lips. Professional Holden. Yep, that's who I am now.

"Figured it was safe to hire you without an interview since you're not a stranger to most of us." I attempt to lighten the mood, and it causes her to give me a grin, with her lips that look welcoming for my co—

"I guess being the coach's daughter has its advantages," she replies, breaking my thought.

Sure, think that, sweetheart. Screw the team rule of not going near her for life. It can go out the window. I'm a grown man anyhow. Wait, why am I even thinking all this?

I can't sit in front of her face to face, because her brown eyes seem as though they will turn me into the smug man I know I can be when I find prey. Standing, I walk to my window to divert my attention to other thoughts. "Everything good in your life?"

"Can't complain. I'm sitting in front of you for a project that's any designer's *fantasy*."

Her tone, I can't pinpoint it, but it causes me to snap my sight to her and find that she has a smirk, which confirms to me that she might have grown into a little spitfire.

And her mind seems to be not as straightlaced as I hoped. That's a relief, sort of. Looks like we might have a few shared interests.

Taking the high road, I keep my wry smile fixed. "And non-work life?"

She folds her hands on top of her thigh thrown over her opposite knee. "Different to last time you saw me. I'm no longer in a sorority, and I keep my weekends busy with sophisticated wine drinking and attempting to find the latest dinner hotspot."

I lean against the window. "Except you've never been here with your boyfriend. I should be offended that the Dizzy Duck Inn didn't make it to your hotspot list."

Lexi's head tips slightly to the side as she purses her lips. "It did. It was before you became owner. No boyfriend. I went with my father." New fact on availability. Noted.

My jaw ticks as her eyes are somehow possessive and cause me to feel slightly uncomfortable. "Of course you did," I mutter.

Her mouth gapes open, and she fakes shock. "Implying I'm a daddy's girl? That's not cool. Back when he was your coach, and even to this day, his team takes priority, and you know that."

I take a few steps back to my desk and hover over it by placing my fingertips on the hard oak, which could potentially be as hard as my cock might be soon. "I'm happy you're doing well." I'm sincere about that.

This time it's Lexi who stands and strolls over to the window to steal a look at the spring scenery outside. "How are you? Lori and Harry?"

I forgot that I brought them to a team holiday party when they were much younger. "Let's see…" I pop my lips and debate the best answer. "Since I last saw you, that messy divorce was finalized from the ex-wife from hell who decided motherhood wasn't for her, and my two great kids cause so much mischief that I'm beginning to wonder if I have Satan as an ancestor. But hey, gotta love them."

My light tone causes her to laugh. "Sounds like you have your hands full and not the way you prefer." Her smirk is sultry. I've been around enough women to know the differences of mouth positions.

And damn, she's at it again.

Does my expression make it that obvious that she can read that she's caught me off guard and isn't what I expected? My head retreats back as my cheeks tighten and rise up. I don't remember her having this sassy boldness, but it's quite a positive attribute to have. "Something like that. But it seems like that might change soon." That's my subtle warning. This time it's her face that has surprise or concern, I'm not sure which, but her brows rise. "With this project, of course." Bullshit, but I do need to discuss the re-design.

She clears her throat and returns to the chair in front of me, and we sit down. Our eyes lock in this unusual meeting. I'm not sure what's in the air that surrounds around us, but I'm doubting it's professionalism.

The thing is, sometimes you have an instant click with someone. That's how attraction works. Noticing someone across the bar isn't a made-up lie. Being familiar with one another just adds that extra element. In a way, it's added value to the flirting game. And I see no problem with flirting as long as the door to exploring that flirtation is deadbolted shut when it comes to my younger interior designer. I didn't think of her this way before, but now she's sauntered into my office as a woman grown and changed.

"Okay, so, I have clear steps to attack the re-design," she begins.

It seems one of us can shift to work mode as fast as a light switch.

I shut my laptop screen that I forgot I left open. Might as well save some battery, right? "Take me through the steps."

"First, I already sent suggestions to your staff manager so they could arrange logistics, and she sent back some feedback on your behalf. After we have a walkthrough, I want to start by bringing in samples. I understand we need to attack the lobby first. Already noticed the moose head on the wall." She cringes.

I chuckle. "You're not a fan of Caesar?"

She chuckles, and it's cute. "I doubt anyone is, especially if you named him after a salad."

Swiping a hand across my rough but short-shaved jaw, I fall into a more relaxed state. "Although a tradition to the inn, nobody is a fan, so you have my full permission to knock him down before an animal lover sends me an angry letter."

Her shoulders lift up then down. "Perfect. No debate there then. So, after samples—"

Lexi is unable to finish her sentence because my phone vibrates on the desk. I reach to ignore the call and turn my phone to silent, but I pause when I see the name across the screen.

I hold my finger up. "Sorry. I just need a sec."

She doesn't hesitate. "Of course."

I hit the green button as my entire body fills with dread. "Principal Johnson," I attempt to sound pleased for her call.

"Mr. West, we seem to have a little problem at school," she begins on the other end.

I clench my jaw in an attempt to keep myself calm. "And what might that be?"

"Today it's Lori. She made quite a scene at afternoon pick-up. Lori decided to speak… disrespectfully to one of her classmate's moms when Lori and her classmate were in a little… debate." I can hear that she's trying to be delicate in her approach.

I snicker while my sight lands on Lexi who patiently waits. "Seriously? You're phoning me because my daughter spoke about a parent outside of school hours?"

"Mr. West." Principal Johnson sounds surprised. "Everyone by the sixth-grade door heard her. It left Gemma McClearly in tears that her mother was being called such things."

Damn it, Lori has been having issues with Gemma. From what I hear, she's a little brat with parents that could use a parenting book or two. And her mom? The parent committee president on a power trip to make up for her recent divorce.

"I'm sure she had a reason. You're well aware they are not the best of friends," I highlight.

"She called Ms. McClearly a gold digger looking for a husband, then decided to add that plastic isn't the look you go for, which means she must have been referring to you." Her tone is unamused.

Even my jaw drops from this incident. "I could see… how that might… be a…" Ah damn, I have no words.

"Mr. West, Gemma was in tears, and the other parents who heard were none too pleased with Lori's lack of manners. Lake Spark Academy, of course, upholds our values of kindness and respect very seriously. Lori is in my office, and you need to pick her up. I'm losing my patience with her, Mr. West."

I blow out an exhausted breath. Great, perfect, swell, exactly what I need today. I pinch the bridge of my nose, attempting to avoid an oncoming headache. "Of course, I'm on my way."

Hanging up my phone, I hear the clearing of a throat, and I glance at Lexi who's awkwardly sitting there. "Everything okay?"

I stand and grab my keys off my desk. "An urgent matter has come up."

"Oh, I hope it's not too serious." She sounds concerned as she stands, realizing this meeting has reached a close.

"Nothing but the usual. I need to get to my daughter's school. We'll have to finish this meeting tomorrow. Let's do the morning so you can get started. Stuart at the front desk will get you your room key, as I know you wanted to stay here for your creative flow."

Her hand flies up. "Don't worry. I'll figure it out. And tomorrow sounds like a plan. I'll meet you here when you figure out a time."

A near sinister sound escapes from my throat. "Not here. Meet me at my house. Early. Seven even."

"Your house?" she questions the unusual request.

I walk to the coat rack and grab my jacket. "Yeah, Stuart can give you my address."

"Your address?" she repeats, as if she's checking that she heard me right.

Throwing her one last grin, I kind of enjoy that I've thrown her off. "Don't worry, I don't bite... at least not at breakfast, anyway."

Her eyes blaze with slight fear. And that's fair enough, because a vision of bending her over my desk just flashed into my brain.

Tomorrow. I'll be on my best behavior. For sure, it's possible... I mean, impossible.

Shit, tomorrow.

2

LEXI

P lease don't let Holden wear a tight button-down, and his eyes that probably pop with a forest-green shirt with jeans.

I stare up at the clouds in the sky at seven in the morning, as if someone is listening and can save me. *Please just do that*, I wish. Nor can he wear that cologne that is crisp to the nose. And as an extra hope, maybe he got rid of that wave of brown hair that I want to rake my hands through.

Anyone in the sky, please. I beg of you.

Holden must know that I'm here, as the security guard of the subdivision let me past the gate to a street with gorgeous lake houses. I raise my finger to press the doorbell, but before I can touch the button, the door soars open, catching me by surprise.

My eyes drop to a little boy that is the spitting image of Holden. His face is soft as he stares at me, then the corners of his mouth hitch up. He's a lot taller than I last saw him when he was maybe two or three.

"You're pretty." He smiles.

"Uh… thanks." I return his smile, as he is cute.

"Don't throw your charm at our guest." Holden arrives behind his son and sets his hands on Harry's shoulders, and oh no, it's a white t-shirt today, giving me a glimpse of the muscles on his arms. "Hey, Lexi, come on in."

I follow and take in my surroundings of a big modern house with an open staircase. It's all industrial feel and clean, with the floor-to-ceiling windows overlooking the lake. Holden continues to walk toward the kitchen, and I seem to follow in tow.

I'm always up for spontaneous adventures. It's why I've spent time traveling and going where life takes me. If there is something I like, then I make a point not to hide it. I'm not a shy person in the slightest, nor am I afraid of many things.

Walking into Holden's house after he got my pussy excited yesterday? This has me slightly nervous.

"Are you sure this a good time to talk about the Dizzy Duck?" I ask, skeptical, as Harry hops up onto the stool at the kitchen island.

Holden opens a cupboard to pull out a box of cereal. "I don't have many options today. I need to head down to Bluetop to sample new wines at the Blisswood winery for our new cellar at the Dizzy Duck," he explains as he hands Harry the box of chocolate cereal. "Besides, I lost a nanny last week, so I need to get the kids to school."

I blink a few times, attempting to absorb the situation happening around me.

"Lori, on the double," he calls upstairs.

"You'll have more luck calling her on her cell," Harry says with a full mouth.

Holden drags a hand through his hair. "Except, she lost phone privileges due to yesterday's little stunt." Holden looks in my direction, as if it's normal that I'm here. "Coffee?" He points to the machine.

I haven't even taken my coat off. "Uh, no, thanks. Again, are you sure about right now?"

His chuckle is low, humorous, and sexy as hell. "No choice, remember? Now tell me the game plan." He grabs a carton of juice. "Lori!"

I shake my head, accepting that this is how this is going to go. "So, uhm, I need a room to keep samples to compare to the existing fabrics and colors. I'm thinking we need to minimalize the use of carpet and focus on area rugs and use bright wood for the walls."

Holden checks on his son who is chomping away. "Lori, seriously, we have twenty minutes!" His attention returns to me. "Timeline?"

I survey the scene of chaos then question the thought in my head about why Dad Holden makes my stomach tighten below my navel. "Right, timeline. We will start with the lobby, which could take a week if we have the right team of contractors. It's just that furniture orders can take a while."

"We'll pay for priority orders," he notes.

"The bedrooms will take the longest, as we will give the larger rooms more of a luxury suite feel. I think the rooms will need a month. We can work in a wave so you still have a few rooms available at all times."

"Great."

Is he even listening?

"Are you going to say yes to everything?" I wonder.

Holden's eyes slice straight to me as he pauses in preparing his kids for their school day. "Probably. I'll trust you with this, just tell me when the budget goes haywire." His gaze snaps to the clock on the oven just as a girl with braids set on the top of her head passes me and grazes my arm without concern.

"I'm here. Can I have my coffee now?" Lori slides up onto a stool next to her brother.

Holden smirks to himself. "No, because you're only twelve."

She scoffs. "So unfair. I'm no longer a kid."

He gives her a doubtful look. "Oh, I know. You've been trying to prove that for weeks. Hence, why we lost the nanny last week."

"Ugh, not my fault. She wouldn't let me have my space," Lori protests.

"She was nice," Harry voices his opinion.

"You both put her bras in the freezer," he deadpans, and my eyes bug out. Then Holden smiles tightly. "Well, we get nobody new since the wonderful antics of you two have gotten us banned from the agency list." I'm beginning to feel awkward standing here. Then Holden remembers I'm present and his demeanor returns to normal. "You have the budget, and the contractor will meet you later today to go over initial ideas."

"Great," I say flatly because I'm still trying to digest this show in front of me.

Lori glares at me. "Who is she?"

"The hotel's new interior designer. You don't remember her, but you've met her before when I played on the ice up in Michigan for the Golds. She's Coach Moore's daughter," he explains.

I give her a weak smile and a curt wave which causes her disdain to intensify.

"Fantastic. Another one to put you on a pedestal," she says sarcastically.

Holden brings his hand to the back of his neck and tries to de-stress with utter failure.

"I need my recorder for school. We have music class today," Harry reminds Holden.

Holden now rubs his hand over his face. "Maybe… in your room or the TV room? Check there."

Harry stands up, ready to search. "Don't forget my lunch." Harry runs off while Holden looks like he is about to melt in frustration.

"Fuck me, lunch making. What the hell goes into that? The nanny normally did it," Holden says to himself, and he massages his temples.

"Well, look at that. Someone curses and sets a perfect example for his kids," Lori berates him.

My eyes gawk because this girl has some attitude. Now I understand why Holden is about to lose his cool on a daily basis.

"Okay." He snaps his fingers. "Let me think. What does the nanny throw into a bag?"

Really? How does he not know? It's simple logic what a child eats for school lunch. Isn't it?

Ah damn, I shouldn't get involved, but I know Holden well enough, and I'm bold in my life encounters, not always needing approval. Which is why I step forward and walk straight to him then search for the lunch bag and spot it near the fruit bowl. I'm going to assume Lori buys her lunch at school since there's only one bag.

He doesn't seem to notice what's happening, as he is in a daze. "So yeah, just do what you need for the Dizzy Duck. I want to have a reveal in a few months and invite a few photographers and writers for blogs and magazines."

I throw an apple into the bag then grab bread from the bread box. My eyes scan the kitchen for where a knife might be. Maybe I should be questioning what I'm doing more, but thinking can happen later. "In the moment" is my philosophy.

But I should examine why I'm working in sync with the man in the room.

"We're still on the deadline that you indicated original-ly?" Now I'm the one caught in an odd moment of multi-tasking.

"Three months," he states while I pull out a peanut butter jar from a cabinet.

Spreading jam and peanut butter on bread, I continue our conversation. "Fine. We should have weekly meetings to check in, too."

"Sounds good."

Now I'm attempting to find some other snacks. I spot the pantry and head straight there. Opening the door and walking in, I examine the shelves then find a granola bar, water bottle, and small bag of crackers shaped as fish.

We say nothing as he watches me, unsure what is transpir-ing. After tossing everything in, I zip the bag then pass it to Holden by slamming it into his chest. "Here. How can you not know how to make a school lunch?" I'm brazen with my astonishment.

His eyes are saucers, unprepared by my tone of slight disapproval.

Harry walks to his father and takes his bag, oblivious to who worked their lunch-making magic and assuming his dad suddenly became a sandwich wizard. "Thanks. I'll meet you in the car."

Holden and I seem to be in a stare-off, ignoring his chil-dren as they slide backpacks off chairs and walk toward the hall where I think the garage is.

I cross my arms, not sure why I'm not afraid to level with Holden, even if he is my semi-boss.

"Wow. Someone isn't afraid to be bold." His eyes remain locked with mine.

"I'm not some shy girl, if that's what you remember of me. In fact, I've never been scared of everything I do in life," I defend, speaking my mind.

He scoffs before his tongue darts out to sweep across his bottom lip. "Everything?" The innuendo is there, I'm not reading it wrong.

Heat swims through me. I wasn't thinking about the broader spectrum of everything, including the X-rated kind, but it's also the truth. Standing taller, I will own this moment. "Yes, *everything*."

Holden snickers. "Thanks for the insight, and just FYI, I know how to make a lunch. You've just caught me on a day when my mind is somewhere else, and last time I checked, we're all allowed to have one of those mornings. Come on, meeting done. You can leave via the garage." His tone is curt before he turns on his heel, and yet again, I trail along, not sure if I pissed him off.

But then halfway down the hall, he stops in his tracks, causing me to bump into his back and get a whiff of the cologne that I'm sure will soak into my coat fabric. His instant turn brings us close, with our bodies brushing as his eyes dip down, and I peer up.

"You owe me," he says, his tone serious.

I frown in surprise. "I owe you?"

"Yep." His P is sharp. "Remember, one of us has an IOU, and it isn't me." I'm confused, and he must see it. "I believe I was out with the team once, and I caught you at the bar when you were twenty and you were attempting to buy a drink with your friend. The bartender was about to card you, but I stepped in and told him that you were a friend of mine so he wouldn't ask."

I do remember now, but still my mouth opens at the ridiculousness of this. "And?"

"I joked that you owe me, and you agreed."

"That was said in jest," I rebuff.

His finger comes up to wave side to side as he shakes his head. "Nope. In your appreciative state, you asked the bartender for a pen then wrote on a napkin." He pretends to search his memory. "Oh yeah, 'I owe Holden West a favor one day, signed Lexi Moore.'"

Crap, it rings a bell and is something I totally would do. "What? Nobody would take that as fact. It was having fun in the moment," I justify.

Holden gives me a satisfied smirk. "Putting it in writing kind of cements it. *So,* Lexi, I'm calling in that favor now."

My entire face squinches from adjusting to the feeling that he isn't joking one single bit, but still I play along. "What might that be?"

"I don't think staying at the hotel for so long is ideal, especially with the room next to yours getting a leak fixed. It could get loud. Treat the hotel more like an office."

"And? Where do you suggest I stay?"

The lines of his mouth stretch so far that his wide smirk nearly makes me want to swipe it off his face by any means possible because it's infuriatingly annoying, cocky, and a little too sexy for seven in the morning.

"My guesthouse."

My entire body must show that nothing about that sentence feels normal. Especially as his tone is so simple.

"Why would I do that?" Because seeing him a bit more than I should feels kind of dangerous.

"That favor you owe is the reason. You can pick up Lori and Harry at school for me once in a while, maybe even do a few drop-offs. I need to find more permanent help, but I have to find a new agency that doesn't know the history of the employment turnover in my house."

I'm nearly dizzy from shaking my head. "No." I continue to shake. "I'm not a nanny, and that's more than one favor."

"You owe me, and we'll count this as the IOU," he repeats.

Returning to a normal stance, I hold my hand out low. "Here's you helping me buy alcohol when I would have charmed my way with the bartender anyways." Then I bring my hand up high. "And here's you asking me to drive your kids around. Not exactly even on the favor front."

Holden tsks. "Lexi, if you could have charmed the bartender, then why didn't you?"

"Because it wouldn't have been as enjoyable. It is by far better to say a 27-year-old pro-hockey player bailed me out. My sorority sisters had a thing for you." I'm maybe too honest around him.

"Well, you did rely on me, so a favor owed is where we are. Plus, with all the redecorating happening, then I could use all the extra rooms I can get for guests, and not to mention that your dear old dad mentioned you were once an au pair in England. See? You love kids. There are many reasons why this isn't a big deal. I might even throw extra budget your way for redecorating and give you a reference for an upcoming hotel deal that I might have."

My eyes widen, and my hip tips out with my arms crossing over my chest. "Bribing me now?"

"Call it extra incentives for following through with your favor. So, what will it be, Lexi?"

Hearing my name on his tongue seems to swirl desire, and everything about him in this moment is a turn-on. I don't need that. My brain even bypasses his mention of extra budget and references, which is an added bonus for my dream job. I desperately need a clear mind to get out of this situation.

But that's not in my cards today. Instant clicks with people are a weakness to me and always sink me into full commitment mode.

Because I blurt out, "Fine."

What the hell? I'm free-spirited, but this? I clearly don't have the backbone to use a one-syllable word that begins with N.

My finger comes up to point to him, as I feel the need to justify my impulsive decision. "I'm doing this because I'm a good Samaritan to civilization and a caring, thoughtful person. Not to mention I hate being bored, and I doubt that happens here."

He claps his hands together with an overdone smile. "Wonderful. You just dropped into my life when a hotel refresh is essential and I still need to balance my little heathens, aren't they cute?"

My fingers come up to rub my temples. "This is…" I have no words.

That exhilaration inside of me bubbles again, especially when Holden steps once forward and it closes our space. "Totally not a good idea, but I'm kind of out of other options right now." He's straightforward, at least.

"Wonderful. Bad ideas," I deadpan.

His grin is full of accomplishment and trouble. "I love how you are very agreeable."

"Well, I aim to please." I'm being sarcastic, but it's too late. I close my eyes at my choice of words. This is, oh no. I blow out a breath and open my eyes to find Holden eyeing me up and down, which isn't helping me keep my body from crossing all the wires.

"Duly noted." He tilts his head before he turns and heads straight to the garage, and I trench behind.

Duly noted. Yeah, let me just add a warning in my head and between my legs to that list.

3

LEXI

"*Poof.*" I gesture with my hands. "All normal human logic just vanished in a few seconds."

As I explain my situation, Summer smiles weakly at me. We're sitting in Jolly Joe's, the local hotspot that fills our needs, from coffee to burgers to ice cream. A throwback to a soda shop, complete with a jukebox in the corner. And Summer? We've been friends for years, and whenever I visit Lake Spark, I head straight to her.

"Remember when you were in Austria and you met those two backpackers, then later that day you ended up paragliding? You've always been spontaneous and impulsive," she reminds me.

I sigh as I stare at the menu to keep myself occupied. "I know, it's just… This is on a different level. Damn, I haven't seen Holden in a couple of years, and suddenly in the span of 24 hours, I've nearly drooled at his hot dad look and complied with his ridiculous demand."

She snorts a laugh. "Well, if it's any consolation, I've heard every single mom in a ten-mile radius is trying to discover his favorite food so they can casually stop by and offer him a store-bought cookie that they pose as their own baking. So, the sexy look doesn't seem to be in your imagination."

Licking my lips, I tip my head slightly to the side. "I hope it's my brain going on a break, because the vibe between us just seems… I can't pinpoint it."

Summer smiles softly before glancing out the window onto Main Street. "That's a good thing to have. I can't wait to watch this all unfold."

"Nothing. It's nothing. Besides, Holden has a chaotic life. His kids? Holy crap, wild."

"Well, it makes staying on his property all the more entertaining. You're still the woman who has no desire to settle down, so maybe that can be your strength to stay in line."

"Hopefully. Besides I'm not sure what I'll be doing once this project finishes. My lease for my place in the city was up long ago, and I've just been housesitting various places while I traveled. I'd love to be near you more and have a change of scene, I'm just not sure there are many opportunities for me here."

She clucks the inside of her mouth. "Ah yes, Lexi is still a wandering soul. Still, I'm excited for the unfolding of your predicament." Summer has a cheeky smile.

I scoff at that encouragement. Then it dawns on me that my ludicrous change of events in my life are minor compared to her life. After a pause for a few seconds, I lean across the table to place my hand gently on top of hers.

"Uh, how has it been?"

Her eyes slide to me as her lips quirk out. "You mean, with a husband?" Summer eloped with her best friend, Zac, for reasons even I don't quite understand. It was recent and sudden, and all I can do is give her an ear. Coincidently, her now in-laws used to own the Dizzy Duck.

I shrug. "Yeah, I guess."

A wry smile emerges. "I'm not exactly sure what I dragged myself into, but for some reason, it feels right."

Squeezing her hand one last time, I then let go. "I don't know what to say. One day you're going to have to explain."

"When it's clear to me, I will let you know." She sounds at peace with whatever is happening.

I don't press her further, especially when Summer's gaze seems to tip up and over my shoulder, with the corners of her smile lengthening. "Someone just arrived, and this might be my entertainment of the day."

I turn my head to catch a glimpse of what she's looking at. Or rather who she's looking at.

An opportunity to pull in some clarity to my brain just vanished as Holden slowly strides to our table with a sly grin. "Grabbing a coffee to gather strength before you pick up your suitcase to move on in?"

Summer snorts a laugh as she watches this scene progress.

"Why, of course, dear master."

Both Summer's and Holden's eyes grow wide at my sarcasm. Because, of course, when it's me, then everyone takes my words out of context.

Holden now keeps his smirk fixed then tips his head behind his shoulder. "The usual," he tells someone behind the counter.

My face puzzles. "You get coffee here?"

He looks at me as though I'm crazy… and maybe I am. Holden even shares a look with Summer who seems to agree.

"It's the best damn coffee around, and I need one for the road before I head down to Bluetop," he explains.

"But you own the Dizzy Duck, shouldn't that be the best

coffee around? You're a traitor to your own hotel?" I'm bewildered.

Holden chuckles as he crosses his arms. "Nah, ours *will* be the best. Just ordered new machines, and I'm waiting on the import of beans from Colombia. They need to have a soft taste for cappuccinos but a sharper hit to your tongue if it's an expresso."

I nod in agreement. "That's fair enough. I guess you must need to consume a lot of coffee after what I saw this morning."

Noticing the way his tongue darts out to sweep to the corner of his mouth, it draws my eyes to his lips, and it causes a simmering warm wave to travel through me. "Well, problem soon solved by your presence," he reminds me.

"Not a nanny," I firmly inform him yet again.

"Of course, you're not. You will just be living on my property—"

My palm flies up. "*Guest* on your property."

"Sure. A guest who might casually notice morning routine gone to hell and say, 'Hey, Holden, anything I can do to help before I head to the Dizzy Duck?'"

"Absolutely, because compliancy was on my resume when you hired me to *interior design* your inn, *not* nanny."

Holden grabs the to-go coffee that one of the staff hands him, except Holden doesn't give the woman even a drop of attention because his eyes are fixed on me, or rather, glued in a gaze with mine because I can't tear away from the view either.

Then he leans down, every inch closer causing my nipples to peak even tighter. "But I believe your words were… I always aim to please." His voice is nearly husky with his breath even breezing into my space.

As much as I should be scared because it feels like a

caution, I only smile. The kind that informs him I'm having fun, although my words are difficult to muster in this moment.

Holden stands and switches his attention from me to Summer. "Good to see you."

"Surprised you noticed I was here." She chortles a laugh.

Holden finds that amusing as he takes a sip of his coffee. "Any chance your brother-in-law has broken his radio silence and might actually return to Lake Spark to take interest in his 10% that your in-laws were so intent were mandatory for the hotel sale?"

Summer's face hardens a tad, her smile strained. "I'm the last person to ask about Nash," she grits out. "And you probably know just as much as I do."

Mentioning Nash's name around Summer always seems to cause her to tense. Nobody knows why, and that unfortunately includes me, too.

Holden doesn't pause for a tick because maybe he too noticed Summer's demeanor change, but then he brushes past the subject anyhow. "By the way, we have a job opening coming up. I need someone to handle the staff and the bookings. It's part-time, but the last manager is moving to California due to her husband's work. When your father-in-law dropped by recently, he mentioned that it might be your forte."

Her lips quirk out. "Huh. Maybe. I kind of like working for the city council, though."

Holden shrugs. "Well, if you change your mind."

"First I need to see how you treat your interior designer, since you are her current *boss*." Summer flashes her eyes at him.

Holden's jaw tenses, and he smiles awkwardly. "I like to

think of Lexi and me as equals in a partnership… to improve the Dizzy Duck."

I want to hold onto the table for stability because I think my mind just tricked me into hearing allusions of underlying meanings. My eyes sideline to Summer, and her look informs me that it is not in my mind.

"Well then, good luck with that, or rather her." She indicates me with her head.

Holden's sexy smirk is back. "I think that I can keep her in line. See you around, ladies." He walks toward the door. "You even sooner, Lexi," he calls back.

When the bell dings to inform us that he's left, I notice Summer's mouth has gaped open. "Uh-oh, someone is in for a wild ride. Wow, you guys have chemistry."

I roll my eyes. "Yeah, I know. His sweltering gaze needs to be locked in a box."

Summer brings her cup of coffee to her lips. "I'm sure you will find a box for that… probably in his bedroom."

I huff a breath. "Well, now you know my predicament."

"This is going to be fun. I get to be the bystander that watches from the offside." Now she has a bright smile that's good to see.

Sliding out of my seat, I say, "Happy to provide entertainment. Now, if you will excuse me, I need to get to the inn to talk with the contractor."

"Keep me updated."

I wave her off.

———

AFTER INFORMING the contractor how I want to redo the fireplace mantel in the lobby, yet preserve the stones and also keep the original wood where we can in the inn but paint over or polish, I feel good about where I can take this immense project. I have so many ideas, but my vision is clear for what will make the best statement when someone walks through the door.

But now I find myself closing the door to Holden's guesthouse behind me. Stuart at reception gave me a key. To be fair, this little place, although missing a kitchen, is a great location behind the house, getting an even better view of the lake. The interior is simple but with a few added colored pillows so the white is taken down a notch.

Again, my mind is spinning with how fast the last day has transpired, but Summer was right when she reminded me that I am a spur-of-the-moment kind of person. I'll just go with the flow and follow the direction of where this rollercoaster takes me.

Opening my suitcase, I search for clothes. It's getting late for dinner, but I'll just order something in, although I'm positive when Holden is back from his meeting he will welcome me to his property like the gentleman I'm sure he isn't. My instinct tells me that he won't let me go to sleep without a reminder of his smug assurance that he has me wrapped around his finger, or at least in his head.

Walking to the window, my eyes wander to explore my surroundings. There is the lake with a dock for a boat, and there's a hot tub near the house. Then there is a tire swing on a big tree and a basketball hoop near the back of the garage. When I admire the stone patio, my eyes draw a line up and I land on a window upstairs. A big window with the curtains open.

The same window where I can see Holden walk into the room. He must have just gotten back, and he quickly yanks up his t-shirt. Oh no, my entire body energizes in a way that seems to be on repeat lately. My eyes refuse to take my sight and mind back to my own room, and instead, my feet stay planted as I study his shirtless chest. The man keeps himself in shape, that's clear.

I hear my soft gasp that I get to see this, but then I deeply question if I owe him privacy when he unbuckles his jeans. Fuck that, I deserve a prize for doing this favor for him. His black boxer briefs appear when he slides down his jeans, and I see his thick and toned thighs.

Am I drooling yet? Nah, that's not me. I'm a confident woman who has no problem allowing herself a peek. He isn't a stranger to me. Although it's been a while, I've known him for years, I guess. Back then, of course, I thought he was hot with a lot of swagger. It didn't matter that he was a dad by twenty-five, he still went out when he could just like any other guy in their twenties. Now? He's aged well, and he still has an aura that pulls you in.

I should question this appraisal more, especially when he turns around and the boxers disappear too, which means I have a clear view of his ass. My brows rise, as I'm not at all complaining about his body. My fingertips glide down my neck, unsure if I should touch myself or hide further behind the curtain. Holden grabs a white towel, and the pool forming between my legs is my sign that I too should hit the shower.

Desperately, I now need relief, but I'm scared that I'll imagine him in the shower with me. His lips cascading down until he's on his knees, his tongue eager. I wouldn't last long because I'd want to be on my knees before him too.

Shaking my head, I walk to the bathroom and whip off my shirt and notice the stack of folded towels next to the sink. I reach out to twist the knob in the shower.

Nothing comes out.

I twist the other direction.

Nothing comes out.

Strange. I turn and do the same thing with the sink knob. Nothing.

Grumbling, I'm not happy about this. More because I have no clue where a switch or something might be to turn the water supply on. He must have turned it off to ensure water doesn't freeze the pipes in the winter if nobody uses this place.

Okay, I'm not going to be able to fix this by myself. Throwing my yoga pants back on and a fleece sweater, I head to the house. I hug myself because it's nippy out as I cross the patio.

Opening the sliding door, I hear pop music is getting overshadowed by a squeaky recorder that might hurt my ears, even though the kids seem to be upstairs. Man, does Holden have to listen to this every day? Another point of sympathy goes onto the scoreboard.

Remembering that Holden was in the shower, I walk to the kitchen to wait. I might as well steal a cookie; I notice the chocolate chip ones from the Dizzy Duck. The ones they leave on guests' pillows at night or offer as a welcome. It's a great touch to the inn, and the cookies are damn delicious and soft, too.

It's a few minutes later when I hear someone come down the stairs as I sit at the island. I know it's Holden because the steps are heavier than what a child's might be.

Strolling into the kitchen, he greets me with a smile, but my eyes only dip down with dread because he's in a fresh pair of jeans and a white fitted t-shirt. "What brings you in? Everything okay?"

I snicker but give him a smirk because I do love our interaction. "Actually, the water doesn't seem to be on in the guesthouse, or at least no water is coming out. I'm not sure where the pipe nozzle is outside."

He licks his lips, and his grin is tight. "This isn't good."

"Why?"

Holden walks to the fridge and pulls out a bottle of beer then pulls out wine to offer to me. Waving my hand no, he places it back in the fridge. Opening his beer, the cap snap fills the silence between us as I patiently wait for his answer.

He takes a long sip as the line on my lips stays permanent with entertaining fear that his response won't be easy.

"I thought for sure that had been fixed," he begins. "I guess not. The plumber did mention if the water doesn't come out, then it's blocked somewhere, and the water can't get through."

My head falls into my hand because this kind of feels like bullshit, but I'll play along. "Is that so?" I cast doubt.

He shrugs his shoulders. "Plumbers don't lie."

I stand up and begin to walk toward him as he leans casually against the counter near the fridge. "Hmm. So, what is the solution to this issue? May I please go back to the Dizzy Duck?"

One step closer and he doesn't flinch; instead, he casually takes another sip. "Nope. I have alternative sleeping arrangements."

My journey lands me close to him, desperate to reach out and touch his chest. I loll my head to the side, ready to soak in this tension between us, except it isn't tension… it's a game where we're on par in our equal level of flirtation.

"Where might that be?" My voice is a soft husk.

He leans down because I'm shorter. "Congratulations, Lexi. The guest room near the laundry room is calling your name," he whispers.

I feared something like this was coming. "Lucky for us we have your kids as the perfect middle line to keep us on good behavior."

A sound escapes his throat. "Is that a 'yes, Holden. What a great idea. Please can you get my suitcase?'"

My mouth seems to dance around his but not enough to graze. "It's a 'yes, Holden. Get me…'" I pull back, and my voice grits out, "A hell of a lot of wine."

We both create space, and his hand combs through his hair, and I notice that he frowns. "There wasn't a please," he teases.

I laugh to myself. "Just move me in because logic doesn't exist around me anymore, unless it's related to paint colors and shellac walls."

He reaches for his cell phone on the counter. "Good that you stay focused on the Dizzy Duck. Now, do you take extra cheese on your pizza?" Now he is ordering pizza for everyone as if the last five minutes didn't happen.

Throwing up my hands, I figure I might as well eat. "Get me whatever. I have a feeling your kids won't be happy about this."

Holden's demeanor completely changes to a sort of fondness, but it isn't for me, it's for his children. "They'll be okay. You're not actually a nanny, so that's a positive step in their book. Lori will be feisty, but that's with everyone. Harry is actually quite innocent. Having you around will be better than me running around like a headless chicken anyhow. Don't get me wrong. I've got my shit together, but *lately*…" He winces. "I could just use even the smallest of favors to relieve some pressure."

His jaw slants to the side and holds as he registers what I'm completely interpreting his sentence to mean.

"Relieve pressure… huh." My nails tap against my hips.

He returns his focus to the screen of his phone. "I can be tame if I choose to be. It might be good for me to have a breath of fresh air in the house that doesn't involve a disgruntled nanny."

"I'm not a breath of fresh air," I point out. He looks up at me. "I'm a hurricane that's about to turn your life upside down."

He laughs. "I can handle you. After all, in the span of 48 hours, you've called me Master and Sir."

"Wine, Holden. Get me that wine faster," I answer dryly.

"Say please and I will."

I shake my head ruefully.

Most fires only start if you light it.

I should probably hide the matches.

HOLDEN

My daughter flops her piece of pizza onto her plate, her frown never fading. "So, she's just going to stay here?"

I set another piece of pizza onto Harry's plate while Lexi observes everyone, not saying much. Fair enough, I've dragged us down a hole.

Something snapped when she showed up yesterday at my office. An immediate inkling to push her limits, and there is nothing to rein me in. I didn't lie, I'm desperate for a little help when it comes to Lori and Harry. Losing another nanny created a total shuffle of my schedule, and I'm struggling to figure out the little things, such as what the hell goes into a lunchbox, because that was a lie when I told Lexi that of course I know how to. But, truthfully, lunch-making is my nemesis, and it's such a simple task too.

"Lexi will stay here for a little bit. She has to work on the Dizzy Duck, but we're short on rooms there, and now the water in the guesthouse is off. We're lucky enough she can give us a hand or two, and she isn't a stranger to us."

"But I'm not a nanny," Lexi chirps, then sinks into her seat in case she's out of line.

Lori and Harry shoot her a stare as if they forgot she was here even though we've been talking about her.

"It's cool. She seems nice." Harry isn't fazed as he enjoys his pizza. My son has a kind heart, and even if he pulls a prank, it's because he wants to make someone laugh and not out of vengeance… but if it pushes a nanny away, then he doesn't mind that either. He has a softer personality than I ever had. Sports don't really seem to be his thing, and sometimes I'm not entirely sure if I'm getting it right in trying to relate to one another.

He continues to speak with a full mouth. "It'll drive my teacher crazy when a not-ugly nanny shows up to pick me up." God, his single teacher who lays it on thick at parent-teacher meetings.

"Not a nanny," Lexi reminds us all again, her tone now exhausted from her repeated memo to the table.

Lori shakes her head and grabs her cell phone that somehow made it out of my discipline attempt. I said it was only for communication to text *one* friend for the night before taking it back. But that plan went to hell when every kid her age uses their phones for everything, and it's my lifeline to connecting with her. Lori is perhaps my biggest challenge as of late, but she's also not, because her stubbornness and independence are good attributes as she grows older. It's just… can't she give me one clue that we're alright? At least before boys enter the picture? Give me an opportunity to save up a little energy before we have to deal with the teenage chapter?

Lori doesn't even part from her screen. "As fun as this little conversation is, I'm sure our *guest* is aware that my room is off-limits."

Lexi quickly answers, "Of course. Besides, I have no

plans to be here every second of the day, so do your thing. I'm only sitting here right now because pizza seemed like a way to refill my strength and hopefully bring back reason."

I'm on board with Lexi's humor, it means not a dull moment that isn't exhausting. My hand slides across my face, not allowing myself to think any more about Lexi as I deal with my daughter. "No, Lori? Can't even be polite for maybe three minutes?"

She studies Lexi up and down, then she grumbles before sliding off her chair. "I'm going upstairs. My nail polish color doesn't match my outfit for tomorrow." Off she goes with her signature hair flip as a statement. I hate it, as much as I try to suppress a smile that wants to form. My daughter has a backbone.

"Great conversation," I call out and unenthusiastically give myself a little fist pump. Glancing to Lexi, she offers me a pained sympathetic look.

"Will you make me a peanut butter sandwich for school lunch tomorrow but use cashew butter?" Harry plays with the cheese on his pizza.

"Why cashew butter?" I'm confused, he loves peanut butter.

"Because Mrs. Crawl said it's a new school rule in the email you should have read that we need to use cashew or almond butter because of allergies."

I snicker as I see Lexi contemplate that logic. "Sure, let me dig it out of the pantry."

"What a bummer. They're ruining a classic American sandwich," he groans.

I reach over to nudge his arm with my fist. "How about we make peanut butter and jelly cheesecake soon?"

His face instantly lights up. "Really?"

"Yeah, it's the only thing I know how to make, and lucky

for me, it happens to be my son's favorite." I smile because it does the trick every time. It's a pain to bake because it takes hours, but I always knock it out of the park. Not even sure how I found the recipe in the first place, but it's my golden ticket. "Anything else?"

He shakes his head, still smiling. "No, I'm going to go read my book now."

"Sure, kiddo." I'm both relieved and sad that we're past the whole storybook and tuck-in phase. It was a time drain, but now I'm wishing I could turn the clock back. Those were guaranteed moments of bonding. I watch Harry leave as I recall it all.

It's only when I hear a stifled laugh that I turn to see Lexi desperately trying to suppress a laugh.

"Yes?" I wonder what the hell could be so amusing.

"No offense, but your kids are hysterical and are totally giving you a hard time because they can. I even have a feeling that one of them will add something awful to my morning coffee, and still, it's kind of funny."

"Are you serious?" Lexi nods up and down in response as she stands to collect plates. "You don't need to do that."

"Oh yeah? You know where the dishwasher is?" Her joke causes me to break out in a smile. "By the way, what is this sorcery of peanut butter and jelly cheesecake of which you speak?"

I follow her in clearing the table and head straight to the sink with pride on my face. "It's my gateway to happiness for children and adults. If you haven't had it yet, then your life isn't complete."

"It sounds delicious and the last thing that would have been on my radar of what to expect from you. But peanut butter squishes all doubts."

"As it should. You know, I… have no clue why I'm dragging you into this."

Maybe it's a game? Everything in my life might feel like a mess, but this is a fun escape I still deserve. Except I'm not sure where our blue line is. Flirtation is okay, but crossing the lines, probably not.

Lexi clears her throat, breaking me away from my thought. "Can I ask, Holden?" She seems to hesitate, and I think I know where this is going. "I know that you were married and the divorce was kind of ugly, but…"

Grabbing a kitchen towel, I turn to lean against the sink. "It was more than ugly. Michelle was, well… a bitch, to put it bluntly, and I don't use that word lightly."

Her lips roll in then her boldness returns. "Was it always that way between you two?"

I scoff a sound and stare ahead of me at the wall. "It was. Lori was an accident, and I will always be grateful it happened. But marrying because of an unexpected pregnancy isn't always the right move. I learned that the hard way," I reflect.

"But you stayed together long enough to bring another child into the world."

"Damn, Lexi. You're not afraid to be forward. But to answer your question. We always lived separate lives in our marriage, as in even separated. Michelle didn't have much interest in being a mom, but I still wanted it to work for Lori's sake. Still, it got to the point when divorce was the only way, but one night I had a thought of pure desperation that we could try one more time to make it work for Lori, and then Harry entered the picture. And I'm 100% sure that Michelle planned it that way to string me along. After Harry was born though, I still asked for a divorce, especially when she…"

She gently touches my elbow. "You don't have to say. You've already shared a lot."

Why am I? I don't really talk about this. Especially with a woman who dropped into my life. Still, intuition has me knocking down a block. My eyes whip to hers. "You're easy to talk to."

"It seems so."

"Michelle didn't want to be a mom. Simply said, she got pregnant with the hope that it would bring her the life of luxury she wanted. When motherhood hit, then reality came crashing down. How someone can walk away like that, I don't know. But I had hoped co-parenting could still happen. So, yeah... that divorce was fun." My head drops, and I bite my bottom lip from the recall of events. "Funny how people are. She has no interest in being a mom, yet she wanted a hefty settlement in order for me to have full legal custody of the kids. I thought that would at least keep one door open if she asked or made an effort to be involved."

Lexi winces at my story, and her hand slides up my arm to land on my shoulder to give a few squeezes to show comfort. "That never happened," I state somberly.

But even though I'm talking about the misery of divorce, a weightlessness comes over me, and I think it's because of her touch. I can't help but follow the path of where her palm traveled.

"I'm sorry that happened. Lori and Harry?"

A long exhale escapes me. "Harry was too young to remember, and Lori was almost four. Maybe it's why she's a little extra... difficult."

Lexi smiles gently. "Oh, I assure you that it's pre-teen angst too. You're not the only parent to be going through this. I was rebellious and utter hell when I was her age... well, until now too, but you know what I mean."

I chuckle and enjoy that her hand hasn't left my arm, even if it's platonic. "I'm sure your dad loves that."

Now she lets go, and her gaze circles to the floor. "I think we can all agree that hockey is number one for him, and I'm a distant second. My dad, I mean sure, he loves me and is protective, but his time is consumed by hockey."

"Protectiveness, for sure. The first pep talk of the season was always for everyone on the team to stay away from you. It's supposed to be a lifetime oath." A small grin forms on my lips.

Her mouth slants halfway up as our moment holds from my words. "Well then, oaths are not meant to be broken." It feels like she is testing me.

I'm not sure what to say except, "Want more wine?"

Lexi softly shakes her head. "Nah, it's okay. I'm going to go use a shower that actually works and get some shuteye. The carpet guy is meeting me at nine tomorrow."

If my kids weren't here, then I would storm right after her to help her undress and join her in the shower so I can get a little relief. I'm not immune to having someone on call for physical gratification, but it's been a solid few months since I got laid.

Attempting to gather some composure, I decide to be the exemplary older one. "Of course, and thanks."

"Anytime. Communication isn't breaking an oath… even if it's dirty. Night-night." She wiggles her fingers at me, pleased with her closing sentence.

The moment she's gone, my upper body collapses over the counter, desperate to do everything to her that's in my mind right now.

———

WALKING into the Dizzy Duck after school drop-off, I debate if it's good for morale for my staff to see me carrying coffee from another establishment, but I think they understand the need for real caffeine.

I glance at Stuart behind the reception desk as he's typing away on the laptop. "We're going to switch to tablets soon to give this place a sleeker feel."

Stuart looks up. "I know, but some things only really work on laptops."

"Solid point." I have to agree. "I'll be in my office," I say.

Starting my walk, I only manage to get a few steps before I backtrack to look at the empty spot on the wall. "What happened to the moose?"

"Lexi had it taken down. You know, she really has great ideas. She should have her own television show. She's hot enough for—" I shoot him a sharp glare, and he must get the sentiment of my scowl. "Or not." He swallows.

Pursing my lips, I decide to find the woman of the hour. It doesn't take long, as she's in the hall that leads to the private reception room. I missed the detail that she's in skinny jeans and heels, since she left before I made it downstairs this morning. The carpet guy is getting a gift to his eyes since Lexi's ass is in the air as she leans over to check two swatches against the wood.

She's completely unaware. "No, let's still do wood. The carpet doesn't work."

For some reason, a wave of protectiveness hits me. Partly because I am a territorial motherfucker when it comes to a woman that I shouldn't pursue but probably will anyhow.

Clearing my throat, carpet guy looks at me and meets my warning glare. He adjusts his posture and slides his eyes away from Lexi.

"Lexi." Saying her name seems to surprise her, and she

looks over her shoulder from the samples that the man way below her league is observing.

"Oh, hey." She stands up to greet me with a smile.

I crook my finger to gesture her over. "A word."

Lines form on her forehead. "Excuse me for a second," she tells the guy. Her saunter to me is nearly in slow motion. "Yes…" she leans in quickly, "Master," she whispers her taunt.

My face remains stoic, trying not to let her have the upper hand. "The moose is gone."

"Yeah, because you said it could go."

"Where is it?"

"A closet, why? Does it deserve a ceremonial funeral or something?"

I'm being absolutely ridiculous. "No…" *I just need a reason to bother you.* "Let's just save it for sinking it to the bottom of the lake or something when the Dizzy Duck is all remodeled."

She nods. "A good idea. We could even get a special buoy to mark his resting place." Is she teasing or is she serious? I can't tell.

"The room warm enough for you? Enough bounce to the mattress for your special time? The drawer the right size for your supplies to get you through the moments when you have some frustration to work out?"

Lexi's face flushes red, with her eyes blazing as I stand in front of her casually drinking my coffee.

"Uh…"

"The old first-floor guest room of the inn for your designing stuff, of course." Absolutely not. "You wanted to keep your supplies and samples there. I can imagine you just use the bed as a shelf and probably tuck some scissors and tape measures in the drawer. Naturally, being a good boss, I wouldn't want you to freeze in there. Why? What did you think I mean?"

She attempts to avoid my gaze, but I only step closer. "Do I make you nervous, Lexi?" I speak so only she can hear. The tension between us causes a shiver for us both, but we try to keep our bodies in check.

Lexi partly opens her mouth but only a croak escapes, then she gathers her thoughts. "No."

My voice turns rather chipper. "Thought so, considering you were spying on me yesterday when I went to take a shower." I get to enjoy a second of her jaw dropping before I turn to leave on that note.

Because yeah, I've been holding onto that fact.

My phone dings with a reminder, and I swipe my screen while juggling my coffee. Lucky me, each of my kids are at a sleepover with friends tomorrow.

Oh, look at that. Seems to mean I'll be alone with my house guest.

My nails thrum against the desk in the large bedroom at the Dizzy Duck. Most definitely, I'm going to refurbish this. I've surveyed the inn to see what pieces of furniture we could keep and revamp with a new look. I'm really going to bring in the elements of history from around Lake Spark and tie it into a mix of farmhouse and cabin feel, using whites and painted wood to keep it bright. There is a park nearby, literally called Pioneer Park.

But my fingers change their beat because of a lightbulb moment of finalizing my plan forward. Instead of celebrating, I have irritation. With certainty, Holden is now adding me to his flavor-of-the-month list, or at least, that's what it feels like. Every word that slides off his tongue is a torturous taunt where it feels as though he has the upper hand.

It's fun, sure. Doesn't mean I want to give him a piece of my mind any less.

I breathe to myself, trying to inhale a relaxing breath as I straighten my shoulders, before I glance at my phone lying on the desk to see the time. It's nearly two, which means it's time for a break.

Leaving the room, I walk down the hall then the stairs to find myself in the lobby, but instead of heading to the table that offers refreshments for guests at all times, my feet plant down, unable to move. I tip my head back to get a glance of the office near the hall and the private party room, I guess because I'm subconsciously thinking of what to do with the fact that the door is ajar, and it's Holden's office.

Oh, fuck it.

I charge in his direction with my heels clicking against the wood. Storming into his office, I close the door behind me without a thought. My abrupt entrance catches him off guard as he glances up from his laptop, with lines creased on his forehead.

Pointing my finger at him, I stop due to the desk being a barrier. "So what? I watched you undress and head to the shower. I am sure it would happen if you used the sauna in the spa here too. No big deal."

Amusement gleams on his face, a fine line stretching on his lips. Ugh, why must he have a little rough stubble today?

No, Lexi, I will not be distracted. I'm confident.

He holds a finger up as he leans back in his chair, relaxed as can be. "One, Lexi, a towel is a necessity in the sauna here at our spa, it's optional if you use it to cover yourself or sit on. And two, you know it's not exactly *not* a big deal. You've seen the goods, and it's quite the opposite, it's a large deal."

My lips part open, entertained by the repartee being tossed around between us. "Holden, I only saw your immaculate ass, so the size of your dick is still a guess."

Holden licks his lips as he chortles. "Are we really going to go back and forth about this?"

I bring my hand to my hip. "No. I just find it interesting that you didn't tell me yesterday that you knew I saw you."

His hands come behind his head and his chest stretches,

which has an added benefit since his button-down is fitted, so I see a few outlines of his muscles. "It's more fun to catch you off balance."

"I'm sure. Let's just keep everything aboveboard, shall we? I have your hotel to decorate."

Holden stands, completely unfazed by my request, as he bypasses me and heads straight to his coat rack, and my eyes follow him. I'm intrigued by what he's up to now.

He swings his coat off the hook then slips it on. "Sure. Anyhow, I need your help if you don't mind. I need to take Harry to get his supplies for his science project, and Lori needs to get to the ice rink for her figure skating lesson. Would you be a doll and help me?"

"I'm not a child carer," I reiterate for the thousandth time, my tone flat.

Holden has a droll smile. "So you've said. But please, can you help get Lori to her lesson?"

I blink a few times. "What does this entail?"

"Pick her up from school, listen to pre-teen angst for ten minutes, then drop her off at the ice rink. I'll pick her up later," Holden explains as he steps slowly in my direction.

I have a weakness for helping people in a crisis, and in a flash, I remember the disaster of his morning routine with his kids. Maybe it's pity. "Fine." I don't sound enthused, but I am agreeable.

Holden reaches with his fingers to touch my arms, sending a buzz throughout my insides, especially when I notice his eyes dip low to my body then jump right back up. "Thank you."

I roll my eyes but then nearly laugh to myself that he keeps wrapping me around his finger. But this time, it's me invading his space, reaching out to his open coat. I pull on the fabric to catch the start of the zipper. His eyes become glued to my fingers that are maneuvering his zipper. Slowly, tooth by tooth, I drag the zipper up as our eyes meet. I do my best to give him a sultry look because I know it drives him crazy.

The sound of the zip stops when I reach the end of the line, and I bring my palms to his chest. I smooth out the fabric, pretending I'm sweeping off some lint, then pat near his shoulders. "I would hate for you to get cold." I pretend to pout with concern.

Holden purses out a breath, fully invested in our tit-for-tat. He caught me off guard with his knowledge of what I saw, and now I'm causing his pulse to pick up a beat because I have the power to weaken him purely by a tantalizing touch.

He clears his throat, but his straight-lined lips that have a hint of entertainment returns. "You're so considerate," he comments dryly.

"I know, and that's just me being a completely normal person." A breathy husk comes out of me. "I'm a giver, what can I say?"

Holden clasps the tip of my hair resting on my collarbone, and he rubs the strands between the pads of his fingers. "I'm a taker, so it seems we have a match."

After a brief pause, we both lock our eyes with soft smiles appearing.

Breathe, I remind myself. Everything inside me wants to be touched, and I'm desperate to pull him close to relieve me.

"Thanks again for helping with Lori."

"Sure."

It feels as though neither one of us wants to leave, but the clock keeps going even if you want it to stop.

———

Lori slides onto the front seat of my car, closing the door a little harder than I would prefer. Even though Holden texted her about my limo service, she still looks none too pleased.

"Hey there." I do my best to attempt to start out with a hopefully pleasant conversation, even offer a smile.

Her eyes roll to me as she snaps her seatbelt in with aggression. "He roped you into carpool duty now?"

"No," I answer, as though her question couldn't be further from the truth, even if she's right. "I'm happy to help, and your brother has a science project."

"Because he's a nerd like that. Bet my dad wishes Harry would play hockey."

I turn the engine on, and we get on our way. "But figure skating is pretty cool. I did it myself when I was younger."

"Really?" There almost seems to be a faint sound of interest, but I can't tell.

"Yeah, did it for seven years actually. But I didn't like competitions and somehow lost my interest in skating." I focus on the road.

"So, you're a failure." Lori seems to be happy about my revelation.

And here is why I knew a pleasant conversation wouldn't be happening despite my best efforts.

"Aren't you honest," I say, sarcastic. "I don't think I'm a failure, I just grew up and found other interests. Anyhow, how long have you been skating?"

She begins to play with the buttons on the dashboard for music in the car. "Since I was seven. I think I'm good."

"So modest," I mumble to myself. The sound of pop-country fills the car. "Nice choice in music."

"Tell that to my dad. I've been begging him to use his connections for concert tickets for my birthday."

I shrug. "Sounds like a reasonable request."

Lori rests her head against the seat then throws me a look. "You know, he loses interest easily. Just because you're staying with us, that doesn't mean you're different."

I nod, trying to think of what to say. "Your dad and I aren't like that." Somewhat true. No kiss or further bases have been taken. Fucking via eye contact doesn't count.

I glance quickly to my side to see that Lori is studying me, then she hums a sound. I'm sure she has a theory or opinion; she seems very intuitive for her age.

"You're weird."

My eyes pop out from her forwardness. "Uh, isn't that a good thing?" My voice is uneven from lacking certainty.

"Maybe. You're the one chauffeuring around kids you barely know."

"I've met you before, you just don't remember. Your dad would always show photos of you guys growing up too. It's just been a while since I've seen him. And I'm not a child caretaker." I feel like I need to get a sign to hang around my neck.

"Fair enough. I'm an adult anyhow. I think my dad still tries to have someone care for us because of Harry. He's a bit sensitive."

"Really?" I focus on the turn on the road.

"I don't know, I'm not a therapist," she responds.

I chortle to myself. "We're almost there. Do I need to come in with you?"

"Of course not." Lori looks out the windows to investigate where we are. "How did you know how to get here?"

"My grandparents used to have a lake house here. I'm not new to the area."

A sound escapes her lips. "So you actually know the area and knew us from before. I'll give you points for that. Most women start from zero when they try to grab my dad's attention."

I come to a stop outside of the rink just in time. "Oh, but I'm not—" She's already opened the door with no interest in hearing my defense and grabs her bag from the backseat.

She leans in through the open window. "Thanks for the ride. See you at home. Remind my dad that I need new cucumbers for my eyes, he always forgets. Something tells me that he'll listen to you."

"Why is that?"

"He actually lets you near us. That's rule number one in his book, don't let his *friends* around his kids."

She walks away, and despite her attitude that needs a strong adjustment, Lori is quite... insightful.

And I'm not sure why a sprinkle of a special feeling forms somewhere within my body.

6

HOLDEN

I watch Lexi as she compares paint samples against the wall next to the fireplace mantle in the lobby. Last night, I think she was hiding from me, as she went to Summer's for dinner then retreated to her room as soon as she was back. Like any sane person, she avoided breakfast in my house before school, too.

But now I do owe her a few words. I approach her slowly, as she seems completely unaware that I'm behind her. My inkling has me believing that we both experience a sort of electricity around one another that heightens the tension in the air, but it only causes us to have relaxed smiles because we both enjoy it.

"Hey there."

I startle her, and she drops the paint sample sheet. "Oh, hi, I was lost in my thoughts and didn't notice you were here."

We both lean down to save the swatch, and our arms graze in the battle of who will pick it up first. Our eyes connect, and I hiss a breath. "Thoughts about me?" I tease her, and her cheeks heat.

Even though I managed to beat her at collecting the

swatch, we remain kneeling, lost in a simple touch and my enjoyment of the gleam in her eyes.

"Wishful thinking, Holden, since my thoughts normally only include how to use mason jars in staging a room or debating in my head what *is* the best position for nighttime activities." Her breathy rasp is a taunt that I'm here for.

"Mmm, if it is designated to only nighttime, then he is the wrong man for you." We both stand as she stifles a laugh, and I hand her the paint sample. "Anyhow, before my indecent thoughts go any further into the gutter, I should probably keep us on neutral ground."

Lexi looks at me with interest. "Oh yeah? That's a sudden one-eighty," she flatly states.

I love when I smirk, it's good for the facial muscles. "The thing is… I owe you a massive thank-you for helping yesterday with Lori. I know she's, well…" I love this kid, but I need to accept her current state. "Feisty and moody. She probably even slammed the car door for extra effect."

Lexi relaxes in her stance as her enjoyment of my presence doesn't seem to fade. "It's… not a problem, and I hate to be the one to remind you, but it might only go downhill from here until she heads to college. It's the joys of pre-teen and teenage life."

Blowing out an exhausting breath, her words instill fear in me. I really need to step up my plans to prepare for all of it. But I have no plans, I'm just going with the flow. I bring a finger to my chin and rub for a few seconds while I follow Lexi to the couch in the middle of the lobby and then notice that the coffee table is already gone.

"You're really speeding along with everything," I compliment.

"Of course, you need the lobby done ASAP. It's your statement room for making first impressions. Plus, we're packing up so they can sand the floors and walls before they paint. I managed to get some of the furniture to arrive next week, a friend owed me a favor," she explains as she grabs her coat slung over the back of the couch.

I really am impressed with her ability to dive deep into this project. "Sounds great, a lucky friend to have, I guess." I fill my jeans pockets with my hands to keep them occupied and in check, because how I would love to touch her ass right now.

She begins to button her coat. "I guess. I went on a few dates with him a couple of times, and I assume that helped." Lexi isn't even attempting to keep me on edge, she's simply relaying a fact.

My body tenses, and for the life of me, I'm not entirely sure why a wave of possessiveness is like a match when she said that. "Oh? Is this recent?"

Lexi stares at me and then nearly snorts a laugh. "Subtle, are we? And no, not recent. Like, two years ago maybe."

Stepping forward, I want her whole body to feel my presence, which is why my hands come up as I invade her space, and her breath hitches. I even sense a shiver when I reach around to grab the belt of her coat. Slowly, I wrap the fabric around her waist.

"Good. That topic's closed." Our eyes are fixed to one another as I continue to tie the belt. "Any plans for tonight? It's Friday, but it is Lake Spark, so…" My voice drops low, and without regard for Stuart at reception who is our audience, I tie Lexi's belt.

Lexi gulps a breath. "I think I'm going to take it easy, you know a glass of wine or read a book."

I yank on the knot to tighten, and it causes her to press against me and yelp from surprise, and her hands can't help but find a resting spot on my shoulders to ensure she doesn't lose her balance. "There is a hot tub at my house if that's your thing."

Her head tilts slightly, and here we go, I know that sexy-as-fuck look forming on her face, her mouth about to retort with a comment I will appreciate. "You own a spa here at the Dizzy Duck. I think I would rather use the hot tub and pool here."

"*Yeah*… but tonight is an unusual night at my place."

"Why might that be?" Her voice is hoarse.

"I'm going to order in Chinese food if you like that. You must get hungry for dinner."

She rolls her head and looks defeated yet doesn't let go. "That is true, and I do love sweet-and-sour chicken."

"Great, I'll order."

"As long as Lori and Harry enjoy it then sounds good."

A gruff humorous sound rumbles under my breath, and it causes Lexi's eyes to flood with alarm, clearly waiting for an explanation.

"Except Lori and Harry are away for sleepovers at their friends' houses."

She backtracks at record speed, creating space between us as she steps away. "Come again?" She blinks.

"Again? Geez, let me first make round one happen."

Her eyes roll at my demeanor that must be driving her crazy. "This is not…" Her face falls into her hands and then appears again with her lips in a grin. "What the hell, fine. Dinner, and then our best behavior in the hot tub, and we can talk furniture ideas."

I begin to walk away without even looking back, instead taking satisfaction from my triumph. "Agreeable as always."

———

With hesitation, Lexi walks down the hall then slows when she reaches the kitchen. I don't give her much notice as I'm unpacking white boxes from the bag, the smell of Chinese food hitting our senses.

"Here I am." She's still in jeans from the day but has replaced her blouse with an old Hollows University t-shirt.

"Got eggrolls and fortune cookies."

She grabs the packet of chopsticks to prepare. "Then I won't be running away."

I circle around the island to join her on the high stools. Sitting at the dining table would be too formal, and the couch would just be a mess.

"You weren't going to run away anyhow," I confidently inform her.

Lexi's eyes have a glimmer of something that I can't quite describe, but it feels positive for me. "Maybe true. Now pass the eggrolls before I get cranky."

I do as I'm told, and we decide to ditch plates and just eat from the boxes. "Eating Chinese food without plates. I feel like this calls for sitting on the floor, eating behind a coffee table," I state.

A peculiar look floods her face. "That is not what I expected you to say, but I couldn't agree more."

"Want to do it then?"

Her shoulder lifts. "Why not, the rug is the perfect material for sitting on," she notes.

We both grab a few things and head to the living room. I manage to grab the bottle of wine and glasses too since she's carrying the brunt of our dinner.

Once we are settled on the ground, I pour some wine for us, and then an odd silence hits us when our eyes catch, and her face turns soft and shy.

"What are we doing, Holden?" She gets straight to the point.

Honestly, I'm not sure. It's just too fun and exhilarating to have a connection that streams between two people. I know I have kids relying on me, and I shouldn't be distracted, but…

"There was an instant click between us, and you're familiar with my situation. In a way, it's refreshing to have someone who doesn't assume I'm one way purely because they've never met me."

Lexi swirls some food with her chopsticks. "It has been quite a few years since we saw one another, and it's different circumstances, but I do like this time around better."

I take a sip of my red wine before setting the glass back on the table. "I'm an asshole for flirting with you. I'm not sure why you're not running."

"Because a retired hockey player doesn't scare me." This conversation doesn't even faze her as she brings a piece of chicken to her mouth.

"The thing is, it's okay to flirt with someone; it's crossing the parameters of flirting when things can get a little murky," I warn her.

She buries her chortle while she swallows her food. "Is moving your flirtation into your house not beyond the parameters already?"

My head bobs side to side. "Meh. I need the help right now, and you're up for the challenge."

"A few days and then I will go back to the Dizzy Duck. I'm not sure us being around one another is good for either of our blood pressures," she explains while she picks up another piece of chicken.

I shrug. "Your loss."

"Maybe. I do appreciate how you threw my father's demand for the team to stay away from me out the window."

I intervene. "As much as I want to be loyal, I also don't give a fuck. I have other issues to deal with, in case you haven't noticed." I don't frown about it, and instead smile.

"You most definitely swagger around to your own tune. But what I mean is Lori and Harry are around, and that's where your attention lies, as it should. I'm not sure us adding underlying innuendo is the way to go."

Neither is being lonely in the coming weeks when I don't need to be.

I look at her with fondness, as she has strong shoulders with realistic expectations, and more importantly, she cares about how my life revolves around my kids. In the past, the women I might have had a hookup with were always well away from anyone and discreet. Now? Lexi is in close waters… yet still, I'm ignoring the lifesaver that I should probably consider using.

"You are extremely right, except tonight, they are not here," I remind us.

Her face swings in my direction. "I've noticed."

I nudge her shoulder with mine. "Relax, we can eat and have adult conversation. Other than eating with Stone, my ability to have adult discussions at dinner is limited. This is a refreshing change."

"I ran into him this morning when I stopped by to hit the gym. He gave Stuart a hard time about cookies."

I chuckle. "That's always the case."

"It's a little insane the number of athletes, retired or not, that live in this town. I know the Spinners train here, but still. Do you miss playing?"

Nobody has asked me that in a while. "Hmm, let me think," I pretend. "No. Which might sound strange, but I feel like everything was meant for that chapter. I always knew that I would retire young, as most athletes do, so I made those the best years possible. Not to mention that fatherhood hit me earlier than I probably would have planned. But now I have a completely different life. Do I wish Harry would be more into sports? Sure, but he has other interests. Do I get excited when Lori is dancing on ice? Yeah. Because the ice brings good memories."

Lexi steals some of my sesame chicken, and I appreciate that we're comfortable enough around one another to do something like that. "I would never have expected you to end up owning the Dizzy Duck Inn, but it's a great story." She gently swats my arm in excitement. "Actually, I have an idea that I wanted to run by you."

"Shoot."

"I was thinking we could hang some photos of all the athletes and sports stuff from here in Lake Spark. I could get some frames to match the feeling of the Dizzy Duck. Everyone appreciates those little touches."

"I like it, and I'm sure our guests would love it, including the owner of The Spinners when he eats there with his wife. We have a lot of team dinners happening all the time too."

"Perfect." She sounds accomplished with her thought before she picks up her wine.

I grab an eggroll, but I'm eager to keep our conversation going. "Other than design, what has life looked like for you in the last few years?"

"Well, I worked on a few projects. Homes mostly, which I love, because your home is where you return to and it's the base of your life, therefore you should make it cozy and full of personality," she gushes.

"Heart in the home or something like that."

She's completely enthusiastic. "Totally. And after a few projects, I backpacked around Europe and then Costa Rica. I even went up to do a tour of Alaska. Basically, I'm not afraid to get lost somewhere in Austria because I ended up on the wrong train or ending up in unusual situations that find myself eating Chinese food on the floor in Lake Spark." She smiles proudly before popping food into her mouth.

"Don't worry, adventurous and self-assured were the first two things that came to my mind when you walked into my office."

Her grin turns shy as she sets the box down, deciding not to eat. "I guess you're kind of my client. And yes, I have no qualms admitting that I wasn't going to keep quiet about my attraction, it would have been obvious anyway."

"You were not subtle, nor was I." Setting my food on the table, we both have empty hands, and we should probably efficiently use them for other activities. "Again, I feel obliged to point out that I'm the guy that plays games, and I just haven't figured out which one I'm playing with you."

With purpose, Lexi leans across me, ensuring her body presses against mine as she reaches for something. Her eyes sizzle with a sexy glint that is roping me in, only made worse because her mouth is within inches of mine. I take in our mingling breaths and debate if my hand should slide up the side of her body, but I don't get a chance to decide because she begins to drag her body back to sitting next to me.

Lexi holds a fortune cookie up. "My favorite part of the meal." Her voice is a hoarse whisper.

"Meal, sure, but once that goes into your mouth then the meal is over."

Her brows rise to throw caution at me before she cracks open her cookie to read the paper. "Run while you can or accept your fortune."

I lick my lips, completely enamored by her humor that is on par with my own. "Fitting," I say before I nab my own cookie. Breaking it open, I read aloud, "You should touch the woman sitting in front of you." I throw the paper over my shoulder and move in to glide my hand along her cheek, urging her to move closer.

"It didn't say that." She grins.

"You're right. It only said, 'you will have a good year.' But my version is better and by far more likely to come true."

She presses her lips together but doesn't let go of her smile. I'll cross the line because I'm completely tempted by her. From her fun personality to the way she tucks her hair behind her ear, I'd be angry if I never got the chance to touch her the way I want.

"I've walked into your life when I probably shouldn't," she chides.

"Don't think, Lexi. We're all allowed a little escape," I whisper.

She breaks away and stands abruptly, with her palms smoothing over her clothes. She busies herself with cleaning up the table which disappoints me and confuses me, but I follow her lead.

Walking to the kitchen, she sets the boxes on the counter with her back to me and her hands planted on the edge of the quartz counter. She appears to be in deep thought.

It doesn't feel like I should say anything, so I don't. Which is good, because Lexi spins on her toes, and the speed of her eyes flicking to me transmits the message perfectly.

I'm not sure who makes the move first, but we both take the step to crash our mouths together, her hands quickly finding their way to hang onto my elbows as my hands discover the curve of her hips, because we're in for a long kiss.

Maybe even more.

LEXI

Was he really anxious that I would just walk away and avoid a kiss?

Nah, I just wanted to keep Holden in suspense a little. Draw it out to ensure he doesn't get cocky with the idea that I would be easy at the click of his fingers.

Our ability to play around one another is equal. We both have that skill and on the same level.

Holden's lips are near bruising, and I love it, which is why I give back as good as I get. My arms slide up his then slow so my hands can trace the curve of his shoulders until I link them behind his neck. He is a little taller than me, so I rise on the balls of my feet. The ability for my body to find the right position of its own accord while I kiss Holden is a talent because it means I can sink into this heavenly kiss.

We both seem to murmur when our mouths tilt together to get more. His lips are firm but caress mine just right. The short afternoon stubble around his mouth is the perfect combination to remind me how much of a man he is.

Sparks fly through my body, and my heart quickens as we gently part to gather some air to breathe, right before our mouths find each other again, a little slower this time. The tips of our tongues greet one another with a little dance. Heat skims down over my obliques to settle on my waist, and gosh, his hands framing my body is what I was craving. It brings stability to the kiss that has me wanting more.

Holden almost growls when we pull away, with his eyes connecting with mine, only to dip down to my swollen mouth then strike up back to my eyes. It's sexy and inviting. He has plans for me, and I'm willing.

"That was fun." His voice is gruff but assured.

"Was?" I ask, with a smile covering my fear that this was it.

But he chuckles. "Not a damn chance."

My smile widens right before he dives down to kiss me again. We begin to step together, circling around as we move toward the couch. During this travel of anticipation, he pulls on the edge of my t-shirt before peeling it up with vigor, only for me to take over when his arm wraps around my middle to keep me close. He only takes one moment to admire my pink lace bra, and it seems to fuel him, because the moment we are back at the couch, he lifts then twirls me until I'm on my back underneath him.

"Tsk, tsk, Lexi," he tuts with a devilish smirk. "You made us go to the kitchen, only to return to where we started."

I chortle as my hands play with his t-shirt, wanting it off already a minute ago. "I'm not that easy, Holden. I may be another one of your conquests, but by no means am I falling at your feet."

A wave of uncertainty glazes over his eyes, and I don't have a clue how to uncover his thoughts. "Huh, conquests. But you have the best mouth I've ever seen that spits out retorts at record speed. Now let me touch you more." He sounds desperate, and confidence and excitement bloom inside me.

My leg drives up to pull his body even closer to mine. "Only if you're nice." I fake a pout.

"I'm never nice, but I am demanding, and something blazes in your eyes that you want that anyhow."

I breathe out a knowing breath but don't answer because I don't get a chance. His mouth is trailing down my neck to my breasts, and my entire body lifts to offer him more. I'm buzzing with a need so strong that I really wish the clock would speed up.

Which is why my hands sneak between us to work the button of his jeans. When his mouth kisses and nibbles at the valley of my breasts, his hand joins me in loosening his jeans to slide down his hips. Instantly, my palm covers his cock underneath his briefs, and I softly gasp. His stiff cock feels very big, and that excites me even more.

The feeling of fingers unbuttoning my jeans ups the antic- ipation, but I won't wait and slide them down as fast as I can. I'm not sure that Holden even looks, he just pursues his crusade to fuck me, and I'm ready to surrender.

A moan hits me as his finger grazes over the damp lace near my clit. A few strokes and I'm already halfway on the road to trembling.

"Lexi, your pussy seems to be eager for me to play. My mouth will have to wait, because since you walked into my office the other day, I've thought about fucking you senseless for round one."

A noise tunes a short melody under my breath. "I don't think I'll mind."

Quickly, he no longer hovers over me, and instead, he stands to offer me his hand. "Come on, your room. I don't think the sofa with popcorn stuck behind a pillow is the place for this."

Ah, and he's right. This is where his family spends their relaxation time, and it would be a little odd for him to take his hookup on his couch, wouldn't it?

I comply, and he yanks me up with power. I don't expect Holden to keep my hand firmly in his as he tows me along, but the off-guard sweetness kind of sends a twinkle somewhere inside me. Luckily, the guest room and bathroom are off the study, so we don't need to go far.

He kicks the door shut behind us and then pushes me onto the bed, and we are back to the same position that we were on the couch. My toes now dig into his ass to press his cock to my pussy. I'm not sure if I can wait long.

"Condom," he says into my neck.

"Mmmhmm," I hum.

"No, I mean, I don't have a condom here. It's in my jeans back in my wallet in the other room."

"Oh." I come up to my forearms. "I think I have one in my bag somewhere." He lies to his side to allow me to hop off the bed, and it takes me a few big steps or rather jog to the bathroom to grab one from my makeup bag. Appearing at the door, I hold it up. "Lucky us." Then I dive back onto the bed.

He studies me with concern. "Had plans for your time in Lake Spark?"

I swat him. "Oh yeah. I was totally going to head to Main Street to see who I could convince to join me in my wicked ways, even heard the sheriff is single again," I tease him.

Holden flips me until I'm on my back and he is on his side. "Looks like you upgraded." His hand pulls my thigh to the side, with the back of his finger drawing a line up my skin, creating a sensitive wave throughout my body.

"Don't go off topic, we need clothes off and the condom on," I usher us along.

The corners of his mouth hitch as he's entertained. We both work off any fabric that remains on us, and he rips open the condom wrapper with his teeth, quickly sheathing it on. The moment he settles between my legs, I think my clit is in pain I'm so desperate for Holden to fill me up.

When he begins to nudge his cock inside me, I moan from a release of patience.

"Fuck me," he grunts. "You're perfectly tight yet taking me well." He pushes further and slowly until he's in deep. I twirl my hips a few circles, only for him move up, pin my arms above my head, and open me wide. "No, baby, you'll lie back and watch as I take you hard and deep."

A sound of pleasure draws out from my mouth when I look down to see his cock sliding in and out of me, glistening with my arousal.

Holden pumps and pumps, and I clench and meet him on thrusts. We go faster, harder, until I'm not sure how long it's been because I'm lost. "Fuck. Almost. Fuck. So good," I moan breathlessly.

"I know," he grunts.

His thumb on my clit brings a near scream from my lips as I reach my orgasm that overtakes me as I shake around his cock, and my head spins. It feels like I'm not even on earth when a few moments later Holden follows me with an orgasm that rips through him and causes him to nearly roar.

He takes a few seconds to recover before he withdraws and falls onto his back.

We're both perfectly spent.

———

I LEAN on my side with the sheet covering me loosely and my head propped on my arm as I watch Holden reappear from the bathroom after having taken care of the condom.

There is a droll smile on his face as he walks naked back to the bed and then joins me under the covers.

"That escalated quickly," he jokes.

"It seems so." My lips quirk out. "I don't think you particularly care, though."

He glances at me. "Not really. Should I? I think we both know this was a release for one another, and there will probably be a second time or third."

"Is that what you do with the others?"

He snorts a laugh. "You really have a great interpretation of me." He sounds almost offended, but his relaxed face doesn't fade. "I haven't had sex with anyone for a few months, believe it or not."

"Well, I mean, I guess you still know what to do," I taunt him, and it earns me Holden gently tackling me until he is on his side looking down on me.

"You are kind of a sunshiny, almost annoying woman, so fortunately for you, I appreciate your humor."

I lick my lips. "Likewise. It's nice seeing very adult Holden again. Last time I saw you, well, you were an adult but with a lot of chaos in your life and not the good kind. You were so distracted that everyone kind of gave you some space," I explain, and it's honest.

Sure, even I wasn't immune to his looks, but it never crossed my mind that he would be a contender since he was way beyond my years in terms of life experience. Now? The moment I walked into his office, a light went on, and I could see maybe more in him, completely unexplainable.

"My life is still chaos," he reminds me honestly.

I smile softly at him. "The good kind." We both lie on our

backs, and I tip my nose in the direction of a canvas photo on the wall of Lori in a tutu. "It's a great picture."

He follows the line of my eyes. "Yeah, she was maybe eight there. She used to dance more but figure skating is her hobby of choice now. Lori still goes to one ballet class a week because her coach says it will help on the ice." The smile of affection and love on his face is apparent. "She's good. I'm happy it brings me to the ice rink on a frequent basis, and memories hit me." Holden points to another picture on the wall of his son playing in shallow water at the lake. "As much as I dreamed of raising a little hockey player, Harry is our science and music guy. I've accepted that one squeaking instrument at a time. A great kid when he's on good behavior."

I begin to draw on his arm with my fingers. "You love them. Any fool could see that. One day, you will look back at this chapter and laugh at some of their tricks."

He chuckles as his own finger begins to swirl on my thigh under the sheet, not even in a sexual way. "You're completely right. If you are firm on that theory, then I'm sure you will roll into motherhood with a breeze."

I shrug. "Maybe, not sure I'm ready for that now, though, if ever."

"Hmm."

I roll back onto my side and tuck my hands under my head. "Can I ask? If it's too personal, then don't answer. But do you think they are acting this way because, well, their mom isn't in the picture?"

He ponders. "First off, with you, I don't seem to mind talking about this stuff, which is new for me. But I'm not sure, at least they never mention it. At some point, it must cross their mind that their mom doesn't want any involvement. I sure as hell have tried to make up for that by being two parents in one… You just caught me on a bad month… or year. It's been a wild ride for the last year or two."

"Growing pains," I assure him.

Holden has a serious look when his eyes greet mine. Maybe for a moment I think it's appreciation. "I should probably go."

It's nice not being alone for a night, but I follow his cues because we need to keep this simple. "Yep."

Neither one of us moves.

There's a tension that can't be ignored.

Then he throws the sheets off us. "Fuck it. One more time."

I giggle as we head into another round.

Meaningless sex is not new to me. You just have clear guidelines, and when it runs its course, then you move on. Except staying and working with the man while you enjoy mind-blowing sex?

That's new.

And I'm not sure about the rules or limits.

Even worse, I've been known to only accept intuition when it's too late.

8

———

LEXI

———

Grabbing my glass of orange juice, I notice Lori and Harry looking at me strangely. Is it because they sense that their father did dirty things to me? He just arrived and went straight to the coffee pot. We aren't obvious. We are putting in effort to be the opposite. That's how passion can work in a platonic way. You can switch it off when needed.

Why are his kids quiet? Hmm.

Bringing the juice to my lips, I take a sip and nearly gag. I swallow with great difficulty while his kids laugh hysterically. "Oh God, what the hell?" Holden whips his sight to me to see what's happening. "There is tabasco sauce in here." Seems my suspicion of spiked coffee was a misjudgment, and I should have given care to other beverages.

In unison, Holden and I snap our eyes to his kids, knowing who the culprits are. He begins to shake his head as his mouth tightens.

"This again?" Stern-voice Holden, here we come.

"Again?" I croak out.

Harry shrugs. "It's a classic move."

Holden drags his hand across his jaw. "Great way to start the day." He takes the juice from my hand and walks to the sink to pour it down the drain. "I'm sorry, Lexi. I thought they got the memo that you are *not* the nanny." His kids receive a serious warning glare. "You don't do this when your aunt stays here. Lexi is a house guest, so treat her the same."

"But she seems like she can handle it," Lori explains before bringing a spoon of cornflakes to her mouth.

"Doesn't mean you won't say sorry because A) it's not cool, and B) how am I supposed to ask her to do me a solid and drop you two off at school because I need to meet with my accountant?"

"It's fine, really. I'll just start a tab at Jolly Joe's, and they can send it to you, since I have a feeling that I'll be eating a lot of safe breakfasts there."

Holden looks at me with pleading eyes. "Deal. But I need to ask…" His face squinches.

I sigh. "Fine. I'll take your little criminals and bring them in their chariot to school."

He smirks and brings his hands together in prayer. "Thank you. I owe you one." The glint in his eyes informs me that there is some innuendo there.

I have to ignore it if I want a chance to get on with my day. "Okay, shall we go in five minutes? I need to grab my laptop," I tell the kids.

"Fine," Lori groans.

Won't this be a fun ride.

———

ARRIVING at Lake Spark Academy after a quiet drive, since Lori had earplugs in and Harry seemed to be reading something on his tablet, the conversation was simple, actually minimal, except the random pointing out a deer or sign about the upcoming market. Apparently, Harry loves a good market churro stand too.

Coming to a halt in the drop-off lane, I shiver from the mom holding the sign. She looks like she's completely on a power trip with her ability to call us all out for stopping too long.

Easing up the line after the lady waves for me to continue, before I barely brake, Lori is already unbuckling. "Thanks, houseguest." Now she's just teasing me, which seems hopeful for no future pranks.

"Have a good day. I think your dad is picking you up for figure skating."

"I don't have skating today. I have ballet." She slams the door then hurries to a group of girls waiting on the sidewalk.

I glance over my shoulder to see that Harry isn't so eager to exit. "Enjoy school," I tell him, giving him the clue that now is the time to head out of my car.

He sighs deeply and opens the door. "Yeah, sure. Thanks, houseguest." I guess that's my new name.

Now he's off, and I can head straight to Jolly Joe's because I'm starving, and I need carbs because screw my health kick. I've found myself in a situation that is beyond normal. Probably, I should avoid adding houseguest to my name before this turns into a muddled mess with Holden that I willingly agreed to.

Driving off, I glance in my rearview mirror and notice Harry walking slowly before two boys come up to him, and my stomach churns when I see them shove him. They clearly are not friends.

I shouldn't involve myself. Harry and Lori must already

be confused by my presence, but Holden really does seem desperate when it comes to them.

"No, Lexi, don't do it," I mumble to myself aloud. But that's only a mere second before I decide fuck it, bullying is bullying.

I slam the brakes and swing open my door, not a care in the world that I'm blocking the car line of fearful drivers at the mercy of the traffic cop. As I storm over to Harry, I hear the traffic lady yelling at me to move, but I don't care.

On my approach, I hear one boy. "You should be good at hockey like your dad, but instead you're weird. You shouldn't even be here. This is a sports school, weirdo."

I arrive and place my hand on Harry's shoulder who is staring at the ground. "Everything okay here, boys?"

The two boys look at me strangely. "We were just telling our friend that science class will be great later, weren't we?"

Before Harry can answer, I pull him back closer to me. "Sure you were." My skepticism is in full force.

In my peripheral view, I see another mom arrive, and her tight dress is distracting. I can't even imagine what the guys from the high school football team must think. "Everything okay here? My son and his friends are just speaking with Harry." She throws me a fake bright smile.

"Yeah, sure. These little youngsters over here are holding up the values of Lake Spark Academy to the highest standard." My disapproval runs strong.

The lady holds her hand out to shake. "I'm Kate McClearly, I don't believe we've met."

That name rings a bell, not sure why, but my weariness is on alert. "A pleasure." I'm sarcastic and don't offer her my hand.

Her hand falls, and her face screws up. "You must be the new childcare for the West kids."

"I am not." I don't bat a lash.

"Oh?" She wasn't expecting my answer.

Harry speaks up. "She's my dad's houseguest."

Yikes, that came out with many ways to interpret.

Kate straightens her posture, clearly agitated. "I didn't realize that Holden has a new… *friend*."

I just stare at her and keep my face straight. "Shall we focus on these boys with demon qualities?"

Her jaw drops. "Demons is a little harsh, considering the children that you must be around as Holden's…. guest," she says rather dryly.

I keep my hands on Harry's shoulders to stay calm. "So, what about those Academy values? Would you like me to find the principal to discuss these boys' exemplary behavior or would you prefer to talk to these boys about showing kindness and respect?"

She brings her hair to her side. "We know how boys are at this age. It's just a little back-and-forth."

"If that's what you would like to tell yourself due to your bad parenting, then by all means repeat that mantra. Wait…" I snap my fingers. "Aren't you the mom that Lori had words with?"

Kate's face shades with disdain. "Yes, my daughter is in her class, and it was Lori who exemplified bad parenting." Her smile is now contrite.

"Okay, maybe she didn't say the right things, but she didn't shove you. So swallow your pride about your child's shitty behavior and take the high road, lady."

She gasps, and I notice kids and a group of moms congregating around us. "You have some nerve. You do one school drop-off and now you are the expert of these fine students at our school?"

I bring a hand to my hip as Harry walks to Lori who joined the circle. "Let me guess, you're a PTA mom."

"Head of it, actually."

"Great. So do something about your son and his friend. "

"They are being kids." She raises her voice.

I shake my head. "Doesn't make it okay. So please rein in your son and his friend, because I'm sure Harry's dad would love to chat about this with the principal."

"I'm sure Holden and I could discuss this without the need of the principal." That thought seems to excite her.

I roll my eyes. "I'm sure he will be busy." Her mouth gapes open, and again the interpretation of my words do not give me points. "I think these kids should get to class. Education and all, don't ya think?"

Kate just holds me in a death stare, but I take a moment to glance to my side and see Harry steps out of the way close to Lori, her fingers feathering his elbow, and I'm sure I see the corner of her mouth twitch in approval. I know they can stand up for themselves, but maybe they need to know that someone else will too.

"Go on, get to class. Your dad will pick you up," I offer Harry, and flash Lori a comforting look.

The crowd disperses, except Kate who stays put in her snooty stance. She can't say anything because traffic mom arrives. "You need to move your car, otherwise I will give you a parking ticket."

I look at her, bewildered. "As in a fake ticket, considering your only power is your sign?"

She straightens her shoulders. "We're allowed to give tickets; this is private property."

I look between them. "Shove it."

I blow out a breath and stop when an older woman blocks my way. She doesn't look happy. "I don't think we've met. I'm

Principal Johnson, and perhaps we should have a chat." The moms behind me try to cover their satisfied looks.

Studying the principal's face, I close my eyes for a second, cursing internally.

Shit.

———

WALKING INTO THE DIZZY DUCK, I see Holden waiting for me. He is leaning against the front desk with ankles and arms crossed, wearing a stern look. It makes me feel uneasy if I'm honest.

"Someone is in trouble. The principal phoned, and to my surprise, it's not because of my kids, which is refreshing."

Oh. He's already aware.

I step forward, ready to defend my actions. "I'm sorry, but those two little punks were being such an ass to your son. I couldn't just drive away like nothing happened. His mom just glared at me with disapproval and words of stupidity." I hold my finger up. "I'm like 100% sure she is more pissed that I was there on your behalf, ruining her chances to get in your pants if she plays her cards right."

Holden just stares at me with his lips pressed together. He isn't saying anything, why isn't he saying anything?

My eyes search the room to see if I'm making a scene. Stuart just pretends to be reading mail, and Holden seems to be enjoying his current state of hanging this situation over my head.

But then his stern phase vanishes into thin air as he uncrosses his body to step in my direction. He reaches out his fingertips, and they land on my shoulders to square me off.

"Thank you," he simply states. We agree that I'm not the villain. "I'm happy you did what you did. I want to throttle a few people, but it seems you put them in their place. Most of all, you were watching out for my son."

I gently loll my head to the side, trying to avoid his praise. "It was nothing."

"It was everything." His appreciation is apparent.

"I-I… He's a good kid. You raised a sweet boy."

Holden rubs my shoulders as he half smiles. "Thanks. Maybe I needed to hear that before I storm into the principal's office tomorrow."

I grin. "Uh-oh, someone is going to get it."

"Maybe you too but in a different way."

Now that twisting ache begins to form at full force between my legs, but maybe I should throw in caution. "Don't you have work to do? I should really focus on a few orders of accessories, and I'm not sure where we're going, but… we should tread carefully."

Holden steps back, not thrilled with my sentence. "Maybe you're right."

"I'm sorry if I caused problems. I'm not sure why you send them there."

He tilts his head to the side. "They have had a few tough times lately with select kids, and the principal isn't thrilled with those kids, either. But for the most part it's a positive place, hence why the principal keeps reiterating values to all of us. Harry loves the science club where he has close friends, and Lori has some great friends she coordinates her daily outfits with. You've just caught us all on a bad week or two. Besides, my donations kind of shut everyone up when needed and gets me out of the parents auction too."

That part I can see him doing. "As long as you feel everyone is happy, then…"″

Holden steps forward and plants his finger over my lips.

"Shh, you were calm compared to what I would do. I bet you are kind of hot riled." His finger drops.

"Now that would land you in detention for sure," I respond. He gently shakes his head, and my lips roll in as I do my best to avoid his gaze. "See ya later."

But as I walk away, I still feel his eyes on me.

———

RUBBING the back of my neck, I try to focus, but it's useless as I work in my room office. Maybe I should just take a few hours off, get some fresh air, pack my bags, and return to the Dizzy Duck on a longer basis. I groan from the situation that spins around me. I took another step to intertwine with Holden's life, and I shouldn't have.

The knock on the door breaks my thoughts. I go to open it, and as soon it's even a crack ajar, it's pushed open, with Holden charging for me and slamming the door behind him.

No words before his lips are on me, hands hoisting me up by the hips to encourage me to hold on. I'm in this moment with all previous doubts now dispersed into history. My inner inhibitions win.

We don't break our kiss, even when he lets go with one arm, and I hear him clear the desk with his arm with items falling to the floor. He plops me down on the wood as we tear at one another's clothes, as if we're two lovers who haven't seen each other in years, though it's only been 72 hours since the last time he made me weak underneath him.

"Fuck everything. I'm starving for you." His fingers hurry up under my skirt, and I try to yank him closer to unclasp his belt.

My breath grows heavy, and my face burns as he kisses my neck, with his fingers touching my pussy.

"Don't stop," I plead.

Holden slithers down my body, throwing me a mischievous warning. "No plans to. I need to taste you before I fuck you so hard that the people on the other side of the wall will question if there's an earthquake."

I gasp, desperate for it all.

HOLDEN

This isn't good. Well, this is kind of *excellent*.

But no, I shouldn't be crossing our lines again, but Lexi can handle the reality that we're only two people who have needs and her brazen attitude does something to me. Add in the hint of her caring nature toward my kids, then I'm a man in a crazed state.

I'm on my knees then jerk her forward so she's on the edge of the desk. Everything is happening fast, but we're both feral in demanding each other. I wobble one step to ensure my mouth aligns with her cotton panties. Most guys hate cotton, but on Lexi, it blasts away any impressions of innocence. It doesn't present any obstacles to slide the fabric to the side either.

My mouth prints kisses along her silky skin while her hands run wild through my hair.

"I wanted to do this more to you the other night," I husk when my eyes jump up to check in.

Her sly smirk shows approval. "You were rather disappointing on that front."

Now she's just toying with me, which is why I bite her

inner thigh, and she yelps. "I would spank you right now, but I need to lick your glistening pussy that clearly doesn't look disappointed when I'm around."

Lexi hums a laugh as her body rocks in my direction. The tip of my tongue licks a taste, and she's fucking luscious. I need so much more. I draw a slow teasing line from her entrance all the way to her clit. I hold her thighs wide and feast on her, with my tongue circling and my lips pressing. Adding a finger, I have her at my mercy.

"Fuck, Holden," she moans.

Another flick and I need to be inside of the woman. Fast and hard is the way I like it with her. Not that fucking has been a pattern for us, but maybe it's becoming one. I knock that thought out of my head, especially as Lexi begins to convulse and curses out my name. My tongue doesn't move, and instead I press until she comes down from her orgasm.

The moment she does, with her breath now rapid, I shuffle back on my knees with her wetness on my mouth. "On your knees."

"Whatever you say." She slides off the desk while I stand and unzip my pants where she had managed to already unbuckle me when our hands were roaming of their own accord.

Lexi's eyes appear eager to please, ensuring I'm staring down at her when her mouth begins to wrap around my length, slowly taking in more with her tongue firm underneath to join the journey.

I grab her hair to hold her the way I like it and to have control of her. Her decadent mouth drags from root to tip, sucking and pumping until she's in a rhythm that I'm guiding. She wraps her fingers around me and grips the base of my cock to give her ample playing field.

"That's it. Just like that. I'm sure you can take it a little deeper." I want to push her limits. Does that make me a selfish man?

A slight gag doesn't seem to bother her as she repeats several times, her mouth salivating and her muffled sounds of pleasure mumbling in her throat.

"Want my cum to slide down that throat of yours? You would take every drop, wouldn't you?"

She nods with her mouth full of my cock.

I'm in a dilemma, though, as I want that sassy mouth to make me come, but I need to be inside her pussy, and I'm not sure I have time for both.

"Sit on the desk," I instruct, and the loss of her mouth around my cock is anything but enjoyable, but in ten seconds, I will have something better. Lexi follows orders well, and I search for a condom in my wallet on the floor with my pants. I notice in the corner of my eye that Lexi's panties are at her ankles, and she kicks them off.

Returning to her, our hands run wild again when our mouths meld into a deep kiss, our tongues twisting around one another. We take a few seconds to soak in our kiss, only to part. I glance down to ensure the condom is on correctly, and I feel teeth scraping down my neck, only to latch onto some skin and bite.

"Fuck," I growl, but my grin doesn't fade, even when she sucks and sinks her teeth tighter. "You're a bad girl. Next time it will be extra spankings."

She throws her head back in laughter. "It's not punishment if I enjoy it, Holden," she taunts.

With my cock in one hand aligning to her center, my palm lands on my stinging neck. "Is this payback for going hard the other night?"

"Does it matter? Now fuck me."

She's my undoing. A perfect quick fuck, even if she leaves me longing for another round.

I enter her while our mouths steal each other's breath, moaning in sync from her pussy clenching around my cock. A few slow pumps, but then I'm at it like a wild animal, only encouraged by her legs wrapping tighter around me and the desk shaking on every thrust.

"Is this how you like it? Hard? Your craving pussy has been desperate for my cock since last time."

"Yes," she whispers.

"You touch yourself when I'm not around? Thinking of my cock?" I lock our eyes because I would be able to see a lie.

The corner of her mouth twitches. "Yes."

Slamming my lips down onto hers again, I bring her closer to my body until we are tightly wound and pumping together.

More. I need her deeper and to make her whimper.

"Come all over my cock, Lexi. Get what you fantasize about," I breathe into her neck as heat explodes in my body, traveling down to my navel, and I know what's impending.

My thumb finds her clit to help her ride the wave with me, and we both get what we need until it leaves us draped around one another with panting breaths.

"If that was a thank-you then I'm scared what will happen if I disobey." Her voice is a labored breath.

I chortle a growl. "You'll figure it out soon enough," I warn.

Because I'm adding another round with her. Not sure when, but it's on the horizon.

"Get me naked next time, will ya?"

Her snark makes me scoff. I wonder if she ever has a

moment where she's anything but a woman who takes things in stride with a smile.

Pulling out, I head to the bathroom to get rid of the condom, knowing damn well that I'm late for a meeting with the hotel manager for filling in her closing paperwork, with information for when she leaves.

It seems Lexi is also in a hurry. We both begin to throw on the few clothes that we took off. I should probably explain why I stormed in here.

"Hey, Lexi," I grab her attention, and she glances up from tucking her shirt into her skirt. "Thanks again. With Harry, I mean."

Her smile is simple. "No big deal." Because kindness is imprinted in her personality, so it's a normal day for her, I guess.

"I should get going," she says.

"Me too."

Then that's us.

A quick tryst, complete with no regrets.

"I'll head out and give you a second," I say.

Lexi doesn't seem to know what to say or do. "Yeah, sure, great."

I grin at her because she's kind of cute when flustered.

Leaving, I open the door, ensuring nobody gets a view of Lexi just royally fucked. I'm straightening my collar, feeling a little flushed myself.

"Holden?" I hear Stone's voice.

I glance up and freeze then gulp. "Oh, hey there."

"Uh, what are you doing?" He cocks his head to the side, and his face is puzzled. "Did someone bite your neck?"

Damn, that's a giveaway. I'll need to hide the evidence later.

I clear my throat as I cover the mark for a second, feeling the broken skin. "Just… a meeting."

"You know I'm not buying that." He grins as he leans against the wall, crossing his arms, waiting for a better explanation.

I do my best to avoid his gaze, and my jaw flexes, but he's a good friend, so what the hell. "You know how we have that new interior designer for the hotel?"

"To get rid of that ridiculous moose head, yeah. Lexi, your former coach's daughter."

I tightly smile. "Exactly. I might have…"

The door swings open right on cue. "I'm off, need to meet with the tile guy." Lexi is smoothing her blouse, completely oblivious to our spectator. Then she stops in her tracks.

"Oh, hi." She frowns.

"You remember Stone?" I awkwardly ask, because of course they know one another, even ran into each other a few days ago.

"Yeah, for sure." She attempts to give him a polite smile. "Nice to see you again. I'm not here. Have a great day." She is quick to walk away.

Shit, forgot to ask something about the kids. "Don't forget that my daughter has figure skating practice after school," I call out.

She mumbles a sound and doesn't even give me any attention. "It's Tuesday, so she doesn't, and how many times do I have to remind you that I'm not your nanny?"

"Yeah, but that was the deal when you moved in," I remind her.

She grumbles again before disappearing into the elevator.

My lips push out, and my head tilts because, damn it, despite these circumstances, I still have time to check out her ass. I'm not even trying to hide it. I swing my tight smile to Stone, and he still seems to enjoy my quandary.

"Someone has something to explain."

A long breath escapes me. "I might have… blackmailed her into living with me for a bit."

His eyes bug out. "Wow, she's really getting the five-star treatment on the personal-attention front."

I rub my face. "*Yeah*, so we might be encountering a little problem with that…"

"As in…" He encourages me to continue.

"I didn't exactly blackmail her, more a favor owed. We lost another nanny and needed some help. Not my fault Lexi tried to buy alcohol way back, and she needed Prince Charming to save her. Alas, favor now owed."

"So, she's living with you?" Stone seems confused, as he should be.

I bobble my head side to side. "Yeah. Just to help out every now and then until I can find another solution for my lovely kids."

He gives me a knowing look. "Just so happens you added other favors…"

I laugh to myself. "Can you blame me? She has good banter, and she's hot. We both know what it is. Nothing around the kids either. It's just some fun. I need to destress, and she's the golden ticket."

Stone brings his fingers to his jaw, thinking for a hard long second. "Uh… I give it a few weeks before this blows up in your face. You don't let women around Lori and Harry. Let alone take up residence in the guesthouse."

Shit. My face stills, and I say nothing.

The problem with close friends is they see straight through you. "Yes?" It drags out.

"Guest *room*, the guest room," I correct him, and his eyes widen. "Water problem in the guesthouse."

"Really? This just got complicated. The only way this could get worse is if you turned off the water on purpose or something." He huffs a laugh.

And face freezing moment number two.

Stone's jaw drops. "No fucking way. You turned off the water, didn't you?"

I step forward. "Keep your voice down," I hush him as I scan the hall. "That part she doesn't know."

"Are you a little psychotic? I mean, we've all known that you have wild ways. You're the guy who hands out candy to the kids and alcoholic beverages to the parents during trick-or-treating. You're also an impulsive guy. But why the hell would you do that?" He raises his voice.

I comb my hands through my hair. "Honestly? No clue, other than that woman seems to have possessed me to do crazy things. Hence, why I called in a favor due to a ridiculous bar napkin. And her appeal doesn't exactly lose any points either."

Stone blinks his eyes a few times. "Seriously, Holden, first-glance connections can raise a flag of caution to what you think is a simple situation. Harlow and I were an instant attraction, and here I am with a fiancée."

I take us out of my lecture. "Fiancée, eh? That's great, man." I knew he was going to ask soon; I guess the time came.

He looks elated. "Yeah, she said yes." He sounds so happy, but then his look falters. "Now back to you. This is my warning that feelings are brewing behind a wall that you didn't realize you have. On the other hand..." His lips quirk out. "You seem kind of content despite your hooligans stressing you out. I'm also assuming you've thought about the kids, so… why not. Have fun with whatever odd game this is." Stone gives up.

I rub my temples. "I should consider your sound wisdom… but I won't. Let me ride this situation out while I ride her. When it begins to get gray, then we'll bench this and be done. We can be friends. She and I both know the score."

"Sure, you do." He doesn't sound convinced.

My phone dings, and I bring the screen up to see that I'm five minutes late because I'm standing in a hall discussing my predicament that I think I'm kind of addicted to.

I've always been a little reckless, and it's been a damn while since I've allowed myself to enjoy that trait.

"Really gotta head out. Tell Harlow congrats." I begin to walk away.

"Will do. Let me know when you need a beer to reflect on your situation like a normal human soul," he calls out.

I flex my neck before straightening my shoulders. "It will be fine."

My phone chimes again, and this time I see a calendar reminder for an upcoming business dinner. They are really into making it a family affair, hence why they want Lori and Harry present.

That might be a headache.

So let me just add asking Lexi to attend as another check-mark on my list of things I probably shouldn't do but will.

LEXI

Fumbling with the keys in my bag, I'm only aware that someone is behind me from the crunching of gravel on the ground of the Dizzy Duck parking lot.

"Where do you think you're going?" Holden is messing with me.

"Not that it's any of your business—okay, it might be, but I'm heading to an antique store about thirty minutes from here. It's only open a few days a week, and today just happens to be one of them." *Got them* I pull my keys out and turn to Holden who is smirking under this bright day with a cold nip that hits your skin with a chill.

Lines form on his forehead. "Really? For the Dizzy Duck?"

"No, my billion-dollar house on a tropical island," I deadpan.

He scoffs. "Can't believe you never told me about that. Kind of brokenhearted that you haven't given me an invite." For theatrics, he brings his palm to his heart.

My smile spreads wider as I move away from our playful chat. "But yes, for the inn."

Holden glances at his watch. "How long do you think you'll be?"

"Hmm, I don't know. Probably two hours or so, depends on what I find."

He steps forward and snatches my key fob. "Great. I have time, so let me drive us there."

I take in this change of events. "Drive us?"

He's already heading toward his SUV, expecting me to follow as he pulls his key out of his pocket and hits the unlock button without so much as checking over his shoulder. And, well, I've learned that I'm weak when it comes to his surprise plans.

"Antique stores are a new realm for me, and I have a bigger trunk if you want something. Plus, if it's for the inn, wouldn't you want my credit card?"

All logical. No way to counter.

"Valid points." I eagerly open the passenger side door.

The engine revs up, and he begins to press buttons on the dashboard. "Address, please."

I swipe my phone screen to draw up the address and show him, then he types everything in to the GPS. Off we go, and I'm still trying to grasp what the mood is between us. Friends with benefits means said friend can accompany you on one of your favorite activities, right?

"It's in an old barn that the owners spruced up. We most definitely don't need them, but they even have old wagons and barrels." My voice is cheerful to bring us to neutral topics.

Holden chuckles under his breath. "Then into the corn-fields we go."

"Could be wheat," I quip, and his head turns slightly in my direction, clearly amused. To avoid his eyes, I glance out the window and stare at the woods that circle the lake. The duck-crossing sign reminds me of this quaint town that is a special place for many. "Actually, Illinois is 75% farmland."

"Someone is studious."

"Nah, I just wondered once when I left the suburbs to see an old college friend and boredom kicked in after thirty miles with no change of scene. Unless you get off a highway and go to a small town that is along a river or freight railroad track. There is, of course, Route 66 which has its quirks."

He laughs as he keeps his hands steady on the wheel. "Ah, so you were a nerd by day and party girl by night all those years ago."

My head lolls to the side against the headrest to appraise him. "Eight years ago, to be exact, that's when you got your favor napkin, and yes, I'm highlighting that you're older yet not wiser," I joke.

"Watch it. I'm beginning to tally how many spankings you'll get next time."

Sprinkles of anticipation begin to burst throughout my body. "Looking forward to it."

The corners of his mouth tug in approval. "Let's focus on this drive, shall we?"

"Agreed." Otherwise, we might not make it there without stopping for a quickie in the back of his car.

Another half-hour goes by until we're driving onto the grass and dirt parking lot where only two other cars are stationed. We both hop out and walk side by side. Holden with curiosity and me feeling like a kid in a candy store.

My sight lands on the outside stand selling fresh carrots and asparagus. "Yum. What are the chances your kids would like those?"

"About 25%, maybe 45% if we slather a bunch of butter on it."

I swat his arm. "Then we shall try." Speeding up my

walk, I beeline it to the wagon with fresh apples and glass bottles of cider. This is fantastic, we can use the bottles after the cider is finished.

Holden watches with a blank look. "Didn't we come here for antiques in the large barn?" He steps forward and places his hand under my elbow to guide me away.

Throwing my finger over my shoulder, I reluctantly give up on my crusade, though I still point out the obvious. "But there's jam." I pout.

"Damn, you are like a woman possessed."

He manages to lead us, and we enter the barn where my exhilaration grows. Right away, I spot a few pieces that would be ideal for the inn. It doesn't take long for me to find myself next to a dresser, and my palm slides against the wood.

"This would be great for the large suite." I bend down to inspect further. "Need to re-sand and then paint it white, but it's perfect."

My eyes are unable to tear away from the furniture, but a blurry vision in my side eye shows me Holden picking up a jar and examining it purely to keep his hands busy.

"But there is only one, and we have several rooms," he points out.

I stand up, with my elation never fading on my face. "It doesn't matter, as each of the large suites will have their own feel. We're not going to be cookie-cutter, as every room will be distinctly different."

He sets the jar down, clearly entertained with my enthusiasm. "Who will be sanding it?"

"Me," I state proudly.

"You?"

My exploration goes on, and now it's Holden being

tugged along. "Yes. I sand and upholster all the time. I can even use a hammer."

He hisses a whistle. "Oh, hammering I'm aware you can do."

I throw him a fun glare. "Shall we focus?"

"How? You're all over the place. I'm scared you'll tell me the chest over there is the key to real treasure."

My eyes widen, and then I nearly run. "This one is great." I'm serious.

"Really?" His voice is unsure.

"Of course. Place it at the end of a bed." I set my hand on the curve of his shoulder. "You have great ideas," I add.

His face is purely confused. "I don't sense sarcasm in that." Holden pretends to search around him. "I should probably take you down a notch. Make out with you behind the long mirror over there?"

I step forward, coming face to face with Holden, calming down as my fingers gently crawl up his shirt along his chest. "Could be an option," I say, my sultry voice in full swing. Another step and his body rises to attention, and if we're not careful then his cock will join in. But then I drop the cruelty of leading him along by patting his chest before I return to business. "There are 1920's light fixtures over there, perfect for candles."

Holden groans and steps back. "Don't test me, Lexi. We have an entire ride back, and if we get bored of farmland, then we can stop so I can fuck you in the backseat."

I titter as I survey further. "So inappropriate, in public and in the presence of our elders too," I tease.

He laughs. "I don't think I'm ever going to forget today. On a scale of ridiculous yet entertaining, this, well…" His voice softens the end of his sentence, and it raises my attention, only to see a glint in his eyes. "It's nice. My mind has kind of shut off, and it's been a while."

Trapping my bottom lip between my teeth, I try to dissect his words and what they really mean. "I guess you've been busy with life," I begin, and he nods subtly once. "You're welcome. I guess this is an odd outing. There's even Amish furniture over in that corner that they brought up from central Illinois." I bounce my shoulders as I try to lighten the mood of his realization.

Our eyes hold, in a moment that lets go of the back and forth of our constant wit, and instead, we're soaking in a new atmosphere between us. But it's dangerous, and I'm not even sure that I've blinked.

"Well, how does this work?" Oh, he's going right into the *us* discussion. I nearly lose my balance. "Do we just pay and they can deliver?" A tinge of disappointment hits me when I realize he meant logistics of our outing.

"Uhm." I tuck a few strands behind my ear. "Yeah, we can do that." My returning smile might appear pleasant, but it feels weak to me. "But the asparagus, tomatoes, cider, and jam, plus the homemade bread that I saw, we can take in the car."

"Casually threw in the jam, didn't you?"

We're back to normal us. How we can already have a normal when it's only been two weeks since I entered his life? I'm not quite sure, but I've always been one to ride the flow between people. I'll just continue that.

———

TWO DAYS later after avoiding the man of the week, I return to Holden's for the day. The cleaner is exiting the front door after she finished her weekly visit, and her intense study of me is a bit daunting. I'm relieved with a faint line on her mouth appears before she moves on without any use of words.

"Goodbye to you too," I mumble.

I really need a snack; an afternoon boost is always key to continuing the day. The view of Harry working on his homework is a welcome scene.

"How's my favorite scientist?" I greet him.

His sight jumps up once before he returns to writing in his notebook. "Not bad. Math is too easy. We're working on decimals, but I've been a pro already for a year. I have stocks to maintain."

"What?" I sputter out.

"My stocks," he tells me, as if I'm an idiot.

"Can kids even buy stocks?" I'm now bewildered.

He shrugs. "Not exactly, but my dad set them up, and I just do the heavy work. A bummer that the NASDAQ has been down for two days."

My jaw drops open because this is a complete shock, and I mouth *what the fuck* to myself. What ten-year-old talks finance?

Shaking my head, I make a note to check the internet later about this phenomenon. My eyes drift down to where he's writing. "Cool, kids are still using a notebook these days."

He continues to write. "Oh, don't worry, this is only a list of companies that I'm interested in investing in if the dollar-euro exchange rate picks up. At school, we have to hand all homework in via our portal app. We're entirely digital. I mean, why would you use paper for that?" He shakes his head.

Holy shit, I feel ancient.

I can't handle that realization, and it's going to take a few hours before I recognize that I'm staying with a whiz kid.

This calls for a granola bar, a mini cake in a package, and I might throw in a small bag of crackers too.

Holden enters the kitchen, scruffing Harry's hair in passing. "What's up, kids?"

"You seem far too happy for my liking, there must be a catch." Lori arrives with her mundane tone, expressing that she heard her father.

Holden gives her a contrite smile. "And what if I am, no catch?"

Lori's eyes swim between Holden and me, trying to connect dots perhaps as her nose rises slightly before she drops her demeanor when she glances down at her phone.

Holden arrives next to me while I rip open a snack cake. "Your son has stocks," I say dryly.

His smile is beaming. "Great, huh? In a few years he can probably handle my entire portfolio." Is Holden joking? I'm not sure.

"Right. So, uhm, hey, the delivery from the antique barn arrived." I survey the room and feel that leaving to get another round of fresh air seems like the way to go. "Tomorrow I'll be sanding, so I'm going to run to the hardware store to pick up gloves and a sander. You guys have a yummy dinner."

"You're not joining us?" Does Holden sound kind of disappointed or am I losing my mind?

"Nah, I'm dying for a little quiet time to search the latest blogs for trends while I gulp down a milkshake and maybe throw in a salad."

He stuffs his hands into his pocket. "Oh, yeah, sure. Quiet time."

"Yep. Off I go." My feet are glued to the wood while Holden and I are stuck in a trance.

"Completely ready to get in my car and check off that list."

Blinking a few times, he blows out a breath. "Let me walk you out. I may need to move my car so you can back up. Not enough space maybe."

"Of course." My lips twitch, as I'm not sure how to act right now with extra pairs of eyes on me.

My awkward attempt to leave leads us outside, staring at my car, both of us with hands in our pockets, me in a coat and Holden in jeans. "I guess the cars are good. I did get home after you, as you were well aware of back in the kitchen," I note.

We both continue to look straight forward at our cars. "I did perhaps know that."

A long pause again, the fifth now, but who's counting?

"I heard the ducks are a killer this time of day." *Yikes*, I realize what I just said. "I mean, not that we want to kill the ducks. Or rather they aren't getting killed, just they over-power the roads in the masses, and we have to stop every quarter of a mile because they normally travel with baby ducks as a family," I ramble.

"Yep, those ducks." His tone is neutral.

I roll my eyes because this conversation is a cover for other things.

"Lexi?"

"Yes, housemaster?" My tone is simple.

Even after our assurance that our cars haven't moved, our standstill continues. "I want to kiss you right now and bend you over the hood of your car."

I chortle. "Thought so. Because I'm sure you've read my mind."

"Another time then."

"Indeed, another time. Not when we have little eyes at the

window behind us." The one moment I slightly tilted my head to the side, I saw them in my vision.

He chuckles. "Thought that would be the case. Have fun enjoying your moment of solitude."

"I'm beginning to think solitude is overrated."

That is what breaks our standoff, and we at last turn to one another with wry smiles.

"My chaos of a life is growing on you." He tries to suppress his smile.

"Maybe." Because truly I am unsure, or rather scared that he is right.

His lips push out, and he thinks for a moment. "Be careful. And that's a warning to us both."

HOLDEN

I watch Stuart behind the front desk opening boxes with a box cutter. I'm not sure what surprise will be in this box.

The lobby is looking great, and in the banquet hall, the floors were spruced up with polish, which meant we had to use the patio doors by the restaurant to let the few guests we have in. It's not exactly an issue since the view of the dock and lake are some of the best in Lake Spark, unless you're hiking up in the small hills. But now with the floors done and the walls receiving a new paint color, I imagine furniture can be placed by the end of the week.

Lexi has been busy, which is why we haven't seen one another much the past few days, which is strange considering she's in my guest room. That's probably for the best, so my brain and dick can cool down.

"I think these are sheets," he guesses.

I assess the contents of the box and see the packaged linens. White with a lace pattern. Huh, not my choice, but I will trust the designer's take, as I promised before I realized my interior designer was a woman who sucks cock well.

The sound of two women giggling hits my ears. I glance up to see Lexi gently touching Summer's arm as they walk into the lobby.

"Oh, hey." Lexi smiles when her eyes lift up to greet me.

I step in their direction as Lexi twists her hair and uses the elastic around her wrist to tie it back. Summer… just observes me with a crooked smile. Of course, she knows what new hobby I've started.

"What are you ladies up to?" I play it cool and pull out my phone to have a quick peek and to appear calm and cool.

Summer clears her throat. "Lexi was just showing me one of the finished bedrooms, then we stole a cookie or two that just came from the oven. I love how, hammers aside, the Dizzy Duck is still upholding their fresh warm cookie tradition."

Actually, she doesn't seem to be covering up what they were probably talking about… me. They probably did nab a cookie.

Lexi and I share a gaze again, with our eyes lingering for a few seconds. "There are…" I scratch the back of my neck. "Sheets that arrived."

Her fingers drop from her ponytail, and she claps her hands together in excitement. "That was fast."

"Dated the hotel sheet supplier too?" I quip.

Summer looks between us, and her lips roll in to keep her laugh in.

Lexi doesn't seem fazed by my comment. "Nah, the woman on the other end mentioned you two go way back, so thanks for that," she rebuffs.

Love her little fabrications. It always leads to her face creating a portrait of pure trouble.

"Lucky us then. Anyhow, we need to talk sheets."

Both the women's brows furrow. "I think this is my cue to leave," Summer awkwardly mentions.

I turn my attention to Summer, ignoring the atmosphere that is boiling into a need for me to push Lexi against a wall. "Have you thought more about that job? To be honest, I doubt I'm going to get anyone new in the coming month or two. The job market is slow around here."

"I'm still in the appraisal of staff treatment phase, but thanks, Holden, for keeping me in mind." She smiles warmly at me.

"Any time."

"Well, bye, you two. Good luck with whatever is going… I mean, sheets. Have fun with serious sheet discussion."

I grin. "Towels are somewhere in that conversation too."

Summer smiles then leaves us be. Lexi and I watch her walk away, but the feeling of Lexi's arm grazing mine brings my thoughts back to her.

"I might give her a good recommendation on your boss skills in your effort to recruit," she mentions. I choose not to answer, and I press my lips together as a long pause floats between us. "So, sheets? Is there a problem?" She trails away.

"They're white," I say bluntly as I follow her behind the desk.

"And? You've signed off on it. White with colored pillows. What's wrong?"

I watch her examining a package. "I do trust you, but can't you see every little thing on white?"

"As in?" She stares at me, waiting for an explanation. "A lot of hotels use white. Makeup comes off in the housekeeping laundry, and if red wine is spilled then we have backups. The mood is more important than concern for wine or any other bodily fluid, if that's where your mind is at."

The painter walking by coughs into his arm, clearly

having heard. I turn slightly to ensure nobody else is in an earshot then give Lexi a warning grimace, but she seems not very concerned.

"You just took us down a very inappropriate route."

She smiles tightly as she crosses her arms over her chest. "And you love it." I roll my eyes. "But seriously, is this really an issue? The curtains will match the throw pillows, as will the candles. That's going to be a great splash of color."

"Candles in bedrooms, as in a hotel room?" My voice nearly breaks. "That's a fire hazard that I'm not sure we can get rid of."

"No, Holden, those are the touches couples want when they stay here for an expensive room and romance. This isn't a big hotel, and although there are many great things here, such as the spa and lake, it's still a boutique hotel, and as such should have the qualities of a traditional inn, even with a cabin feel, including candlelight. This is the land of Lincoln and prairies, after all."

"Okay, fine." I give up on our discussion. "You have some valid points."

"Great." Her bubbly voice returns. She kicks the box to slide it along the floor. "I'll ask one of the guys to move this to the design headquarters, otherwise known as the spare bedroom of indecency, which is an HR nightmare should I work here on a regular basis."

Her wit never fades, and I love that.

"I would offer to carry the box, but I need to change and head to Catch 22." The other great restaurant in Lake Spark. It may not have won awards, but it's still a decent evening that is worthy of frequent visits.

Lines form on her forehead. "Eating at the competition again?"

I chuckle and pull my phone out of my pocket to keep myself

occupied with checking my inbox. "I don't want to show this place until the final touches are in place. It's a meeting with an old sponsor, he's in hotel development. Old money who potentially wants to invest in opening an inn similar to the Dizzy Duck elsewhere. He wants to have dinner with my kids included, as he seems to be into wholesome and doubts a former pro-athlete is on the straight and narrow. I thought of asking you to come but then realized that I'm pushing the limits on the not-a-nanny quota."

Her laugh sounds good. How can anyone not enjoy the melody? "That's very true. Could be a great opportunity for you, and if you need an interior designer…" She splays her hands out.

"You'll be the first I ask," I assure her.

Her eyes glint at me, unsure of where to carry our conversation. She slouches a bit as she ponders her thoughts. "I don't want to intervene, so it's better that you bring your very-well-behaved offspring who most definitely will not be bored at the dinner."

I groan at the reminder of my wonderful children who I adore but know this might not be easy. "Thanks." I recoil.

"I kind of want to have an early night, as there's a flea market tomorrow between here and Bluetop."

My lips push out as I understand her logic. "Sure, of course." I'm still slightly disappointed, though. "If you change your mind, then well…"

"I know." Lexi takes a step forward to touch my arm. "Good luck, Holden. My fingers are crossed for you."

"For the meeting or my kids?"

"Both."

Her smile as she parts from our encounter is so incredibly platonic and caring. Because despite her wicked ways, she has heart. Not often do you come across that combination.

WE'RE SITTING at Catch 22 next to the big windows, displaying the dark sky, as we pass around a basket of bread. I glance to my side to see my kids less than pleased to be here. They've dressed up when all they want is to be in jeans, and they're counting down in their head until this dinner will be over. This isn't the first time we've done this. I used to have a lot of meetings with sponsors, but now they're a little older, so saying they can play on their tablets while the adults talk doesn't exactly work.

Ordering their kiddie cocktails with extra cherries only brought me five seconds of hope.

I get it. I do.

I'm able to give them a great life through love… but also money that provides them many things.

"Into hockey, Harry?" John Colbie asks my son. John is in his sixties and as honest and genuine as you can get. That's how I've always remembered him. He's very much a family man, too.

Harry looks up almost in fear of disappointment. "No. I enjoy music."

"Ah, music isn't half bad. It's never too late to start ho—" His attention hops up to behind me.

"Sorry I'm late, I told Holden I couldn't make it but moved some things around." Lexi's voice and her hand landing on the back of my chair is a welcome relief.

When I turn to smile my appreciation, I bite my lip. Because she arrived in a dark red sweater dress with knee-high boots. It's completely appropriate, but the shape of the fit captures the attention of every man sitting in this room.

A bombshell with snark. Lucky me.

Now it's not just my kids counting down the time until this dinner is complete.

12

LEXI

I shouldn't involve myself. I shouldn't even be here. I most definitely need to tamp down my free spirit that seems to want to explore situations that I've never been in.

Still, I'm standing behind Holden with a polite smile coating my face for a man across the table as old as my dad, and Lori and Harry are staring at me peculiarly from around the circular table. But when Holden offers me a faint smile, a mixture of surprise and gratitude, then I know why I'm here. He didn't ask outright, but I could sense that this night might be better for him if I was here. Such a crazy impression considering whatever we're doing.

"Lexi." Holden stands, ready to offer introductions. "John, this is Lexi, our interior designer at the Dizzy Duck. I thought she would be a useful addition to the discussion and your ideas." Holden pulls the chair between him and Harry out like a gentleman, multi-tasking while indicating to the waiter for an extra wine glass for me. Holden and John already opened a bottle and are halfway through a glass of white.

"It's so nice to have you join us. I can't wait to see the end result at the Dizzy Duck. I hear there will be a big grand opening. Holden did share some preliminary photos, and I enjoy what I see." John seems pleasant. I could imagine Lori and Harry wouldn't find him riveting, but these days some folks just brush off any extras to the conversation in favor to talk purely business.

"I'm sure you must be excited for the prospect of another inn. Will it have a spa too?" I attempt to insert myself into the conversation, but really, I am interested too.

Holden's eyes find their way back to me. "No spa, but he mentioned a pool. He wants it to be more family friendly."

"You should have human-sized Jenga blocks," Harry pipes up.

"As opposed to alien-sized blocks? We're all human," Lori snipes.

Holden smiles nervously. "I think what Harry means is large, outside-sized blocks," he attempts, to defuse his kids' bickering.

John chuckles. "That's a great idea, Harry. This is why I wanted you here. I have a lot of grandkids, but they all live out in Colorado."

"Well, wonderful kids are here," Holden gushes. He has hard times with them, but he also relishes every moment he's in. That's the balance of fatherhood, right?

My wine glass arrives, and Holden pours from the bottle. I take a sip, noting to pace myself, since I drove here. "Don't let my arrival disrupt wherever you were discussing," I say. I use taking a sip of my drink as a cover for the fact that there are fingers swirling over my thigh under the table—fingers that aren't mine. A pleasurable ache spreads down my skin.

"We should talk about timelines of what you're thinking," Holden suggests to John.

"I'll be back, going to the bathroom," Lori excuses herself, and nobody takes much notice.

I wink at Harry who picks at his bread roll out of boredom. Grabbing the basket next to him, I offer him one more, but he shakes his head to decline. More for me, I'm a little famished. I search for the butter because who wants a bread roll without it?

"A year and half could maybe be realistic, depending on the construction," Holden discusses, and I clearly missed part of the conversation.

"Are you building from the ground up?" I wonder, as that's quite a project.

John shakes his head. "Oh no, dear, I'm on the search for a historical property. It will probably need a lot of renovations."

My whole body lights up. "Historical buildings are the best for charm. But you mentioned family friendly, which means you would for sure need to be cautious of interior choices."

"No candles in bedrooms," Holden volleys.

My sight whips in his direction, and a mischievous smile ghosts on his face, with his eyes narrowing on me, almost a message to prepare myself for being devoured or spanked later.

They continue their conversation, and after a few more minutes, I notice that Lori has been gone a while. Probably made an escape. Still, I should probably check, as John and Holden seem to be lost in numbers.

I quietly excuse myself and make my way to the restroom. When I open the door, it's quiet, too quiet considering I didn't come across Lori on my travels here. Walking in, I check the lock signs by the knobs of the stalls and see all are open except one. Bending over, I see Lori's shoes and hear a sniffle.

Oh no. Tears. I don't do well with tears. It makes me either cry like a waterfall or become dry as an alligator. There is no middle ground. It always depends on the person.

I bring my knuckles to the door. "Knock, knock, the houseguest I haven't figured out if you like or hate is here," I announce.

"Go away," she says, her voice muffled.

My face screws up, aware that I'm going to have to reach her chip by chip. "No can do. The table conversation is kind of boring, and you seem to have found a great hiding place."

"It's a toilet," she deadpans.

Well, her mood is still the same. That's a start.

"I might as well freshen up my makeup. Want some lipstick?" I offer and meander to the mirror to color my lips.

"Your lipstick doesn't match my dress."

I twist up the stick. "Good point. I ordered the chicken Alfredo. You ordered before I got here. Did you order that or go for the chicken breast with potato?"

"Go away." Her voice is even more disgruntled.

"Not a good idea if I do. Otherwise, I have to tell your dad that you're crying in the bathroom—"

"Don't," she cuts me off.

My eyes meet my reflection in the mirror, congratulating myself for grabbing her attention enough that I can stay. "Okay, then are you not feeling well?"

It's a long silence, but then I hear the click of her door, and it opens slightly. I turn my body to see what her next move is, but nothing happens.

"Do you... you... have something?"

I step forward. "Uh, what do you mean?"

"Something. You know, *something*."

I circle my eyes as I try to decode, and then it hits me. "Oh, I—yeah." I begin to search my purse. "I think I have a tampon."

"I…" Lori sounds petrified.

Then it dawns on me again. "Is this your first time by chance?"

Another sniffle, and I have my answer. I flinch and my body tightens. It's her first period and she's stuck with me in a bathroom. I wasn't prepared for this, nor was she.

"I think it's better if we get you a pad, let me think." I'm beginning to panic because I don't see anything around. Stay calm, Lexi. Do it for the almost thirteen-year-old who is going through a major life event. "I know." I lift a finger in the air. "Let's break out of this place. I have my car here, and we'll tend to important matters instead of listening to an old guy talk about hotel stuff."

The door to her stall opens even further, and her red face seems to accept that this is our only option, and she nods gently.

A line stretches on my mouth in support for her before I search my bag for the key to my car. "Here." I hand it to her.

"Please… don't tell him why we're leaving."

I zip my lips with my fingers. "I won't," I promise.

Okay, it seems the waterfall tears want to form, but I remain defiant and hold them in for her, and she snatches the keys and walks away. This is a big moment for her, and she must be scared. There isn't a woman in her life, but somehow the universe decided it should be shared with me.

Once I can't see Lori, I let out a deep breath that I think I need because I'm surprised we both survived that scene.

Gathering myself for a few ticks, I head straight back to the table.

Holden looks at me with concern and seems to be searching for Lori. "Where is my daughter?"

I lean down with one hand on the back of his chair and the other on the table to ensure I'm only in his earshot. "I think this is a perfect guys' night. Lori and I will be leaving."

"She hasn't even had dinner yet?" Holden doesn't sound pleased.

I smile tightly to him. "Trust me, okay?" I mumble under my breath. His brows lift, not impressed. "Holden, we're leaving." I'm firm in my tone that only he can hear.

He examines my face, only to read the message in my eyes that I'm putting my foot down and he has no choice but to accept it. "Sure. I'll bring home a doggy bag."

I stand and give the table a wide smile. "Forgotten homework, right?" I lift my shoulders.

"It's Saturday," Harry points out.

Geez, can anyone at this table just let it go?

"John, although brief, it was nice to meet you. I'm sure we will cross paths again."

He stands and sets his napkin on the table. "Of course. I'll be sure to get your details from Holden."

I smile in appreciation and turn, only to lock eyes one last time with Holden who has an unusual stare that's new to me.

It's fine. He should enjoy his dinner because I have a feeling he might freak out later.

———

I FIDDLE my thumbs as I lean over the kitchen counter when I hear Holden and Harry arrive home.

"Head upstairs, and I'll say goodnight soon," I hear him tell his son, followed by feet thumping up the stairs.

I dread what's coming, but Holden will figure it out. My

eyes lift when he slowly saunters my way, half pissed and the other half lost.

"You owe me a few explanations. That was one abrupt exit for an important meeting. What has my daughter done now?"

I grab the bottle of wine that I had opened and drag it my way, but then second-guess myself and slide it in Holden's direction and pour him a glass, as he will need it at the ready.

"She started her period," I mention as I close the bottle.

Holden's eyes flutter, and he seems to be registering the information. "Excuse me, she what?"

Okay, disbelief it is.

"Holden." I circle around the island to be close to him because a counter seems too much distance for us. "You know what I said."

He grabs the glass and takes a gulp of wine before setting it down and hissing a breath as he claws his hair. "The time has come."

I nod in understanding. "It seems it has."

He blinks a few times, taking in the fact that his little girl is growing up. "I knew this was coming, I just wasn't expecting it now. I'm kind of unready and surprised here."

I touch his arm to ensure he connects his eyes with me. "Then imagine how she's feeling."

"What the fuck do I do? I'm not prepared. Do I need to go upstairs and talk to her? Throw her party to welcome her to no longer being my little girl?" He's all over the place, as expected.

My hands skim up to square his shoulders to me, and I squeeze the curve of his muscles to assure him. "I took care of it, and if you need to add buying supplies next month to your grocery list then so be it. That's life."

He attempts to escape my hold. "I should talk—"

"*Noooo.*" I shut that down right away. "Just let her have some space tonight, and tomorrow it's a normal day. She wanted me to tell you, and I have."

Another sigh leaves his lips. "Okay, normal day. Yeah, I can do that. I can totally do that." He peps himself up.

I look at him with skepticism. "Really?" My tone is flat. "You're eyeing the wine bottle wondering where you put the whiskey. I can read your mind."

At last, he scoffs a sound of calm. "That's right… Want to have a drink with me?"

"I want my doggy bag actually. Lori and I just ate ice cream, and I need my Alfredo."

His face drops. "Oh shit, I knew I forgot something."

"Tell me you didn't." Ugh.

A grin stretches on his face again. "Nah, but messing with you is a relief right now."

I swat his arm, only for him to catch my attempt. His hand wraps around my wrist to hold up with warmth in his eyes.

"Lexi…"

"Yeah," I rasp.

"Thank you. I'm happy… that you're here. I would have been lost."

"It's nothing."

He crooks the fingers of his other hand and captures my chin before tipping my nose up to give him a perfect canvas. His lips lowering onto mine feels different.

Overpowering yet tender.

It isn't lust but instead a moment with significance behind it.

Holden presses down to suck my air before his mouth seizes my upper lip, softening the kiss. A light feathery feeling floats through my body, sending sensitive ripples from my toes all the way up.

Breaking away, his teeth scrape along my bottom lip. I feel it in my bones that this isn't a normal kiss. When he nuzzles my nose with his, it dawns on me that this is slow. The kind of kiss that leaves you entranced for days.

He reluctantly backs away, still keeping his finger under my jaw. "Truly thank you. You're…" he whispers, and although he doesn't finish his sentence, it feels as though we are on a new line.

A slow chip to a layer that we said we wouldn't cross.

After all, we both know what our attraction only is, right?

13

HOLDEN

I kissed her like it matters.

I know I did.

But it's not a complication. Is it? Now I need to focus on Lori who is about to come down the stairs for breakfast. I remind myself to stay calm and collected. Play it cool. Lexi is near, casually sipping her tea, and Harry pulls out a donut from the box.

The sound of Lori's steps approaching feels daunting, but I've mentally been preparing myself for this all night.

She looks at me warily, but I decide to jump right in. "*So*… it's morning." I have no clue why I just said that, but if it sounds like I'm nervous, it's because I am.

Lexi gently touches my elbow. "I think she knows that."

Lori grabs a donut from the box. "Why do we have donuts? Normally we have donuts on Saturdays."

"I know, but two days in a row is fine. I went this morning to Jolly Joe's to pick them up, they're fresh." Because I couldn't sleep. I clap my hands together. "You know what? Today we'll make peanut butter and jelly cheesecake."

Harry perks up. "Awesome, donuts and cake in the same day."

"Well, the cheesecake needs to be in the fridge overnight, so not exactly all today," I correct him.

Lori stares at me blankly, waiting for whatever blunder might come out of my mouth next.

"How about tomorrow? I'll just let school know that you'll be off for a few days."

The flare of fury erupts on my daughter's face. "Stop acting weird." I try to get us back to normal morning routine, and I drink my mug of coffee. "I'm a woman now, okay?" She's defensive, and I nearly choke on my hot brew.

Lexi intervenes. "Well, I think Harry and your dad can make that cake and you and I can get out of the house while your dad… *adjusts*." She gawks at me as a warning to get it the fuck together.

Harry's eyes dance between us all. "Why is everyone acting strange?"

I pinch the bridge of nose, miserably failing at this morning. "Doesn't matter, buddy."

Lori bites into a donut with glaze, her favorite. "You know now. I'm fine. Let's move on. I want to just lie on the couch anyways, I feel ugh."

I swallow, hating myself right now. A woman's monthly supplies don't scare me, but when it comes to my daughter, I'm a basket case.

"Sounds like a plan. I'll join you. Grab some nail polish and snacks, I can grab you a blanket, and we'll probably binge on some bad reality television," Lexi offers.

It grabs my attention when it dawns on me. "Don't you have the flea market today?"

She shrugs. "It's okay. There's another one next weekend."

My lips twitch from her thoughtfulness, and she recognizes it.

"Thanks, Lexi," Lori says softly and throws Lexi a look that seems to be a sort of understanding that only they have. I guess the name houseguest went out the window.

It occurred to me a few times that there isn't a woman in Lori's life to prepare her for the years ahead. My mom and sister are a few hours' drive too far to play a role. I just never figured out an answer of how to deal with a daughter and only her dad in her life.

I guess Lexi paid me back more than a favor.

———

Lexi's mouth gapes open as she watches Harry and me prepare a cake. "You really swirl strawberry jelly into the cake, that's a heaven of cream cheese and peanut butter?"

"It's the best." Harry is in his element.

I carefully swirl the jam with the blade of a knife. "It's delicious. The graham cracker crust is essential, though. We tried it once with chocolate cookie crumbs, and that was just an insane tastebud explosion on that one. We all mutually agreed that we needed to take it down a notch and go traditional with this recipe," I explain.

Despite the start of the day, it's been relaxing spending time with Harry and Lori, although quiet. Lori nods her head in agreement with my assessment and has a new glow on her face that might even connect us more. The snark went down a level.

And then there is Lexi who observes us all with joy. Maybe she's doubted me and parenting, but today she seems in awe.

"I feel, as the houseguest, that I should get the first piece once it's done." Lexi is dead serious, and Harry and I smile.

"Nuh-uh, I always get the first piece," Harry is quick to inform her.

She brings her hand to her heart. "Then I shall not break tradition."

We're going into the final stretch as I slide the cake onto the wire rack in the oven. Once it's out, then we have hours of cooling off the cake before it goes in the fridge. "Okay, negotiations over then. What are we doing for actual dinner? Stir fry?"

Lexi raises her hand. "I could try to make Sloppy Joes… or rather, find a can of it. But seriously, I can make it from scratch."

"Yes, can we have that?" Harry asks me.

"Yep. Lexi has to prove her cooking skills," I agree.

Our eyes catch, and we're becoming even more relaxed around one another, with Lori and Harry too. Why isn't there a red warning flare in my head yet?

———

AFTER CLEANUP of delicious sloppy joes and with the cheesecake now in the fridge for overnight, I do what I know I shouldn't. I find myself knocking on the guest room door.

It's only a few seconds before Lexi greets me at the door in a tank and pajama pants. "Hey there, stranger. Is this the part when you tell me that someone has food poisoning?"

I chuckle. "No. It's the part where I yet again thank you."

Her demeanor leaves her sarcasm behind. "You did good, Holden. I imagine it can't be easy."

My lips roll in because I agree with her but also appreciate her support. "Yeah, but you were there. Unplanned. But you were there. That's maybe the real favor that I needed. So, thank you for writing that IOU on a napkin way back."

I feel like we both have a giddy look on our faces because this conversation calls for emotion that can't be hidden behind jabs and teasing.

"I wouldn't consider it a favor."

I step closer, but she doesn't budge nor back up into her room. It's better that way since my son and daughter are upstairs. But it doesn't matter where she stands because I cup her face and bring her lips to mine, an instant murmur from her mouth before she kisses me back. We won't get to strip off a scrap of clothing right now, but I still want to kiss her.

It's not even from a debt that I owe her. It's because it isn't a debt to her at all.

We light a fire when we drown in our simmering sexual tension, but there is more to her that is underlying and deserves attention. The combination of attraction and personality opens a weakness within me.

I should run. Close the door and move on.

But her forehead rests against my nose when our mouths part, and she stays put. I smell her flowery hair, and my heart quickens. Lexi should retreat, but she doesn't. There is a wind around us; it should blow us in all directions, but it takes us only in one.

"Hey, Lexi," I whisper.

"Hmm."

My words are lost when all I can think about is asking for a weekend, just us. But something stops me.

"Nothing. Just good night and sleep well."

"I will." She smiles softly as she creates space. "Actually, tomorrow, can we meet? I mean at the Dizzy Duck?" My eyes nearly bug out, and she giggles. "Bad host of the house,

I was purely indicating that I wanted to show you a few rooms that I'll finish tomorrow morning."

"Sure. Just find me when you're ready." I tense when I realize how our brains are wired and where our imaginations are going. "The meeting, about rooms and designs."

"Bedrooms. Not just rooms. Guest bedrooms," she replies with a husky tone, very well aware that we're both acting odd. My only response is to groan as I pivot to walk away.

When I hear her door close behind me, I'm relieved, because tomorrow means that I'll be closer to her again. Me and her.

14

HOLDEN

Lexi is a mix of enthusiastic and proud. She also appears like a jumping bean due to her eagerness for me to inspect her creation. With her hand on the handle, it feels like she's opening a door to a new kingdom.

I'm not sure it's a kingdom without us. Especially when she's in a flared skirt that ends just above her knees.

"I really think you are going to love this. It's the largest suite at the Dizzy Duck, and it's by no means a cheap stay. Ready?"

Her mood is infectious which is why my face is beaming. "I am."

She nods her head. "Great. Here we are."

The door slowly opens, and I guess all those house shows I watch in my spare time feel a little more realistic. I walk a few steps in and then freeze. I need to take a moment to assess the room that is a complete opposite to what it was before, and I'm in awe.

Lexi observes me, with her hands in tight fists against her chest. She's about to burst if I don't say something.

"This is… fantastic," I exclaim.

The natural dark wood floors have replaced the carpet, and instead there is a threaded area rug. Everything in this room is white except accessories and pillows that are the pop of color. The dark blue blends well. A free-standing tub has a tray across it with a candle holder resting on it for effect.

Stepping farther into the room, my eyes focus on different areas. The chest at the bottom of the four-poster bed, the different heightened candlesticks along the mantle of the cozy fireplace with two rocking chairs nearby.

"Like a magazine, right?" She finally lets out her excitement.

My eyes can't stop exploring, but I slow down my track when I land on my destination which is Lexi who is now twirling once as she takes in her surroundings.

"That was the goal," I reply. "It's exactly what I was hoping for and more." Already my mind has marketing plans, and I'm eager to get this room available as soon as possible. I could probably raise the price too.

"I was hoping you would say that." She rushes to me and grabs my arm to ensure she can direct me to where she wants me to examine. "Did you see the table by the window with a feathered pen and glasses with a classic bottle for port? And then there are little things like a hockey rubber duck with a Spinners jersey for Lake Spark's favorite pastime, next to the towels and shampoo. The curtains along the massive window and French terrace really removes the cookie-cutter hotel feel. Out on the terrace we ha—"

I spin to grab her wrist and pull her close. She seems caught off guard as she peers down to my hand then back up. "Everything is great… really," I assure her.

It's honesty, and I also need to cool her down a bit. I won't need any more coffee today, that's for sure. Her hyper state has rubbed off on me.

"I'm happy about that," she quietly answers.

I ease my grip. "Where is the furniture from that antique barn place?"

"I'm using that for another room. Remember? Every room will be unique."

I scoff. "Unique." Just like her. Lexi doesn't seem to grasp that it's her I mean.

She steps away. "Everything is coming along so well. Moving ahead of schedule probably," she continues to babble.

Oh, I know why, I really know why.

"Lexi." I think I need to rein her in a bit. She remains oblivious to my attempt. "Lexi," I repeat.

"I can imagine this will be a prime honeymoon destination, and with matching bathrobes and a welcome basket, then it's…"

"Lexi." Now my voice is tight, and it catches her attention, except she avoids my gaze. I notice that her breath is heavy. "Are you speaking a mile a minute because you're alone with me?"

She chortles. "Trust me, you don't scare me. It's just…" Her head tilts gently. "I'm not sure," she admits.

My journey begins with walking to her while she backs up. "You probably feel how I did last night when I wished you good night."

Lexi licks her lips. "We do seem to align on thoughts."

Closer, but it's not fast enough.

"I must insist on one more thing in relation to your design process." My eyes are hunting her.

"What might that be?" Her voice is thick with curiosity, especially when the back of her knees hit the end of the mattress and she braces her hand on the bedpost.

My arm circles around her waist in a flash to pull her tight against me. "We need to test the bed."

Our mouths meet for a kiss that has more urgency than last night. Not as tender, not as soft. It's a hell of a lot more demanding and reverent.

She squeals when I lift her onto the mattress, creating a dent against the duvet. "Hey," she scolds.

I'm already traveling to her hips with my hands but freeze at her warning. "Yes?"

"What will housekeeping think if they come in here and see a rumpled bed?"

A gruff chuckle rumbles in my throat while I hover over her, causing her to lie on her back. "That's why we should just use the bed all afternoon. Make it worth their time. Besides, I pay them, and they signed papers for discretion of all guests. I get a free pass."

And who the fuck cares? Because I'm desperate for her.

She hums due to my answer, and we kiss as she kicks off her shoes. Her fingers drag the fabric of my shirt up my back, and every inch of my body that she touches spirals me into a man that is about to rip clothes if I can't get us naked fast enough.

Somehow, we get there and I'm naked, and all she has is her turquoise bra that needs to find the floor. I kiss her along her shoulder, dragging the straps down, trying to fight the magnetism to plunge right into her because her thighs align with my hips and her knees point to the ceiling. The mere touch of her thigh against my cock is a dangerous game for us.

Lexi lifts her shoulders enough to enable me to sneak behind her to unclasp the bra.

I imprint the image of Lexi underneath me with hair

splayed against the duvet and a gleam in her eyes of hazed desire.

Maybe I should take her slowly? That's what I'm wanting, isn't it?

To distract that thought, I stand, ensuring her legs stayed glued to my middle, and I grip some of her hair, pulling her up to inform her that I'm in control.

"The last twenty-four hours, all I've wanted is to fuck you."

Her smile indicates that I have no chance of being in control. This is her show, because right now she is slaying me in every way possible.

"Well, Holden, what a funny coincidence." She falls back and her legs loosen until she urges me to return to her, only she fools me and presses her big toe into my chest to keep me at bay. "I've been wanting the same thing. Now before you get comfortable, we need a condom."

"Obviously. While I handle that, how about you get those hands of yours wrapped around the bedpost as you stand, and I'll take you from behind."

She salutes me, and we both do what we need.

With condom sheathed, I bring her back to my front, and she jolts from my force. My lips scrape along her neck, my breath creating a wildfire against her skin. Lexi's arm wraps up behind my neck, with her body now stretched, and she searches over her shoulder for my mouth. Our lips meld together for a long kiss that confirms that whatever we do, we'll walk away as two people who can handle our boundaries.

Lexi hums into my mouth when my palm flattens against her belly then travels down to land on her clit that I circle with my long finger.

"You're soaking. Is that all for me?"

"Yes," she rasps.

Growling into her neck, I want to punish her for creating a man that is determined only for her.

"Those hands of yours better hold on to the post, Lexi," I warn.

Always the obedient one, she does as I say, and I guide her hips back to ensure prime position.

A few strokes of my cock in her arousal and then I'm sliding into her pussy.

"Fuck, Holden." Lexi does her best to scoot back to bring me deeper inside of her while she tightens around my length.

"Be a fucking good girl and face forward."

I press down at the bottom of her spine for a better angle, bringing my hands underneath her to squeeze her breasts and twist her nipples a few times. Everything is heightened, which is why I slam into her harder and faster, her body jolting on every thrust.

"See? The bed isn't even moving. Your designer picked a sturdy piece of furniture."

That comment earns her my palm on her ass in one spank. "Your wicked mouth, Lexi," I taunt. "But I guess it isn't punishment since you enjoy it."

"I do. In fact, I think I earned a few more."

This woman. I move faster, harder, deeper. Sweat breaks out as her body heats and her breathing changes. I spank her once more, just making us like this. Thrusting together with equal temptation to get us to an orgasm because there is no stopping this ride that we're on together in this moment.

The post gets held tighter because Lexi's body is bouncing every time I hit her deep, then I lift her off just enough that only my tip remains before I plunge into her body.

I grunt because we're out of control now. No possibility to slow down. Nor would we want to.

My release comes first, even though she's close. A dizzy spell hits me which is new for me, but then again, Lexi probably has the ability to change my blood supply. I moan and sigh when the very last drop is out, but I continue to pump her slowly and bring my fingers to flick her clit to help her, and it's not long until she's coming around my cock.

We're both completely gone when she falls onto the mattress, and I join her to steady my breath.

"We need to try harder. All scenarios to ensure the bed really can't break," I joke.

Lexi wipes her hand across her forehead. "Let me recover a minute or at least a few seconds."

"You consider your timeline while I head to the bathroom to take care of this."

I force myself to leave the bed and walk to the bathroom.

"Now housekeeping will really know what we did," she calls out.

My smirk only intensifies with perhaps a sense of pride because I don't think I'm afraid about people figuring out that I have a claim on Lexi.

Shaking my head from my apparent new philosophy, I join her back on the bed where she seems to be searching for clothes.

"No, you don't." I shackle her wrist with my hand and drag her back to lying down. "I've literally added another notch to my bedpost."

Lexi snorts a laugh. "Fair enough, that joke was waiting to be said."

I bring my hands behind my head and stare up at the ceiling. "Comfy bed."

"Only the best."

My arm shapes around Lexi, and she inches close to me on her side.

"Give me a few minutes then I need to lick that pussy of yours."

"Seriously, we had our quickie, and now we need to get out of here because this room needs new linens, even though there are no guest reservations."

I roll to my side with mischief on my face. "When you say it like that, then it makes me want to do it even more."

Her grin stays fixed. "Don't you have work to do?"

"Probably, but I would much prefer having an afternoon of sliding into you." Not even that. I could spend an afternoon just staring at her while she's tucked into my body.

"I need a nap," she deadpans.

I laugh to myself. "Not a bad idea either."

Lexi places her hand over mine and guides it along her curves. "Maybe sliding into me before a nap would be a perfect compromise?"

With that I drag her on top of me with full intention to give us this.

———

BLINKING MY EYES OPEN, I'm drowsy. My blurry vision fades when I see Lexi sitting on the side of the bed throwing on a shirt.

"Running away?" I sit up and search for my watch which is lying next to an old rotary phone where you need to spin the dial, an extra touch, I guess.

She throws me a glare. "We've been in here for three hours because we really did fall asleep."

"I guess the bed passes all the tests then."

"Except if it can handle the weight of three." She flashes her eyes at me,

I leach forward and tackle her back to her position on the pillow next to mine. "That doesn't need to be tested," I affirm.

"Anyhow, I'm going to run and grab a cookie on my way through the lobby on my walk of shame when I tell the front desk that they need to send housekeeping here."

I grin. "Let me handle that. I'm sure your excuse would be creative, though."

"As opposed to yours?"

"Stuart won't ask questions. He's a pro. Discretion is key for my staff."

She sputters a laugh. "I'm sure there is a fine line crossed when you have to clean up your boss's afternoon activities that involves sheets."

I ruefully drop my head.

The sheet still hangs around my waist which draws Lexi's attention low, or rather she's unable to move out of this bed,

"Well, this has been a fun afternoon," she says. I nod in agreement with her. "Don't forget that Harry wanted you to check his tablet. It was malfunctioning during his stock update."

I can tell that she thinks we're all crazy.

"Ah, the economy is malfunctioning, so it might not be his piece of technology at all."

"He really is a smart kid."

Pride and fondness come over me. "The math club is starting up again, so he will be in his element."

Appreciation floods me too. Lexi asks about my kids because she's generally interested. They are not a deterrent to her.

"That's good because he will need to count how many

pieces of cheesecake have been stolen because peanut butter and jelly cheesecake is hands down the best thing in my life in the last few weeks."

I feign a scowl. "Sorry for not making you come on a regular basis."

Her smile stretches. "Oh yeah, thanks for the reminder."

We both seem to settle back to sinking into the mattress and take in the air around us that's filled with lust.

"But seriously, the last few weeks have been fun." *Fun*, huh. I'm beginning to hate that word. "I guess I've been so busy in a life of wanderlust and then the spontaneity of every project that it's refreshing to just be steady and having a chance to really observe life floating by."

"Doesn't sound half bad."

Lexi presses her lips together and ponders for a second. "I guess so. Nearly makes me want to put down roots and settle. My parents would be thrilled with that."

Holding her closer, it dawns on me that I haven't really asked. "I keep forgetting who your father is." I smirk to myself.

She points at me. "Good. Most men try to get into my bed because of my sports connection. You're way past your prime game days, so I don't need to worry."

I shake my head. "Great way of explaining that. Love being reminded of my expiration date."

"Oops, sorry. It just makes you hotter." She soothes my chest with the print of her fingers.

We both begin to shuffle. "I'll take that." I spot my clothes on the floor and yawn as I leave the bed.

"Really need to talk to the owner. There are no snacks in this room," I comment.

"The owner was busy today." She smirks.

"That he was." I grin proudly.

Lexi and I acknowledge this moment while she ties up her hair. "I was going to run to the grocery store. Now that I'm comfortable with your kids not poisoning me at breakfast, I can finally buy yogurt and not live in fear. Need anything?"

"You're not scared of them," I state.

She shrugs. "Why would I be? They're kids and great kids. If I run into the PTA mom at the store, I will even run my cart into her for them."

Lexi makes everything sound so simple. It's comforting, it's new, it's… hopeful?

Don't do it. No, Holden, don't go down this road.

DO. NOT. DO. IT

"Hey, Lexi, uhm, Lori and Harry are going to stay at my parents' up north. Forgot to mention." They live just far and close enough all the same.

That hint doesn't count, does it? I can still back out.

Lexi holds onto the post as she slips on a shoe, pausing for a quick second. "That's… an interesting piece of information."

I scratch the back of my head. "Yeah, so we'll have the house all to ourselves."

Damn it, man, don't suddenly have nerves when I'm perceived as the man with a heart of steel.

"Wait… so, we're alone… the whole weekend… together." It dawns on her, and she even gulps in this adorable way.

I work the buckle of my jeans. "Something like that. Maybe we can find an antique store or farmers' market, hiking maybe." Okay, ready to spit it out. "Maybe do adult things like dinner or wine, in case we need to leave the bed."

Lexi has an odd look as she stands then brings one hand to her waist as she tips out her hip. "I hate hiking," she flatly informs me. "But, uhm… the other things are appealing."

We both walk to one another to meet in the middle of the

room, as if we are walking on a balance beam. Once we're close enough, our eyes meet to be certain, and her face softens. From an automatic response that's formed recently around her, the back of my knuckles caress her cheek and her fingers play with my shirt.

"Other things it is," I whisper.

"Yeah… just to be sure I'm not confusing things. You mean, like, kind of spending the weekend together as more than friends with benefits?" She isn't nervous, she is well aware what I said, but she wants to hear it.

"Exactly."

We smile at one another, both blushing. Something new floats between us because we have a fresh horizon.

Because I completely did what I said I wouldn't.

I'm asking for more.

15

LEXI

"**B**ig plans?" Summer asks as she appears next to me. She was in town on errands and saw me.

I stare at Piper's lingerie boutique on Main Street. The owner designs her own creations and just so happens to be married to a football coach that everyone raves about. My head cocks gently to the side as I contemplate for what feels like twenty minutes but is probably only two.

"Not sure it's a great idea. Oh, what the hell. Why not? We have an entire weekend to shake things up, after all." I speak my subconscious thoughts more than directing my sentence to Summer.

She grabs my arm to break me from my daze. "Weekend?"

I wince. "Holden's kids are away which means we're alone. Avoiding one another could be an option, but he kind of suggested… maybe we can grab dinner or have wine together. Stepping up our game."

Her eyes blaze open. "Damn it, I knew I should have picked up popcorn at the grocery store," she teases. I give her an unimpressed look. "I warned you that this could get complicated, except sometimes complications unravel into perfect relationships. A chance you could run with."

I shake my head. "I think it's better that I just see this weekend as purely that. Two people who enjoy one another's company. Besides, he has kids and his hotel. I'm not sure a relationship is what he wants. Otherwise, wouldn't he have had one by now? He has options."

"Sometimes you have to wait for the right someone to drop from the sky."

My sight returns to the window. I do see a white number including garters. White is perfect; it reminds us that I'm an innocent soul who has no intention to complicate his life. Except the low plunging line of the lace bra leaves little to the imagination but an A+ for effort.

"Don't think."

I sigh. "What the hell. I've always been fearless." That thought instantly causes my heart to dip slightly. "He has great children who are excellent at causing trouble which makes them all the sweeter. I would never want to insert myself into his life where it affects him or them in a confusing way."

Summer's closed smile begins to stretch. "Lexi… the fact that you're even considering that is a sign that you can't help but imagine what the future might hold. You want to explore something and with care. So let him lead the way." I smirk to myself, and she notices. "Outside of the bedroom, Lexi. Outside," she clarifies with a tight smile.

My body relaxes and an ease hits me from her sound logic. "You're right. I'll just relax because there isn't really any pressure or anything. This is a big adventure."

"Great. You listen to me. Now, I think you're in luck. Piper has a sale this week." She winks before leaving me.

My feet take the lead and head over to the door to go on in.

———

I BEGIN to smile to myself when my hand turns the knob of the front door, and I let go of any nerves. There is no reason to feel this way. If Holden can be calm, then so can I. We're always on the same level in everything we do, and right now is no different. That's the lucky thing about us; the ease. We keep one another on point.

The sound of someone shuffling around in the kitchen informs me that Holden is already home. He must have finished early with the staff meeting at the Dizzy Duck. It doesn't matter. It's officially the weekend now.

Slowing my pace, I observe him unloading the dishwasher. Who knew a man doing chores would be sexy as hell. I like that not many people have seen that, under his well-taken-care-of appearance and strong presence when he enters the room, he has a domesticated side. It makes me feel sort of special that I've had a front-row seat. Is that odd?

His eyes bolt open when he notices me. I stride to the island counter with a sly look on my face. My nails begin to tap the marble as we greet one another.

"So, this is the weekend it seems," I begin, maybe even challenging Holden.

"The clock does say that." He wants to laugh, I can see it.

My gaze swirls around the kitchen, wondering what our plan of action is. But then I know I'm being ridiculous. "Did Lori and Harry get to your parents' okay?"

He nods as he closes the dishwasher. "Yeah, they live up near Madison, so we meet halfway to make it easy. They normally see one another every six weeks or so."

"That's great. I assume you grew up there?"

Holden shakes his head before he takes a few steps to open the cupboard and grabs two wine glasses by the stems. "Not exactly. Actually, I grew up near St. Paul in Minnesota but by chance my parents wanted to move to Wisconsin to be closer to an aunt who lives there. They then formed a social circle and realized they would be close to their grandkids, and they set down roots."

I accept the wine goblet that he hands me. It's the size of a bowl, but I know we will have white wine which I don't mind at all. "We can start on wine, but probably by eight, I'll have you on shots."

He chuckles. "That's quite a party."

I shrug as I hold out my glass while he pops the cork. "Why not? You can let loose; the kids are away, and you can even be a devil by sleeping in for once."

"Why not." He grins.

My glass becomes full, and we clink our glasses before taking a sip. "Ooh, crisp and not sweet. Smooth," I note.

"It's the Blisswood brand. Midwest's finest."

"I've noticed their wine is on every menu in this town, not to mention the giant display in the supermarket. Right next to the Grizzly Dash maple syrup collection."

He tips his glass at me. "Lexi, you know they are all connected to Lake Spark, and a riot will start if any other brand attempts to take over." I giggle at his answer. "Besides, the Grizzly Dash syrup made special-label mini bottles for our hotel guests."

My hands come together. "I love that touch. Stuart also informed me that the Dizzy Duck has special ticketed seats for Spinners games, only for VIP guests. See? These things set the inn apart. Not only for people who want to leave

Chicago for the weekend but also anyone who is looking for a getaway near or far."

Holden appears proud. "You can stop with the flattery and maybe park business to the side."

I nod a few times. "You're totally right." My lips tuck into my mouth, feeling the next part of our night is about to hit us.

Especially when he leans over the counter, not having a care that he must use his arms to slightly lift himself over to reach me. I do the same, and we meet halfway where our mouths gravitate, until our lips press together with a quick swipe of our tongues tracing one another's lips. It's a quick kiss, but it still scares me slightly. Fast kisses are the kind reserved for couples, or at least they are in my mind.

"I believe you promised me something else. Such as food, no hiking, maybe more food," I list.

"Thanks for the reminder, and I'm happy to report that I picked up some Italian dishes from the deli at the general store. We can just throw it into the oven."

"Solid choice for my calorie intake. Bonus points if dessert is included."

He throws me an enticing look. "Depends if having you on your knees with my dick down your throat counts?" His brow arches because he's playing with me, or not, but it's in jest. "Unlucky for me, you can have leftover peanut butter and jelly cheesecake that I hid in the freezer and am defrosting now so it will be ready."

I point my finger at him. "Perfect plan."

We take the next half-hour to prepare dinner and set some plates out on the dining table. Not taking any notice that we're speeding through our bottle of wine, and not because we need to for courage, it's more due to the fact that we seem to unwind with good wine and conversation.

Sitting down, we both take a few bites. I'm in love with the eggplant parmesan. "I wish I was a better cook. I'm just thankful takeout exists."

Holden looks at me peculiarly. "That's all you really eat?"

"Of course," I sputter, only to hold up one finger. "Wait, not entirely true. My mother is a great cook. She makes a mean brisket, which sounds like the last thing in the world that would be someone's favorite food, and it's not my number one on my dishes list, but when she makes it then I'm there."

His eyes flash. "Ah yes, your parents. I keep forgetting about your dad."

"Maybe because your career is miles behind you. He coached so many players over the years, and I'm not sure he has favorites."

"That I believe. You're not very close with him," he notes.

I cut another bite of my food. "Yes and no. When we're around one another, then yes. When he is away and especially during hockey season, then no. Yet, he still feels that he has a say in my future life as a wife and mother. I guess that's a dad thing."

"I don't even think that far ahead when it comes to my kids. I need to focus on now."

My hand finds his, and I plant it over the back of his hand resting on the table. "That's the perfect answer. Besides, you have to survive the next bake sale at Lake Spark Academy. I even got a flyer when I did drop-off the other day. They were handing them out."

His other hand pinches the bridge of his nose in agitation. "*And* here comes a financial donation. Not going to walk into that den of wildlife."

A loud laugh escapes me. "It's… refreshing, the whole

settled feeling, yet little things bring aggravation for a moment or two. Sure beats the constant travel without much regard for the future, because who knows what the universe will throw at you."

Holden flips his hand with his palm now open to collect my hand. "The universe will throw something at you even if you are standing in the same place."

My head lolls to the side, and I tip my nose up as my lips quirk out. His philosophy makes sense and sends a clap of thunder to the center of my chest. He has a valid point.

"Never thought of it that way, yet it's logical."

He releases my hand to grab his wine. "I'm not even sure why I seem to have wisdom tonight."

I pick up my fork again. "Probably because you don't get many chances to talk about it with someone, I mean a woman, or maybe you have, and it just didn't work out." Yikes, I'm prying for info.

Holden has a gleam in his eyes as he leans back in his chair. "No woman who I actually talked with, admittedly. It's kind of been blank physical fulfillment, except I don't even think it was fulfillment. You have to have the whole package of bedroom and out-of-bedroom interaction, including conversation, to have fulfillment."

His words catch me in a moment. My suspicions are right, and it seems we are crossing paths. "Why am I sitting here having good conversation with you?" I'm serious.

He scoffs to himself before his mouth changes form to a pleasant look. "It seems you've drawn me into wanting it."

Now my pulse quickens. "Holden." I focus on the table but then decide there is no need to hide. "I-I feel it too. But this is my warning to you…" His eyes search mine with great interest. "Only sex is one thing. But I don't do well with crossing the line from sex to beyond. I go all-in once a line is crossed. My ability to separate it is nearly non-existent. The last few days, I can't help but remind myself that you have a different dynamic that is new to me. Your age, kids, and a commitment that I'm not sure you have interest in giving. Not to mention, I'm your houseguest which adds some extra complication to our cocktail of current life."

His lips quirk out, and the waiting for him to answer me is nearly overbearing. Even when his mouth begins to make a sound, I'm anticipating his words, even though I'm aware that I have to accept whatever he says.

"Lexi, I hear what you're saying. I do. And all I can say is I have some strange new inkling that I wanted to spend the weekend with you. Maybe it's selfish," he explains with a softness in his tone.

I take a deep breath and abruptly stand, pushing my chair behind me, then circle around the corner of the table to Holden. His tongue darts to the corner of his mouth, his eyes glued to me with a desire that mirrors my own. He's letting me lead the scene, but his demeanor is eager.

Between him and the table, I lift my leg to cross over his lap to square my body to his. I slowly lower myself until I'm straddling him, with his eyes peering down then back up to mine. I can feel his cock harden against my panties, with my skirt now bunched around my waist and my arms resting on the curve of his shoulders. The feeling of his hands firmly gripping my sides intensifies everything I want in this moment.

"Focus on now, Lexi, and we'll see where this weekend takes us." His voice is a simmering warning. It's also a key to open a door if it's locked.

"I agree."

I lower my mouth to trace his lips, ensuring they don't

touch but skim to tease him. His hands work behind me at moving his plate.

"Don't tease, Lexi," he warns. Using his strength, he lifts us then sets me on the edge of the table, with his glass of wine spilling and neither of us caring. "Now lean back on your hands and take it like a good girl when I fuck you with my tongue before I flip you to fuck you from behind while I yank your hair."

My entire body flares, with arousal soaking my panties.

I nod once as our eyes hold. Then he kisses me as I fall back to my propped arms.

All thoughts of complexity float out of my mind, even when he nearly rips my panties as he drags them roughly down my legs, a growl escaping from deep in his throat. He parts my legs in one swift move and stares at my bare pussy, his entire face hungry.

"I need to fuck you so damn hard here before I take you upstairs to my room."

A strike to my center. I've never been to his room. We've only ever fucked on neutral ground, but now he is crossing us over a line.

HOLDEN

I don't care about the spilled wine, nor the fact that clothes have created a trail as we moved upstairs, arriving perfectly naked at my room.

It was a few licks on her luscious pussy, but then I felt a need to transfer us. Probably, the fact that the living area is not just mine, it's my kids'. Maybe one day we will share it with someone else, but right now doesn't seem right yet. But the true reason, if I'm honest, is I want to lay Lexi down in *my* bed. No woman has crossed that line since I moved into this house. It's far too intimate, yet here I am with an eager desire to have Lexi in my bed.

That's the reason why I throw her onto my bed, only for her to reach for my arms to tug me down to join her. We find our way to the middle of the mattress, and I sit up as Lexi swings her legs around my waist because it must be her position of choice today. She's straddling me again, this time with her glistening pussy rubbing against my bare, hard cock.

Her eyes float around the room when we settle into a little silence.

"This is your room, it appears." She does that cute thing where she slows her speech and states the obvious.

I tuck hair behind her ear, causing her to focus on me again. "You are very wise," I whisper. "I guess it's new for us." My room is large, with a king-sized bed, a lot of gray happening in the simple decorating. A man's room, I guess.

She splays her hand against my chest. We don't say anything more because something so small seems to signify a lot. The simple act of letting her into my room that I normally keep private says enough.

Our lips find their way to meet, and we kiss. A sensual kiss that brings our bodies pressed together and my arms wrapping tighter around her waist, as if tight isn't even enough.

We pull away, and her eyes gleam with sentimentality. "Hi," she whispers.

"Hi," I echo.

She smiles almost shyly, but I'm putting an end to that. I adjust our bodies and roll her back with her head now near the end of my bed, I encourage her to tilt her hips up, giving me ample opportunity to go slow with her.

Parting her thighs open, my tongue finds her clit again, and instantly she gasps. Lexi's limber, and I appreciate that she can hold this position until I have her trembling. I circle her clit and keep my eyes focused on her face and hands that have found her breasts to fondle with. She's even more damn beautiful because she freely does what she craves.

I'm not sure the cause of how drenched her thighs and pussy are, because since I set her on the dining table, I've both licked her and turned her on purely with the tease of what we're going to do. Now I'm adding a finger to her pussy, and she needs my cock.

"Baby, you must be aching and craving my cock to fill

you." I watch her eyes hood closed then open while she thrums with pleasure. I add another digit, and she twists her nipples between her fingers, her hips beginning to circle, eager for more. "Tell me what you need."

"I need you. You make me feel so good," she grates out.

I pop my fingers out of her pussy and shove them straight into her mouth. "You're sweet, Lexi. Delicious, and you're making a mess of your thighs. I've done this to you, and I have every intention of being inside you."

"Please," she begs.

I rumble a sound of pride while I reach for my nightstand to grab a condom. She follows my cues and comes to sit on me again in the middle of the bed. Our eyes lock, and I don't need any words; she slides down onto me. Deadly slow, with every inch taking us deeper into our own world. Her hair falls behind her shoulder as she looks up, and her breasts present themselves to me for my teeth to drag around her nipple and my hands to mold against the shape.

She drags her pussy up then bears down on me with force that buries the tip of my cock as deep as possible inside of her.

Her breath becomes labored. "You feel so good," she whispers.

My hands roam down her spine until I grip the cheeks of her ass in one slap. Her body jolts, but then approval through her smirk informs me that she didn't mind. Using my hands on her behind, I guide her rhythm. She loops her arms around my neck for support, and we seem to be moving closer and closer. Our bodies have nowhere to go as the emotional element of sex only intensifies the ability to become one and move in sync.

That's what has happened. Hasn't it? I care for Lexi, she

brightens my day, and when I close my eyes, I don't see her gone.

I refuse to label this, but I'm allowed to have this time with her.

We're both overheating with a sheen of sweat forming on our bodies. Through our heavy breathing, we still manage to kiss deeply. We slow down our thrusts, and our foreheads touch as we both soak in a few seconds of one another.

"You're so fucking beautiful when you aren't afraid," I whisper.

Her eyes flick to mine. "What should I be afraid of?"

My lips twitch, but I don't respond. Because I'm not sure of the answer. Did I mean her sexual confidence or what's transpiring between us?

It doesn't matter. I pull her flush to my body and begin to piston up inside of her, needing to hit that spot that makes her see stars. She's losing control, and she brings her mouth to the curve of my shoulder to caress and nip.

Our speed picks up with her hand between us toying with her clit. We both moan, and when we finally reach our destination, I'm positive I black out from a mind-blowing orgasm. All her doing.

———

"I SHOULDN'T BE YAWNING," I declare as my mouth stretches, with Lexi in my arms in my bed.

Lexi begins to mirror me. "Don't say yawning. When you hear the word then you automatically yawn." Lexi places her hand on my bare chest. "Old man." She snickers.

"Watch it there." I look at my clock. "Fair point, maybe. It's not even nine and we're drowsy in bed."

"I think we know why."

"Har, har. We were supposed to watch a movie or talk over a bottle of wine. Didn't you have the idea of shots?" I list.

I could get used to the feeling of her lips kissing my pec. Always delicate but without thought. "We can always bring the bottle here, but I feel like that might ruin this sacred surrounding. Tomorrow, we have the whole day. Besides, I kind of like your bed. It's comfortable, there are great pillows, a hot guy, high thread count sheets, and big windows over there."

I tickle her, and she squeals. "Hot guy, huh?"

"Don't get cocky on me. But seriously, I don't need to leave this bed. I'm tired too. I mean, unless you want me to leave this bed." She sounds unsure.

I laugh under my breath. "I'm not kicking you out," I clarify.

"Okay, but I'm a cuddler."

"Then I'll spoon the hell out of you."

"And I wake sometimes in the middle of the night," she adds.

"I'll slide into you and fuck you back to sleep."

She hooks her leg across my body around my hips. "Do I have to sleep naked, or do I get one of your shirts?"

I grin. "You have a lot of questions." Lexi looks up to give me a love-to-tease-me look. "But to answer. No scraps of clothing allowed in this bed."

"Hmm, I was afraid of that." She frowns, but then her entire body perks up. "I guess being at your service at all times will have to do."

My arm sweeps her in closer to me. "Don't say things like that to me."

"Fine." We both simmer in our joint embrace in silence until she breaks it. "Your jersey isn't here."

"Nah, I keep that on the wall in my home office. I kind of need a space with no reminders of the outside world."

Her nails tap against my skin. "Huh… I don't even see photos of Lori and Harry in here."

"I love them, but this space needs to be a blank room so I can gather my thoughts."

"That's actually… a perfect thing to have."

My eyes close because tiredness begins to take over, but I still listen and talk. "That means a lot coming from a professional designer."

"No work talk. Tell me something new. Why don't you have a dog? That makes children's lives happy."

I'm wide awake again and burst out a laugh. "Because we killed Pebbles the fish way back after two days at home. Doubt we can handle a dog."

Our fingers entwine and move together, creating their own shapes. "I had Diamond growing up. A Dalmatian who was pretty cool. Used to sit on my bed when I would do homework or sneak out my bedroom window. She was even exactly where I left her when I returned home. I'm positive she only kept quiet because she wanted my bed to nap on."

"That's ridiculous. Do you ever want to have another dog?"

"I think so. I need to settle somewhere first. Before I was traveling all the time, so it wasn't ideal. Now that life is less hectic with less travel, it seems that a dog is getting closer on the horizon."

I begin to ponder in my thoughts. "Okay, focus on projects, no plans of traveling, less hectic, anything else?"

"Why are you making a list? Something brewing in your head?" She's amused.

But her observation strikes a chord, and I move to my

side to face her. "How do you manage to assess my thoughts?"

A sly smile creeps on her lips. "Because our minds think alike. Isn't that kind of scary?"

"Terrifying," I deadpan.

Lexi's expression turns serious, and she cups my face in her hand, with her thumb tracing my bottom lip. "I know the feeling," she whispers. "Isn't it a strange realization when a strong click that you share with someone has been blinded by the fun you have with them? Turns out the connection isn't just on the surface."

She explains it well. Too well.

"Tell me something that will make me walk away from you, completely uninterested," I request softly. I'm spiraling again, no control of my thoughts or feelings.

Her fingers stroke my hair, a calming smile faint on her lips. "I'll maybe tell you in the morning, but right now, I think you need to find your way back inside of me."

My fingers trail down her body to find her pussy that is wet again. She's trying to distract me, and it's working.

WAKING up when Lexi begins to stir in my arms, I blink my eyes to see the sun peeking through the curtains. We kept true to our suggestion of waking in the night and I spooned her from behind. Now I have every intention of having lazy morning sex with her.

She rolls out of my hold, and I reach to yank her back but fail.

"Holden." She shoos me away. "I need breakfast, and I'm sure there is a carnage of wine over your table."

I rub my face to wake up. "Forgot about that."

She's already out of bed and heads directly to my closet to get lost in, only to return a few seconds later, pulling on one of my old Spinners shirts, and it drowns her but is still hot as hell. "We can come back to bed after breakfast. Or... we could actually do something non-bed related. I was thinking we could head to the ice rink."

My face puzzles. "I'm always up for the rink. Didn't really expect you to say that, though."

She splays out her hands. "I'm full of surprises."

That she is. "Give me a few minutes and I'll be downstairs."

"I'll grab the toaster pastries that are full of artificial goodness. If you have those weird cinnamon ones, then I'll be concerned."

I pretend to be serious. "That's a classic."

"Or we can just pick something up at Jolly Joe's."

"Good plan," I agree.

It's a few minutes later when I arrive downstairs to find Lexi still in my shirt, dancing around the kitchen as she puts dishes away from last night. I don't think she realizes I'm there as she's belting out George Michaels' "Father Figure."

Clearing my throat, she startles. "Have some daddy scenarios that we need to talk about?"

It's not even nine and we're already into our daily rhythm of back and forth.

Lexi waves a finger at me. "Hmm, I don't think so. But I'm all for some chains and floggers."

My eyes grow bold. "Shut up. No seriously, shut up. Every time I know you're serious about your sexual wishes, it only makes me become more curious about what I can do with you."

She salutes me. "Yes, sir."

"Seriously, get in the car in ten minutes, otherwise we

have no hope of leaving this house." I'm growing frustrated with her lack of inhibitions, purely because I want to instantly put them into practice.

Her face goes neutral. "Agreed."

We make it out of the house and pick up bagels and coffees on our way to the rink. I wasn't really expecting her to suggest this, but I'm game.

Lake Spark is lucky that the Spinners' training center here also has a small public rink. It's where Lori has her lessons. Fortunately, it's not busy either, considering it's a Saturday. We should probably give it an hour or two before it picks up.

Lexi and I tie our skates on, and I follow her onto the ice.

"Here we go. Non-inappropriate activities here we come," I say.

She throws me a glare.

And soon I know why.

Lexi skates away, and she doesn't have one wobble. Instead, her speed picks up and then her body circles before skating more. It seems as though she's warming up. I just slowly skate in observation. Then stop in amazement when she jumps off the ice in a turn. It doesn't stop. Leg up, twirls, another turn in the air.

No fucking way. She's not at all an amateur.

I give up on skating since I much prefer the show. She slows down with a smile and skates around me as if I'm a target.

"What's the story, Lexi? I've heard mention that you used to skate. Yet, this talent you still seem to have, you did nothing with it."

Lexi shrugs and tries not to look at me. "It's nothing. Besides I gave up when I was a teenager. My mother wasn't a fan. Felt I'd be better off going to college."

"And your dad?"

"He wanted to go all out on the skating front."

She brings her leg up while her body lines into an L shape. "And me? I guess fate ran its course."

I take a few glides, and she skates away a little, as if I need to chase her, and I do. But then we both reach out and grab one another's arms which knocks us to the ice. Nobody is hurt, though, and we burst out laughing.

We lie on our backs and stay there while our hysteria fades away. Staring up, we just freeze, but she reaches out her finger and invites me to link with mine.

"You still have skills," I point out.

Lexi sighs. "I still practice sometimes for the old feeling. It's been a while, though."

"And how does it feel?"

"Liberating." She sounds at peace.

My head angles to study her face that looks content. "How come you haven't watched Lori, out of curiosity? She loves figure skating."

Lexi meets my gaze and hesitates. "Simple. I wasn't sure how much she hated her new houseguest and didn't want another reason for her to."

Creases form on my forehead. "That's a silly reason."

She shakes her head in disagreement. "Also… when you're her age, the last thing you want is for someone to steal your limelight. Skating is her thing, so let her shine in it. I didn't want to take that away."

My entire body wilts from her thoughtfulness and the way she ignites wants and feelings that I imagined were always locked away.

I don't care who is watching or the feeling of ice on the other side of my clothes. I lean on my side and kiss her softly on the lips then look down at her.

"You keep surprising me. In every best possible way. I'm not sure what to do."

She lifts her head up to kiss me once more. "Me neither."

We both lie back down, splayed out like two octopuses. Not a concern in the world that a few other skaters are circling the rink.

It's a minute of our hands laced and relaxing breathing as we stare at the ceiling.

Until Lexi laughs to herself.

"What's funny?"

"I lied to you."

My eyes snap in her direction, fear now flooding me. Of course, it's too good to be true.

But her smile, it's coy yet promising.

"What did you lie about?"

She hurries and scrambles to standing on her skates, and she offers me a hand to yank me up, which is kind of pointless as I'll just take her back down due to my size. I don't take her offered arm because I would rather have an answer.

"I didn't tell you that I know."

"As in?" I need a clue.

Lexi licks her lips, and her cheeks tighten from a cheeky smile wanting to break free. "I know you turned the water off on purpose, always knew."

She laughs and skates away. Leaving me sitting on the ice grinning to myself.

Because even from day one, she still stayed.

HOLDEN

Tequila. A bottle of tequila rests on the rug near the turned-on fireplace downstairs. I spill some from my shot glass onto my hand as we sit on the floor. A few shots might do that to you.

We both chuckle as we let loose. It's been quite a day and here we are post-dinner—well, a charcuterie board. Lexi brings out a side of me that I haven't felt in years. Sure, I would kick back with a few drinks with friends. However, the constant laugh while we're doing it seems to be different. It's more uplifting, with my cares of the world turned off. And even more of a change is that there is a woman in my house who is more than a platonic friend.

"Last one," I say.

Lexi nods and tosses her empty glass to the side, and it lands on the rug. "Agreed. We have to think clearly." She points a finger at me.

"What? That you are a bad influence?"

A cheeky proud smile stretches on her lips. "Yet you, oh so wise old guy, follow me willingly?"

My brows lift, and I give her a warning. "Seven years.

Only seven years older," I remind her then slide all signs of alcohol to the side. It gives me ample space to tickle her and guide her back onto the floor. We both quickly lie on our sides and rest our heads against propped elbows while we stare at one another. "I'm having fun."

"Good. You should. Take it down a notch on the stress level. You're allowed to do that."

"So it seems."

Our eyes are glued to one another, and after a few ticks, a gentle look floods her face. "We might be tipsy but still we know that tomorrow this is a thing of the past. I should probably go stay at the Dizzy Duck after tonight."

"Is it the alcohol? Or did I just hear you say that you're leaving my house?"

She shakes her head. "Our dynamics have changed, and I don't think this is a good idea."

Sobriety hits me at rocket speed. My lips press out, and I debate for a few seconds. "How is this different to you staying here while we fucked on what was becoming a regular basis?" My free hand lands on her hip and rubs back and forth. I can't not touch more of her.

"It's a little more than physical now, don't ya think?" Her face turns puzzled.

She's right. But I'm too selfish. "What if I refuse to let you leave? I'm beginning to think my kids wouldn't like it either. You can still stay in the guest room."

Lexi sighs then rolls to her back, with frustration clearly growing. "Holden, I am completely on board with Harry and Lori being in the dark. But this. Where is it going? At some point, one of us will want more, and I have a feeling it's not you. Impending disaster is probably looming over us."

An inclination inside me has me ready to be far too honest. "Lexi, you're… I can't describe it, but you are different. I always turned off the possibility to go anywhere with anyone—"

She cuts me right off. "Exactly. You don't even allow yourself to have anyone in your life that could be more. You seem to have thrown away that you're allowed to be in a relationship and be a great dad too. Which is why I think me leaving my captivity is the way to go."

My hand on her hip drags her closer to me. "Will you let me finish?" She rolls her eyes, yet that just makes me even more certain of what I want to say, because her ability to be blunt all the time is a positive to me. "I told you at the start of the weekend about going with the tide. Here we are. What if I'm saying that I'm curious to see if, yeah, I can have what I've been missing, and it seems you're actually that key since you're on the other side." A suave smirk hits my lips as I know I've surprised her.

Her head cranes up with her face skeptical. "Really?"

"Yeah."

"Not tequila doing this to us?" she double-checks.

I squeeze her hip to add a signal that she needs to get with the program. "Nah, this is me. Even if it was the alcohol, people normally speak honestly anyhow, they have no fear suddenly."

Her eyes blaze, and Lexi seems to soak in everything that I just told her the last two minutes. "Then kiss me."

Now I grin, my fingers raking into her hair then gripping the back of her head. "I'll do better than that. I'll take you right here because off-limits locations to fuck you senseless have been abolished."

Her smile is pleased. "Okay, I'm convinced. Now please show me."

I dive right in to kiss her lips.

IT'S Monday morning and Lori and Harry are silent as they eat their cereal at the counter. That's not unusual for Harry, but the fact that Lori is on time and actually eating breakfast is new. Kind of scary, to be honest. Eerily unusual.

"Uh, I'm going to head to the inn to check the delivery of new lamps." Lexi holds up her to-go mug of smoothie she made. "Thanks, guys, for not adding any extra ingredients."

"We could have added laxatives for all you know. You don't taste those," Lori deadpans.

We all swing our attention to Lori. "What?" I check if I heard her correctly.

She shrugs. "Relax. It was a joke."

Lexi releases a smile. "You have some dry humor, but thank you for confirming."

Lori offers her a faint smile that only seems directed at Lexi.

I glance at the clock on the oven. "Okay, team, five minutes until we need to head out." My kids groan but pick up their speed, their spoons full of cereal. "I will walk you out, Lexi. The switch for the garage is acting a little funny."

"Thanks."

As soon as I close the door from the hall to the garage, I break Lexi's attempt to hit the switch. "Lexi."

She looks over her shoulder. "What? This seems to work fine."

The door is already slowly rising. "Of course, it does. But I needed a cover to kiss you good morning."

Lexi greets me with a knowing smile. "I figured. But I like to make you work a few seconds extra."

My arms loop around her waist, and I pull her until our middles touch. Our lips meet for a slow sensual morning kiss.

A few days ago, I probably would have called this sappy. But now? It seems I want my day to start this way. Especially since I don't get to enjoy a shower or morning sex with her. Maybe we can role play that later at the Dizzy Duck.

She purrs a sound as our sensual kiss deepens. It's one long kiss to begin the day on a strong basis. When we pull away, we take a few seconds more to admire each other before she shakes out of my hold.

"Down, boy, I do have to get to my job. Plus, I make Stuart's day by having a morning cup of coffee with him. He's trying to ask someone out that he met at the supermarket. It's kind of cute."

I chuckle. "Phew, had me worried he's a contender."

"God, no. I'm not even sure he knows how to use a key for handcuffs."

She pats my shoulder then is quickly heading toward her car. Lexi is the type of person that always wants to start the day with a smile. It does ease me. I have no qualms that when I head back inside it might be chaotic, but it's looking a little less stressful lately.

But that thought vanishes as soon as I return inside and turn the corner of the hall to the kitchen; it isn't quiet.

"No, Dad has to take me to my music lesson, not to your fufu skating lesson." Harry is standing his ground against his big sister and seems annoyed too.

Lori is unimpressed. "No, he is taking me to figure skating because someone in this family actually has talent. Besides, I have a competition coming up."

My hands come up, trying to calm them. "Alright, relax. We probably have three more weeks before we get another nanny. Or at least that's what the agency said. For now, can we just balance it out? I'll ask Lexi to help so everyone can get to their afterschool activities."

"It's not an activity, it could be my career," Lori says, defensive.

Bringing my hand to my heart, I'm ready to apologize. "You're completely right." Blowing out a breath, I twirl my finger in the air indicating to wrap this all up. I give Lori zero pressure when it comes to skating, but if she envisions a career, then I'm not going to knock her down.

Somehow, we all make it to the car in record time. On the road, Harry is occupied in the back, while Lori is in the front messing with the Bluetooth.

"Can we try to find a middle ground on the music? I bet you would find some bands that you actually like that I grew up with too."

Lori throws me a glare as she sits back, satisfied that she won the music battle with a pop song. "Not today." She crosses her arms, and I give up in defeat, but it's after a little silence that she speaks up again. "Did you fix the garage door?"

Her question causes me to quickly glance to my side while I keep my hands steady on the wheel. "Yeah, just needed a little wiggle." I swallow my lie.

"Sure, it did." She sounds skeptical.

But she doesn't press, instead turning her attention outside, but I can't help but notice in the side mirror that her lips twitch into a closed-mouth smile to herself. Almost as if she has a thought that makes her glad.

I don't try to interpret it because the warmth of her face is something that is far more important because she doesn't do it often.

———

I WAIT for my coffee at Jolly Joe's after school drop-off. I hate school drop-off. The moms always give me an over-the-top smile, even if I don't leave my car. They stand on the sidewalk with a cute little wave or drive up beside me and ensure we catch sight of one another through the windows. My awkward smiles are beginning to hurt my face. But these are the things we do for our children.

Stone and his fiancée Harlow walk into the place, the little bell ringing over the door. They instantly catch sight of me, and it feels like their looks are entertained.

"What are the odds?" Stone grins as he lands right next to me, pretending to read the menu.

"Not really. You know I swing by after the morning school run," I highlight.

Harlow clears her throat. "I attempted to divert his attention to other topics, but it failed." She steps forward to order with the lady behind the counter.

Stone turns to me with that grin still smacked on his face. "But while I'm here, we should catch up since you've avoided me the last week. Then, our boy Stuart—"

"You hate Stuart. You try to have me fire him every week." My tone is flat.

Stone slaps a hand on my shoulder. "Well, I look at him a bit more positively since I did a cookie pickup yesterday for Harlow, and Stuart shared some fun information."

I take a step forward to grab my coffee order that is ready. "And what might that be?"

"Shall we take a seat? This might be a few minutes."

Sighing, I give up. Plus, I could use an ear now. We find a booth by the window, and Harlow joins us. They both sit across from me with bright smiles.

"Stuart informed me that you seem awfully happy lately, and Lexi seems quite chipper too. Any coincidence?"

"You know that answer."

Harlow seems ecstatic. "Is this the part where you move on from the only-benefits plan?"

My cheeks puff out while my finger taps the side of my to-go cup. "Yeah, okay? Yeah. We seem to be doing more than that."

"As in? We need more intel to advise you correctly." Stone thanks the man who brings their coffees and a plate with a cinnamon roll.

"We spent the weekend together when Lori and Harry were away. Now we are, ya know…"

Harlow and Stone wait patiently, both with arms crossed on the table and their backs straight.

"Lexi and I enjoy one another. She makes me laugh and doesn't seem to mind the kids, either. In fact, I think with every antic they pull she likes them even more. It doesn't feel as though she's out of place when they're around. I can't seem to shake that we're more than a fling," I admit.

Harlow's face lights up like a Christmas tree; she writes romance books, after all. "The realization phase has hit you. Go for it." Her palm comes up to face me. "Go for it. You've sworn off relationships in the past, but she's the gamechanger, and if she has a great connection with Lori and Harry, then even more reason to keep exploring this thing."

My eyes land on Stone with a plea. "Calm her down."

He gently touches his fiancée's arm. "Go a little easy, even if you are 100% correct." His sight sharply turns to find mine again. "Holden, for fuck's sake, you seem happy."

"Which is why we are going to see where things go."

"Perfect. As long as fear doesn't become a barrier, then this could be something special."

I smile to myself. "That's the thing. I'm not sure there is

any fear, other than it scares me that there is no fear, you know what I mean?"

Harlow sips her coffee and remains elated. "That's your sign then."

I snicker a sound and throw my hands up. "Everyone here is speaking logic, congrats to us."

Stone and Harlow hold up their coffee mugs and meet them in the middle for a toast.

"Fast or slow, you have a chance at a relationship worth everything," Harlow announces before we clink our mugs.

Stone sets the little spoon for his coffee to the side. "Now just don't fuck it up when it comes time to tell the kids," he casually mentions.

Because one day, when the time is right to share the news, then they could be the dealbreaker.

"These cookies are so damn good." I nearly moan as the gooey chocolate chip cookie bends easily in my hand.

"There is something about Dizzy Duck's welcome cookies that is like a psychedelic experience," Harlow says with her mouth full.

We're sitting on a couch in the lobby of the Dizzy Duck. The finished lobby, if I may add. Harlow is someone I recently met. But she's around the inn a lot, as she and Stone stayed here for a bit while their home was getting renovated. They are a perfect couple, and it's nearly infectious to see.

I put my cookie back on the napkin then set it on the coffee table in front of us. "I really need to figure out what it is about the recipe," I mention.

"Nah, they're only excellent because someone else bakes them." Harlow nods then looks at me funny. "Uhm…" She's trying to keep a smile in. "I saw Holden the other day."

Ah, I think I know where this is going.

"*And*?"

Her smile breaks out. "He's close to Stone and me. I

consider him a good friend, and maybe I shouldn't be talking to you about him. But my mouth won't stay shut because he seems different. I think it's great that he is opening up with someone. I've even heard his kids have calmed down a bit. Seems that you are a good influence on everyone."

I shrug my shoulders, brushing off her proclamation. "Nah, just a distraction for most. Something new."

She shakes her head. "Except, you know that you're no longer just a distraction to Holden."

A feeling of pure joy explodes inside me. "I'm not sure that I should be talking to you about this, but I believe so, and if I'm honest, he isn't to me either. I'm just not used to a connection with someone like this."

Harlow gives me a look of understanding. "But you like it?"

"Love it."

"Then maybe as time goes on the bond will only get stronger. You're up for that?"

"Is this an interrogation?" I volley but lightheartedly.

She laughs then scans the room before her gaze falls on me again. "Maybe or maybe not. I just love to see two people with a clear connection letting it grow. It doesn't seem to scare you that he is a bit older or has kids, right?"

I think about it for a second, because nobody has confronted me in this way, but I have no hesitation either. "No, it doesn't. Should it?"

"If it isn't an issue for you then not at all."

Reaching forward, I pick up the remainder of my cookie. "But you know we're kind of keeping everything on the downlow, right? I mean, I'm almost finished here at the Dizzy Duck, although it never really crossed my mind that he is kind of my boss." My head tips to the side, and I wince.

"It's more we have a few factors, so we need to be sure before being more open."

Harlow sputters then throws a thumb over her shoulder to the empty reception desk. "Trust me, reception is well aware what shenanigans are happening between Holden and you. Staying ambiguous can only last for so long. Plus, what the hell? You're staying in his house?"

My finger whips up. "Only until the water is fixed at the guesthouse he rents out… which he might have turned off on purpose."

She roars with laughter. "Ha! No way is that ever happening. Besides, then you would just become his neighbor. Want my advice?" She slides a little closer to me, prepared to speak softer.

"I think you will give it to me anyhow."

"Just continue the living situation as it is, then when it's clear there is a serious next step in the relationship, you're already where you need to be. Besides, you've already tested the co-habiting with his family. Don't need to practice on that part."

My lips purse out, acknowledging that her plan is worth pondering. I just want to repeat the obvious. "First we just need to be… us."

Harlow begins to stand, while she throws the strap of her purse over her shoulder. "All positive thoughts. Now, if you will excuse me, I have a Zumba class to attend. Cookies and Zumba is just how I roll."

I raise myself up and off the couch too. "That sounds like a slogan for a t-shirt."

"Totally, right? See ya soon."

We both say goodbye as I walk to the reception desk, slightly unnerved when Stuart has a day off. It's just not the same. Jane puts in the effort, but she seems to fret about little things, as if she's scared that she will be fired any moment. Before I can be polite to say hello, a hand that I've become familiar with touches my elbow.

"I believe you need to update me on the last of the guest rooms and the timeline for completion." Holden sounds way too playful, even though his sentence is a fact.

Turning, I'm faced with his smoldering gaze. "Is that so?"

"Completely."

"You're going to have to wait. I want to make a few calls."

"I'll live."

I cross my arms over my chest while I give him a wry smile. "Oh gee, I was greatly concerned."

He steps closer and that thin layer of sensitivity creates a wall between us, and I believe he knows that. "Caring, as always."

"You should really be more professional here," I tease him.

But then our moment of flirtation is subdued, and we just stand in the presence of one another, still synced together and unable to part.

He drags a knuckle across his jawline. Holden always has a little bit of short stubble on his chin, and I love it. It only adds to the flaming look he has.

"Thanks for handling school lunches this morning. I'm kind of thinking they prefer yours over mine."

I lick my lips. "I do make a mean cashew butter and jelly sandwich."

He stifles a laugh. "Maybe tonight after they go to bed, we can open a bottle of wine?"

"I would like that."

We're frozen with one another, feet planted on the floor.

"I heard we've both been cornered by our friends over our latest developments."

"Oh, we have." His body completely relaxes from the humor of all this.

"The moms at school have already been assuming for weeks, but if they ever receive a fact, then I'm positive they'll be grabbing the pitchforks. Don't really care. I still get to fuck you, not them."

Holden breaks out in laugh. "I… I love how you always present life in a positive way, minus pitchforks."

I feel like I'm melting. I don't need to kiss Holden or have sex. Just being in his presence weakens everything inside of me.

"I should probably get to those calls." I make it not even half a step before Holden touches my arm to ensure I can't pass. "Is there something else?"

His face changes to a shade of vulnerability. It only ups the ante of connection because it's a side I'm aware not many people see. "You're still satisfied with what's going on between us, right?"

I just want to throw my arms around him and kiss him. "Do I look like someone who isn't? I am completely happy and satisfied," I assure him.

Relief floods his face. He's just as scared as I am in this exhilarating rollercoaster that we're on. But his relief twists into something else. His eyes send a straight line over my shoulder, and he freezes.

"Why do you look like that?" Now fear hits me.

Holden clears his throat, almost nervous. "There is someone here for you."

"Like who?" I only turn halfway and a startled shriek bursts out of me. "Daddy?"

My father stands a few feet from me in a windbreaker and

long khakis. It doesn't matter because his outfit most definitely doesn't match his cold glare directed at the man now behind me.

"Coach Moore," Holden greets my father.

"Holden," he replies, a little too firm for my liking. His eyes float between Holden and me.

Maybe Holden gets a hint or he just wants to escape, but he is quick to say, "I'll leave you two to catch up. Good to see you, Coach Moore. Feel free to grab lunch or drinks in the restaurant or patio, on the house. Maybe I will join you later to talk about old times."

"Good to see you too, I think."

My head spins between them until Holden smiles tightly and leaves us be.

I prepare myself for my father's unexpected arrival. I do my best to form an excited smile. "Daddy, this is a surprise." I walk to his open arms for a bear hug, because although we sometimes have odd moments, that soft spot as Daddy's Little Girl is always there.

"I wanted to surprise you while we have a little break on the team schedule, even if this town doesn't have the right team when it comes to hockey." Of course, the Spinners are his rivals. "And you've been too busy for time with your old man. Your mother sends her love, but she has her book club meeting that happens only once a month."

"I forget that she's still doing that. Ever since I was a little girl," I reflect. It takes me a moment for my bearings to return. "Come on, let's go grab a drink out by the lake. The weather is great."

"Sounds like a plan. You have to show me some of your work first."

I interlace our arms and begin the tour. In the end, I only explain the lobby and show him a few touches near the private party room. Mostly because it's still a little frenzied with a few contractors scattered around, and housekeeping is busy working their daily rounds. But in all honesty, I wanted to speed up to our conversation.

We grab two iced teas and a bowl of nuts from the bar and go outside to sit at a table on the patio.

"Everything looks great. I'm proud of you, Lexi."

My father's praise causes me to smile. "Thanks, Dad."

His gaze turns firm in my direction. "Must be fun staying here while you're busy with the project."

An ice cube falls out of my mouth. "Did I not mention… I'm staying with Holden. In the guest room since the guesthouse had a water issue, and there was a leak here, but they still need a few rooms open for guests…" I quickly sew together a sentence.

My father's eyes darken. "How convenient." Not one ounce of sincerity is in his tone. "It was only a few years ago that he was on my team, and I coached him. He had a lot of drama in his life. Kids, divorce, a lot of attention from women and the press."

A need to defend Holden hits me in a boom. "Well, his kids are great, maybe misunderstood, but they are kids with a warm heart. Plus, Holden's not in the media anymore, and I'm sure Holden from years ago is not the same man as now."

He rests his arms on the table. "Except now he's sleeping with my daughter."

My face drops. "Daddy!"

My father shakes his head and grabs a handful of nuts from the bowl. I feel as though I'm about to be lectured as if I'm no longer an adult.

"It was obvious the moment I walked through the door that something is going on."

"I-I…" I don't lie to my father unless I'm sixteen and sneaking out to a party. "What if I am? I'm an adult."

Leaning back, his cold look gives me no clue of what he must be considering. "You're right. Doesn't mean I can't voice my opinion. You're younger than him, he has kids, and his life is quite different to yours. You travel and look for adventure."

Anger is flaming inside of me. "What if being with Holden *is* an adventure?"

A near sinister laugh hits my ears. "What if you're infatuated?" He takes a moment to admire the lake view and maybe calm a smidgen. "I'm just watching out for you."

I twist my hair and plump it on the top of my head to tie into a bun. "I get that. But, please, just let me figure out my life on my own."

"He doesn't even have the decency to speak with me about this."

Throwing my hands up in the air, I'm exhausted. "We're new. Going slow. We're being sensitive to his family situation," I explain. Watching them is more a picture of a family than I had growing up.

My father's eyes grow big. "Moving into his house? That's not going slow."

"Not that it's your business, but we weren't this way when I moved in. He needed a little help with his son and daughter since the nanny quit."

He scoffs a sound of further disappointment. "You're a nanny now?"

The humor in how this must all sound brings a smile to my face. "No. I'm not the nanny," I grumble. "Now, can you be the dad that I've always remembered who would let me be and discover the world for myself?"

"Daddy bear has to come out when you're dating an older

man who I happen to know quite well." He is half serious, which makes it all the more endearing.

Throwing him a pout, the kind that causes him to remember the days when I would skip around with piggy tails, his entire body falters.

A sound of hopelessness fills the air. "Fine, Lexi, I'm not one to tell you what to do with your love life. I can only warn you and hope you don't get hurt."

"Thank you." I pick up the bowl of nuts and offer it to him. They're his favorite, slightly salted with a few sugary coated peanuts thrown in.

"Any other shockers I need to prepare myself for?" he queries.

I shake my head. "Not that I can think of."

"Great. Will you do me a favor then?"

"Of course."

My father rubs his face. "Text your mom about this. Because if I have to tell her, then I'll have to listen to her shriek for half an hour straight."

Warmly, I smile. "No problem."

The next half-hour, we talk about the team, a vacation he is planning with my mom, and possibly redoing their BBQ area in their backyard. My father has an uncanny knack to continue conversation, even if a thousand thoughts are running in his head.

By the time we are hugging goodbye and walking through the lobby, I take notice of the clock on the wall. It's nearly the end of the school day, which for some reason now makes me wonder how Lori and Harry's day went or what homework they have.

It's also the time when Holden walks through the lobby because he needs to go pick up the kids, as he is doing exactly now. The faceoff between my father and Holden is instant.

"I'm expecting you to contact me for a talk. My daughter isn't hockey." My father's voice has a lot of bite to it, and it causes my body to jolt and my brow to raise. I'm not sure if I should chortle or be scared. He storms off before I can solve it, or before Holden can reply.

Holden strides my way, his face pained. "Figured it out, huh?"

"Oh yeah. Call it my father's instant assessment of situations."

He rakes his hand through his hair. "Well, almost feels like we should just throw up a billboard at this point."

I step forward and touch his chest with no care in the world about our surroundings. "It's okay. We will take a little more time for Lori and Harry."

A bitter laugh hits him. "If they don't hear it from somewhere else or figure it out for themselves."

I lift my shoulders. "I don't know what to say. It's your train to drive."

He leans in to kiss my forehead. It's chaste, but to the world, obvious enough that I'm his woman and he's my man.

"Need to get the kids. We'll talk later."

I reluctantly remove my hand and nod in understanding, watching him walk away and wondering what is the next step in relation to our families and should I be scared?

19

HOLDEN

The calendar on my desk taunts me with the days ticking by. After a couple of weeks, everything is complete at the Dizzy Duck, and although fantastic for business, it does mean one thing. Lexi won't have a reason to be waltzing into the Dizzy Duck on a daily basis as if she owns the place. Making demands of what she needs, all while delivery men smile and Lexi shows kindness to the staff that adore her.

Leaning back in my chair, I tap the wood, very well knowing that my concentration for the day has gone to shit. It's been a week since her father showed up, a week of a weighty awareness that this small town has a tiny bubble of gossip that may no doubt reach my kids before I do.

The sound of my door cracking open causes me to smirk. Lexi doesn't even bother with knocking, and even if we weren't sleeping together, I'm positive she wouldn't knock anyhow.

"Holden, the magazine called, and they want to take photos of the inn a few days earlier than planned. We can make it work, I just will need to order two rounds of flowers, and we need to up the ante on little trinkets to hand out. We'll need to do everything now…" She looks up from her little notebook that she carries around and stops in her ramble to notice me.

I'm always amused by her adorable fits of speed talking. My elbows rest on the arms of my chair and my fingers steeple together.

"What's up with you? You seem grumbly," she adds as she strides my way, approaching me as though I'm her target, ready to relax me.

"Not grumpy. Just lost in thought."

She clicks her fingers. "Well, snap out of it. I only have fifteen minutes until I'm supposed to pick up Lori and get her to her lesson. Her coach has been sick for the whole week, and to my surprise, Lori asked me if I could… monitor, help, give tips…" She's doubting what to say, but Lexi seems fully invested.

I spin my chair slightly and reach out for her wrists which causes her to flop her notebook on my desk. I give her a tug until she lands on my lap in a perfect fit. "Thank you for doing it." She shrugs, because to her it's nothing, which is why a simple smile graces her lips. "You've kind of become a staple in the not-a-nanny-but-a-houseguest role."

Lexi gently smacks her palm against my chest. "How are you doing with that? You better have not put that nanny search on hold. Although, I'm positive that a pre-teen does not want a nanny, nor needs one. You really should consider other options, otherwise you'll only have more angst to deal with, and I'm positive she's switched your normal coffee with decaf just to test you." Again, her long-winded sentences return. Lexi does that when she's invested in things.

I bring my hands up to cup her face then quickly crash my lips onto hers to quiet her… and also because her lips look luscious today with a pink gloss. It does the trick, and she eases instantly with a purr and her wrists resting on my shoulders. In truth, these kisses bring us both back to a stable foundation here on earth. Sometimes we're stronger together.

Pulling away, I lick my lips to taste her. "A shame we only have fifteen minutes," I say in a near-rough voice, desperate for more in this moment.

Her eyes pop out. "Really? Fifteen minutes is stopping you? I'm sure that's not an issue."

I laugh and quickly peck her mouth once more. "It will have to wait. I kind of want to talk to you about something."

A slight fear forms in her eyes. "Oh…"

To ease her worries, I smile at her. "It's nothing bad, except we seem to be avoiding the detail of what to do once the inn finishes…" Lexi's chin lifts up, waiting for me to say it or to give her own assessment. "It will kind of feel like a step back if you move out. Which is crazy, as we probably should go back a few stages that we skipped over. It's just…"

"Yeah, of course, I totally get it." She nervously tucks hair behind her ear and her eyes avoid mine.

"I don't really want you to leave, and I'm not sure Lori and Harry would want you to, either. They've become accustomed to you."

Her eyes whip back to me. "But if I get a few projects around Lake Spark that I've been asked to do, then I can take the guesthouse with working water, but it's not… You know, if we're moving too fast. We are moving fast."

"The guesthouse? It's not the same."

Lexi's lips begin to curve up, but she can't quite commit. "I'm not sure what to say…"

I begin to rub her arms that fell from my shoulders, coaxing her to continue. "The truth."

Her eyes blink a few times. "The thought has crossed my

mind… the slight sadness of leaving. Even if I'll be banished to the guest room downstairs."

My finger is quick to shush her lips. "Then it seems we have a predicament." She nods in agreement with my finger never parting. "Lori and Harry should probably be clued in on this change between you and me." She bobs her head again, nearly mesmerized. I break out in a wide grin. "It's settled. I will tell them tonight, maybe alone is best. This is a change they've never had before. I've never had a girlfriend in the picture really."

Lexi laughs. "Really? I should probably dive into that mystery a little more, but fuck it. Holden, we are at a point where my feelings for you are an attachment that will be difficult to break. Everything we are doing, I hope it's because you feel it deep within you that we're going somewhere on the long-term. Because the last few years I've been floating around life, one place after another. But I'm ready to settle down in a way, and that's an adventure in itself."

To cement my agreement, I kiss her. Long and firm. Promising too. "That's what I wanted to hear, Lexi." My thumbs follow the curve of her face. "This is new to me, but it feels right."

Her smile breaks out, and she gives me a quick kiss before bouncing up, leaving my lap. "Then we're on the same road. It's clear. Which is great because I'm out of time right now."

"To pick up my daughter, which hits me somewhere unknown within me. You're special, Lexi."

She winks at me. "I couldn't agree more."

I shake my head because she can take soft moments and bring us back to our normal day in a split second, and that's what I need, because pondering in my thoughts for too long sometimes leads me in all directions.

Lexi went to have dinner with Harlow and Summer to give me some breathing room to talk to Lori and Harry who are staring at me while we sit in the living room.

I uneasily scratch the back of my neck, wishing I had rehearsed this a little bit instead of choosing to wing it. "It's good that we can spend a little time together. Nothing like pizza."

"On the couch. You never let us have pizza on the couch. This is a little weird," Harry highlights my rule.

Meanwhile, Lori sits with arms crossed and her face neutral. "Probably because he is trying to butter us up."

"Oh man, is this the part when you say that I can't get a dog for my birthday? That sucks." Harry flops his piece of pizza on his plate, his garlic stick falling off onto the couch, which is the least of my worries right now.

My head tips gently to the side. Huh, I forgot about that request. It also seems that this conversation really is normal to him. But Lori's eyes? They're waiting for me.

"The thing is, as you know Lexi has been staying here, and with the inn almost done and the water fixed in the guest-house, then it means…" Now Harry's attention is grabbed. "I've asked her to stay… here."

"And why is that, dear father?" Lori's face shades to one I'm very familiar with since it's a mirror of my own when I'm waiting for her to confess her past tricks. She thinks she has the upper hand right now.

A sound escapes the back of my throat, now aware of Lori's play. "Because we're together."

My daughter has a satisfied smile at her win and drops her arms. "No shit. This conversation wasn't obvious at all," she muses with sarcasm.

"Really? Like, you have a girlfriend? That's a little…" Harry contemplates.

It's a little worrying, as my children's opinions matter to me. They will always come first in my life, that's how parenting works, how I want it to work. There is no other way in my book. My attention turns back to Lori.

"Care to elaborate on your no-shit expression?"

"Which you won't care about my use of language because you're probably freaking out about my opinion." Damn, this daughter of mine keeps me on my toes, and in other circumstances, I would be a little proud she has my genes. "You think I'm an idiot? As if you cut your neck while shaving. It was totally a hickey."

"That was weeks ago."

"And your over-the-top concern what we might do to her at breakfast was another clue. Then there is the ridiculous cover of checking on cars and garages." Lori sits back on the sofa, grabbing a pillow to hug because this appears to be a casual discussion.

My eyes tear away from Lori to my son. "You okay there, buddy?"

He hums a noise and brings his finger to his chin to contemplate. "I guess it's fine. I do like her. This means we have to see all of this cuddly stuff, don't we?"

"That's kind of how relationships work," I highlight to my son.

"Fine. But this doesn't mean she gets to eat all of our cheesecake when she wants. We all get equal shares. Speaking of which, we really need to talk about your stock portfolio. Lexi let me explain to her why she should invest the other day. She may be richer than you one day if she invests the way I tell her."

I snort a laugh because I can envision Lexi's perplexed

face as she listened to him. But it seems business as usual with them, not bothered about my news.

Which brings me back to the apple of my eye, and she notices. "Now I have someone to take me bra shopping, I need one of those."

My hands claw the arms on my chair, with my entire body tightening and my face attempting not to show my total freakout that my little girl is no longer a little girl. "Oh yeah, I'm sure she'll help with that," I nearly squeak. Deep breath. "But why didn't you tell me you knew about Lexi and me?"

She shrugs her shoulder. "I wanted to see how this ship would sail, and here we are. I'm fine. It's cool. You can even focus on her more and let me have my space."

I groan at this girl's ability to wrap me around her finger and keep me at her mercy. "Delightful." Another deep exhale. "Is this conversation done? Any questions?"

"All good." Lori stands and flicks her hair. "Off to my room to call my friends to tell them that this conversation has happened. They had timeline estimates and now need confirmation. Bye."

I can't even with her. In my peripheral view, I see Harry has cheese strung along from his mouth to the plate, only to have it break and land on the couch cushion.

Guess we're all going to be alright.

20

HOLDEN

exi gives me a peculiar stare as we stand in the reception room of a country club outside of Chicago. Lake Spark may be a hockey town, but sometimes sponsors like to get away from the ice for a children's charity and find neutral territory for athletes from all teams to come together for a cause. These events can be fun. Still, my team at home are not impressed, which is why Lori's stare is more a near scowl—but still cute.

"I'm not sure this counts as a family outing?" Lexi chides but then touches my arm and completely relaxes and smiles because she's joking.

I snicker. "I can't get out of it. It's a sponsor that I still have a contract with. It's why I still appear at sports functions. At least it's a family-themed event and you got to watch me attempt to golf one hole, no?"

"*And* you should just stick to hockey," she mumbles but then stands tall. "My dad is here, and I spoke to him for a little bit. I'm surprised I didn't need to chain you up and drag you here because of that. How could you not want to fake a sickness and get out of this?" Lexi refutes.

"I'm aware." I sigh. I need to face him eventually. After all, with my kids now in the loop about my relationship status, then it's a step into the not-casual-dating category. I owe Coach Moore a chat. I missed the traditional train to ask for permission to date his daughter, but I can still make an effort.

I study my kids for a second. Lori scans the room while Harry is already beelining it to the snack table. My face turns pleading when I face my daughter. "An hour or two tops, then I promise we can do something just the four of us."

"Does fun include shopping?" Her tone is flat.

"Not exactly." But the four of us, for sure. Since everything between Lexi and me is out in the open, everyone seems a little happier. Lori in particular seems to have bonded with Lexi, which is refreshing to see since Lori could use a strong female figure in her life to look up to. It also brings Harry and me closer because the pranks have died down and I don't have to spend time defusing fires.

Lexi plants her hands on Lori's shoulders and guides her in a new direction. "Come on, I hear there are cute junior hockey players visiting this event, and we can go look at them over there." Lexi flashes her eyes at me as they leave.

Still, I manage to hear them as they walk away. "Does it matter? I see the Spinners practice at the rink all the time," my daughter reminds Lexi.

Ruefully, I shake my head as a guy calls my name. I turn to see Trey, an old buddy from my team.

"Hey, if it's not Mr. Entrepreneur himself." His hand comes up to shake mine. A strong hold because it's nearly a side hug.

"Hey, Trey. Long time no see. How's life treating you?"

He hitches a thumb over his shoulder. "Pretty damn awesome. Kim is over there talking to a few of the other wives. She's holding baby one, and baby two is on the way. Gotta have those kids close together in age. Complete the diaper phase in one big swoosh." Trey shines, and it's great to see.

"Congrats. My kids are around here somewhere."

"They must be big now. I still don't know how you managed to play hockey on little sleep. Respect." He squeezes my shoulder. "Miss the team life?"

I place a hand on my waist. "Nah, it was a great life. A little wild at times. Eventually we settle down, or at least I wanted to. I need the energy too, for my kids. It's like the first years are chaotic, then you get a break age six to ten, and then it goes back into the unruly phase where you want to grit your teeth far too many times to prevent words you shouldn't say from leaving your mouth."

Trey chuckles. "Thanks for the warning." He nudges my arm. "And… might have noticed that you didn't come alone today." He raises his brows. "Man, the coach's daughter? Didn't see that one coming. But does it count when you're no longer on the team and have retired? Surely, his cold glare coming straight for us is a signal that it isn't a big deal. Even if you and Lexi look pretty damn good together."

"I am lucky. Easy on the eyes, younger to keep me rejuvenated, and an absolutely great personality."

He smiles to himself. "Hope luck is on your side because Coach Moore has arrived to talk to you." Trey winks to me and then gives the man behind my shoulder a smile. "Hey, Coach, we still have it in us. See how our team came together to golf? A reflection of your fine leadership. It's just some of us forgot about certain rules pertaining to your daughter." He's proud of himself as he pivots and leaves. Trey has a good heart, and everything he does is in a positive jest.

Maybe he even just lightened the blow because I turn to face the man that I need to speak to.

"Coach Moore," I greet him.

"Holden." His tone is stiff, and he indicates that we should step to the corner out of earshot, which I feel is probably a great idea.

Nervously I smile, reminding myself that I'm a grown man who was always determined and fearless. "I've been wanting to reach out and talk to you. Life has been a little busy with the Dizzy Duck and my kids."

"Not to mention my daughter. You seem to be busy with my daughter." His cold demeanor is nearly scary as shit, but in the corner of my eye I see Lexi giving me an encouraging thumbs up.

"Listen, you can doubt my intentions or believe I'm not the right fit for Lexi, but I won't hear what you have to say about it. All that matters is that Lexi and I believe that we're something worth building on." I'm firm in tone, my stance strong.

His eyes survey my body up and down. "I'm concerned about the experiences you have. You've been through a lot, when Lexi has lived one big carefree journey, even if it means ignoring the negatives. If you two are strong and have a future, then even if you're nowhere near there, it still must've crossed your mind that one day she will want her first and hopefully only marriage, probably a baby too. Anything about that scare you? Because you've already experienced both, except the wife who is long-lasting. Would you do it again for my daughter?"

I take a few beats because everything he says is a stark reality that maybe I haven't thought about this all enough. Still, it's not a scary warning that I should run away either.

Lexi is younger, and of course one day will want things that are already part of my life story.

"Yes, sir. I've thought about all of that, yet here I am."

He lifts his chin, debating if I'm worthy. One thing that is different to our dynamic than any other normal relationship is that Lexi's dad was my coach and through that we learned how we both react to situations. He knows if I'm being honest or not.

"Lexi raves about your wonderful children. Good kids normally means that someone in their life is a strong influence. They've had you, which indicates that you're responsible. That counts for a lot in my book. You know I value strong family dynamics."

My hands splay out. "Then look no further. You also know that I can support Lexi too."

Coach chortles. "Now you're sounding like this is a marriage talk. Don't get ahead of yourself."

My body relaxes, as he just made a joke, that's a good sign at least. "What will it be? Skepticism or an attempt to accept us? You know I'm not one to settle for anything less than a win."

He glances over to the other corner where Lexi suddenly appears to keep herself busy with something else, having clearly been observing this scene.

His lips stretch slightly. "This is taking a little bit to wrap my head around. You broke my token rule to stay the hell away from my daughter. Which means you are even more persistent in getting what you want. I'm assuming you're not doing this for kicks, and my daughter's blatant joy right now is because of you."

"Hopefully so."

He sighs. "Fine." He deflates. "She's an adult and can

make her own choices, even if it means that upcoming family dinners might need to defrost my opinion a little."

My lips press tightly together, debating what else I should say to plead my case. "Thawing of opinions it is," I concede.

We stare at one another for a long few seconds, standing our ground and wanting the same thing—for Lexi to be happy. I offer my hand; he hesitates, but we shake. An agreement between two men.

That's another checklist item done.

When he walks away, I sigh in relief as Lexi nearly skips to me, overly joyous, and she claps her hands together.

"See? Not so bad. I made him promise that he would go easy."

I rub my face in doubt. "I guess it could have been worse. Remind me to sit on the other side of the table at Thanksgiving."

"A perfect idea."

I wrap my arm around her shoulders, and we begin to walk through the room to find my little heathens that I love beyond the world.

"We should head outside. There are some games for the kids. Then I can also sign some stuff for the children from the foundation."

"Sounds like a plan."

After a few more chitchat conversations with a few people, we move outside. Harry and Lori run ahead of us to the candy-apple making next to the face-painting tent. Lexi and I keep our fingers gently linked as we walk. I spot the area where my former teammates are signing things for the children who anxiously wait with glee, and I'm happy this event makes their day.

"I want to give some time to this, so if everyone can be a little patient a little longer," I tell Lexi.

She nods then tips her head in the direction of a face-painting stand. "Of course. I totally need to get a unicorn painted on my cheek anyhow."

We both lean in for a kiss. God, it feels good not to have to sneak around. We're in the open with no worries in sight.

That's how it should be.

―――――

LORI THROWS some popcorn at her brother while we're all set in our places in the living room. Harry and Lori on the other ends of one sofa and Lexi and me on the other. We all have a blanket and snacks as we watch a movie. I should be a little stricter with what Harry watches, but I agreed to PG-13 since it was his choice to pick, and he wanted to watch an action move.

Lexi rests her head against my shoulder as she snuggles into me. Never thought I would see this scene where someone else joins the three of us for casual family time. Nor did I expect to have a woman in my arms who isn't just instant gratification behind closed doors.

This feels like a right fit for all of us.

My phone vibrates on the side table next to the couch, and I feel compelled to answer it to ensure that everything is fine at the inn, as I haven't checked in all weekend. My screen only shows me an alert related to news… on me. Probably not the brightest idea, but long ago I set up alerts about my name in the news. It was more to ensure Lori and Harry wouldn't have to be blindsided by anything from others, although I do my damnedest to keep them out of the public eye. Another reason that I appreciate Lake Spark Academy; they take these kinds of things seriously, especially as there are other high-profile parents too.

Swiping my screen, I'm not sure I want to smirk to myself or be kind of pissed.

"What is it?" Lexi asks as she notices my interest on my cell. Her eyes travel down then move in different angles. "Is that us?"

"Yeah, seems it is. I forgot there was a photographer at the charity event yesterday."

Holden West in a Relationship with Former Coach's Daughter.

The photo only shows us holding hands, but it shows enough to make assumptions.

Lexi pops her lips. "At least it's a good angle," she quips.

It's been a hell of a long time since I've appeared in any photos this way, but I guess I don't seem to mind.

"Ooh, someone is going to get some glaring eyes on them at the next school drop-off." Lori seems excited.

"Yep, my life's goal," I joke.

Lexi yawns. "Just roll with it."

"It's fine. Nobody will care tomorrow, and there are no photos of Lori and Harry."

Stretching her arms, Lexi gives me the clue that she's tired. "Guys, are we sure we're close to the end?"

"Five minutes," Harry informs us.

"Okay, I can cope with that," Lexi promises.

But it felt like a long five minutes, even for me. The movie dragged, and after picking up kernels of popcorn that seemed to have scattered everywhere and folding blankets, everyone was ready to call it a night, as tomorrow is a school day.

Every night lately, it's been the same routine. Harry and Lori to their rooms. Harry to check his financial portfolio on his tablet and me promising to actually talk to my financial advisor. Lori scrolling her social media on her phone, and me reminding her to turn her phone off. They both make their way to sleep on their own, and it works.

Lexi? It's a humorous scene every damn time. I lie on the bed waiting for her, and she hesitates in the doorframe of my bathroom, doubting what she should do.

I offer the same easy and assuring smile every night. "Come on, woman. I'm getting impatient."

"Are you sure this is a good idea?"

Shaking my head, I'm not sure how many times I need to repeat this. "Yes."

She takes a few more steps, slowly adapting to the idea. "I mean, it must be a little weird for them to know that I'm in *here*."

That's why I'm waiting as a man ready to pounce her. "Trust me, Lori and Harry don't seem to notice or care."

Lexi twists the ends of her tank top because regular sleeping with one another entails normal pajamas now, just in case we have any family mishaps. "What if they're scared to say something? It must feel odd that suddenly there is a woman sleeping in their father's room."

I pat the bed, inviting her in. "I think we've been over this a thousand times. Now get in here."

Finally, she drops her shoulders and nods in agreement. "You're right. I'm being silly." I lift the duvet, and she slides underneath. "I mean, I know how to be quiet anyhow." There is her assertive spirit returning.

"Damn straight you can, now pass me a condom so we can get a step ahead on this train."

Her mouth forms an O shape, and a sound croaks out of her mouth. "It's okay. I'm on the pill, and I want to feel you completely, and I'm positive that you want that too."

I take hold of her body and drag her on top of me, our

eyes connecting with a new significance. There is something about this that only binds us closer.

"Lexi, if you're truly comfortable with that then there is no going back, because the first taste of the way you feel will be the only way I'll ever take you again."

She lowers herself and murmurs against my lips. "I want you to come inside me."

I'm completely hers, and it's true… there is no going back in all aspects of us, because she's completely mine too.

My toes dig into the mattress while Holden's eyes gleam and cascade down my body for inspection. There is something about a woman wearing white lingerie with garter belts and stockings; it brings innocence when we're the opposite. The fact that I'm sitting on the middle of the bed in the luxury suite of the Dizzy Duck Inn is even more special, I think.

I crook a finger to invite Holden to join me. "Surprise," I whisper.

A sly grin appears on his face as he steps forward while he unbuttons his cufflinks. "I thought we were having a meeting about last-minute touches for the opening in a few days." His knee dips into the mattress while he approaches me.

My palms smooth next to me over the duvet. "All the more reason to enjoy this room before others get to. Consider it my present to you for reaching a professional milestone in your life."

With his shirt now on the floor, his lips find mine, and I lose my balance only to land on my back. Holden joins me on his side, breaking our kiss, and his eyes strike below to watch his fingers feather along the lines of the lingerie.

He hisses a sound, very satisfied with this situation. "I completely approve of this outfit, and I completely approve of what you're going to do while wearing it," he warns.

"Oh yeah? What might that be?" I rasp.

His kiss on my lips feels stronger; it's the type that draws out my breath every time and also a kiss to remind me that, for the next few minutes, his mouth will be elsewhere. I'm correct when his lips begin to slither down my throat, skimming my skin, with my entire body curving up to offer him more. Sensitive ripples float through me like a wave, and the ache between my legs begins to make me feel impatient.

"I plan on inspecting every inch of this lace." Oh yeah, I asked him a question. His lips cover one nipple while his hand squeezes my other breast for attention. "The lace covers far more than I prefer, but it's so damn sexy on you."

"Mmhmm." I close my eyes when he travels below my bra, and I feel his hand sliding up my thigh to explore the edge of my stockings. My panties are already soaked because he's drawing on my navel with his tongue, pausing near the band of the garter to taunt me.

Snap. His fingers flick the thin straps holding up my stockings. "I think these might need to stay on when your legs are wrapped around me," he murmurs against my skin.

"Holden." I begin to beg as I'm desperate for a touch on the spot that will give me only a tiny bit of relief, eager for more.

A moan hits me as his fingers skim over the drenched lace between my legs and along my pussy. I'm mad now that I'm even wearing panties because I want his bare touch. I want all of him. Always.

"You are dying for my cock, clearly."

His fingers slip under the fabric for one long sweep through my arousal, but that's all I get as he abandons my pussy to bring his fingers up, ensuring that I'm watching him, with his eyes possessive as he sucks and hums, the sound of his fingers popping out of his mouth. "Sweet as always."

I nod once, mesmerized by his ability to lead and dominate us without my body or mind wanting to challenge.

He captures my lips for a soft kiss, his lips tracing mine side to side, and I know he wants me to taste myself on his mouth. "I taste good."

Holden laughs under his breath. "Damn right you do, but I want you to taste me."

I know my cue, which is why I urge him to lie back, and he obeys. My best sultry look appears on my face as I swing my legs over his hips to straddle him, with my hands working on his pants to open and slide them off his legs.

The moment my tongue darts to swirl around the tip of his cock, we're both nearly gone. I always love the sound that he makes when I begin to take more of him into my mouth. Wrapping my lips to suck, my eyes flick up to watch his face with that pleasured smirk. I release my own moan into my filled mouth. Our senses heighten when I bring him in deeper near the back of my throat, and his hands claw into my hair to guide me to ensure I give it to him the way he likes. Pumps that get harder, then slow, then harder. Every time he escapes my salivating mouth, I lick along his length before I repeat my actions.

But unless we are only doing a quick blowjob when we steal a moment, he always pulls me off his cock because he prefers to come inside me.

Holden scoots to the headboard. "On my lap but face forward."

"I think I like the sound of this," I tell him as I take action to get in place.

"You should."

My back is to his body, but we are tightly bound together, his hand roughly parting my thighs to ensure he has an open canvas before he tucks his hand into my panties from the top and instantly circles around my clit, bringing his other hand to cup my breast.

"You like that? Playing with your clit." His voice is thick and raspy in my ear, sending new tingles to my pulsing nub of nerves.

I cover his hand on my breast and bring the free fingers of my other hand to my untouched nipple. "So good. You always know where to touch me." My voice is heavy and my breath changes.

His movements on my pussy become more frantic, with one finger inside of me and the other rubbing my clit up and down, nearly punishing me for being so aroused.

"I think we've played enough." Both his hands abandon my body, and he drags my panties quickly off before he squares my hips to lift me slightly to ensure his cock has room.

The moment he aligns his tip, he plunges me down onto his length, and we moan together. His hard cock is snug in my body, and I need him deeper. I bounce on him, and he thrashes up inside of me. Neither of us want slow right now. We want our incinerating desire for one another to indicate the way.

Our moans sync, our bodies sync, and something else between us syncs too, but I can't pinpoint it.

But it becomes clear when he directs me off his cock and cues my body to lying on my back. In no time, he's over me and back inside of me, deep... but slower. My toes rest against his ass to keep my thighs wide. One arm gets pinned to the bed while our eyes connect.

A new gust blows in my body, but it's surrounding my heart—no, it's taken over my heart. I swear the sentiment that's flaring inside of me is mirrored in his eyes.

Our lips meld, and we move together as our foreheads touch. Both clearly about to fall in the same place.

———

"WELL, THAT WAS…" I pant along with Holden as we rest on the bed, trying our best to come down from our high.

A breath sighs from his mouth. "It was."

Neither of us can find words to describe it. "Different?"

"A little beyond our usual savage tactics in the bedroom," he attempts to lighten the reality of the axis of our relationship changing.

I roll off the bed, holding my index finger up. "Hold that thought. I need to take care of something."

After cleaning up, I open the bathroom door and suddenly seem shy as I walk back to the bed. "Hi." My voice is etched with gentleness I'm not used to.

"Hi," he returns the sentiment.

Sliding back into his arms, we stare at the ceiling and there is silence, but it doesn't feel uneasy.

"We have to stop this," he mentions.

My head whips to look at him but remains set against the pillow. "What do you mean?" I must sound concerned.

But then the corners of his mouth hitch up. "Me asking housekeeping for a discreet favor because we keep using this room for our escapades… although worth it."

I smile in relief. "After tomorrow, we are passing on the

torch to couples who will have a romantic night at the Dizzy Duck Inn."

Holden squeezes me tight against his body. "It's okay."

My lips press together and roll into my mouth. I've never been one to refrain from speaking my mind, but now I am. "Excited for tomorrow?" I cop out and talk as if it's an average day.

He chortles a laugh. "You want to talk about mundane subjects when we should be discussing this hot-as-fuck outfit you're wearing?" Holden looks down at me to capture my gaze.

I lift my shoulders. "I was saving it for a special occasion, and I felt that the mundane topic you just mentioned is actually kind of a big deal. You're really going to have a finished inn that is ready to shine."

"Because of you. I sure as hell didn't pick out paint colors or take down moose heads."

My fingers crawl up his chest. "It was one moose, and I'm not exactly sure why you didn't do it before."

"It was a statement piece that got people talking when they arrived."

"Solid tactic." I begin to stir out of his arms. "Now if you'll excuse me, I'm freezing and need to get out of this."

Holden sits up, disappointed, but then slants his head. "I guess we need to leave this room eventually today." His eyes pin on me with that devilish grin forming. "Can I have one picture of you like this? For my eyes only?"

I glance away, both honored and entertained that he would ask that. "How do you want me?" I agree.

He stands up and walks to his pants lying carelessly on the floor to grab his phone. "We can do several so I have options."

"Now this is a photoshoot?"

His eyes draw up from his phone. "Well yeah, I need you standing up, lying down on your back and belly, on your knees too. Would you squeeze your tits together once?" he quips, but I'm going to give it all to him anyway, which is why I'm crawling back onto the bed.

"Here you are, sir."

Holden stalls for a second, his eyes glowing with a shade that I can only describe as fragile. A thought seems to cross his mind, and I don't believe it has to do with dirty pictures.

"I like this surprise." It floats off his lips.

Our eyes linking together only confirms my suspicions. The thought in his mind has everything to do with us, but beyond the bedroom.

———

I EXAMINE the lobby once more as various guests chat while trays of champagne and nibbles travel through the room. My fingers wrap around my wrists to keep busy, causing the fabric of my long-sleeved black dress to move. The lines of the dress follow my curves, and Holden fully approves, judging by the once-over I got earlier when everyone was placing the final touches here before guests arrived.

After discussing with the event planner, I asked that we have a few options that are a homage to the history and design of this place. How she mixed pioneer with 1920's flare, I'm not entirely sure, except I see champagne in classic goblets. I'm too nauseous to eat, but the corn-inspired food looks delish. The pride I feel for my work, I want to be validated. The other day when the press did a walkthrough for photos and to ask questions, it seemed positive. But now close family and friends, plus the Lake Spark mayor, are here.

They will kill me if I got it all wrong. This is a place of history for the town. It's special to all for so many reasons.

The line of my lips moves from straight to curved when I see Lori and Harry next to the snack table. Of course, they go straight for the pecan squares. Lori even seems invested in the night, with a smile on her face.

"You did great," my father mentions as he stands by my side with whiskey in hand. He quickly stopped by, even though the team needs to be in San Jose tomorrow. My mother already had a girls' trip planned with friends in California.

My head turns to the side with elation from his comment. "Thank you. That means a lot to me. Also, that you managed to stop by, even if really quick."

His lips snag up. "Sorry about that, but hockey season calls."

I shrug my shoulders. "I know, it always does." I think I've become accepting of that fact. When I was younger, I didn't quite understand his absence due to his marriage to hockey, but it now makes sense.

"I wish I could stay for the toasts and grill your boyfriend a little, but that will be for another time." He's actually teasing me.

I chuckle at him. "More accepting now?"

"A higher percentage than last time." His mundane tone represents truth yet skepticism all in one, and I throw him a pretend glare. "I said hello to him and congratulated him on the opening. Even shook his hand. We're progressing."

"Best present of the day," I reply dryly.

My father leans in to kiss my cheek. "As long as he doesn't break your heart, then we'll be okay. Might even let him cut the turkey at future holiday dinners." I give a side hug, pleased with his comment. "Congratulations, sweetheart. Sorry I have to run."

"Thanks, Dad. I'll see you soon."

He squeezes my shoulder once in passing before he moves in the direction of the entrance.

My eyes scan the room yet again, but it doesn't take long for someone else to say my name.

"Hey, Lexi," Harlow's voice breaks my daze.

My eyes sideline to her. "Hey, nice to see you here."

Her welcoming face returns the sentiment. "Well, since my boyfriend has invested in this place and wants to do nothing with it, then I have to make an appearance." She's half sarcastic.

"Have to get his money's worth, right?"

"Totally. I love everything about the design of this place."

The compliment causes my face to brighten even more. "You had the whole tour of everything, including the bedrooms?"

"The master suite, oh my, gorgeous. I'm jealous of whoever books that," she gushes.

"Thanks, Harlow. It's nice to hear that. I mean, I've had a few new clients reach out even here for Lake Spark, but it's even better to hear from friends and family or at least, you know, from Holden's circle."

She looks at me amused. "Yeah…" She sips from her wine glass. "Heard that ship is sailing into calm seas. He also seems extremely happy. I've also noticed his eyes keep tracking you down. Saw it when Stone and I briefly chatted with him, and well, right now, he seems to have a hard look that's a cross between possessive and sentimental. *And* he's walking over here. Ciao."

My entire body thrums with excitement because it's a type of bliss unknown to me when someone in your life appears blatantly happy and it's your doing. Plus, he is extremely hot when he's wearing dark jeans with a white button-down and blue blazer. I could melt purely from seeing his image. Even though he strolls my way, it surprises me when he stands next to me to lean in to whisper in my ear. Everyone in the room can see us, and we very much appear as a couple, especially when he places his palm on my lower back to keep me close.

"Everyone is raving," he reminds me.

"I think so too. Oh hey, why is the principal of Lake Spark Academy here? Figured she would be last on your invite list."

Holden chuckles low. "Because it's strategy. First off, she's on the list of the essential Lake Spark people who consider themselves crucial to the running of our small town. Plus, I need to schmooze her for my kids."

I snicker a laugh. "Very smart."

"Want to get some air before I give the toasts?" he suggests.

"Sure."

He tips his head in the direction of the hall to the bar. It's the closest room with a door to the back of the inn for a view of the lake and the patio. We step on the stones from the patio to the bench swing that gives us a little more privacy.

Facing one another, with the sound of the party distant in the background, my heart beats fast.

"Lexi…"

What kind of conversation is this going to be?

"I love you." It just bursts out of my mouth without thought.

We both realize what words are now in the air, unable to be forgotten.

Maybe that's why Holden stares at me, frozen.

Which only makes my body weaken from fear.

22

HOLDEN

Lexi's eyes twinkle, and although petrified about what she just said because she doesn't think I was expecting it, it was honest, and I'm not surprised. There was a shift yesterday in bed with one another. The air is heavy, but it feels as though we can only lift up.

Still, I blow out a long breath, and my eyes swim side to side.

Her lips part open. "I-I'm sor… No, I'm not. It just rolled out of my mouth." I stand there just listening with my entire posture and face blank. "It's just, I can't control this giant ball that keeps rolling and rolling, taking me into this future, that crosses my mind." She's talking fast again; my nervous Lexi is back.

"Lexi." I state her name, attempting to break her chain of thoughts spewing out of her mouth.

It falls on deaf ears. "I'm sure you don't, you don't, you know… feel. But I can't hold it in. I have feelings for you. They're strong, and I feel connected to you and your family. It's warm and caring. So it slipped out of my mouth, and we know my mind and mouth have little control—"

"Lexi," I attempt to stop her again as the line of my mouth stretches up. Her chest is visibly moving up and down. "Lexi? Is the third time's the charm going to get your attention?" It does, as her eyes rocket up to meet mine. I step forward, and my fingertips embrace her elbows to ensure she can't run. "I love you."

Her face falls with relief before completely brightening with a smile. "You do?"

I nod. "I would say so, since I asked you to come out here to talk because it was getting kind of unbearable."

"This is crazy, right? Everything we do seems to be big steps ahead. Yet, looking back, it all makes sense, and we haven't missed any."

My grin is in full force. "Crazy sounds about right. Now, can you shut up for a hot minute? I believe we have something to do." I step closer and dive my mouth down to cement our new state.

That's what this kiss is. Lexi has this uncanny capability to break down my walls, causing me to believe that I'm allowed to feel things that haven't been on my radar in years. I'm not ignorant to the practical fact of that. I'm in this new state because of her. I want it to be her. It is her. Now she's mine.

Her arms circle around my neck and my own loop around her middle to pull her flush to my body. She sighs in relief against my lips, not wanting us to part. "We have this click, the kind too overbearing to ignore. And you shouldn't because it will only get better," I tell her.

How can it not? She molds into my life, with Lori and Harry included. Most of all, I'm alive in the way that brings constant excitement for what the day ahead will look like. It will always be an adventure. That's a pretty damn good way to live.

"It kept building inside of me, this feeling. Maybe it's because I've intertwined in your life, houseguest upgrade included. But none of that would have happened if you and I didn't have a flare between us that grew into a fire." She nuzzles my nose, completely content with melting into my body and ready for what time will bring to us.

I cup her head, my thumb circling her cheek, ensuring her eyes gaze up at me. "Sound like we're aligned. Does this mean I get another gift like yesterday's show?" I tease her, and she pinches my stomach to cause me to flinch. Lexi knows that I'm playing with her.

But we calm, and she burrows her cheek into my palm while she calmly inhales. "I love you," she repeats in a rasp.

"I love you too."

We stay firmly in place, not wanting this moment to end, but it has to.

"We'll have a long night ahead in bed, but right now, I have toasts to do."

She creates space, with understanding seeping across her face. "Of course."

A quick kiss and then she pivots, only for me to yank her back for one more fast, decadent kiss.

Watching her walk away, I examine her sway and notice that it has extra pep to her movement, and hopefully that's my doing.

This is a big step for us, but it's our direction.

Now that the knot that was inside of me all day is untied, I can focus on the rest of the night with ease.

Walking back inside, I mentally switch gears and remind myself about my speech. Everyone has been waiting for it since they arrived before sunset so they could see the inn in two different lights.

Returning to the noisy lobby, everyone seems in good

spirits. When I see Lori and Harry talking with Harlow, I know they're in good hands. They look freaking adorable. Lori in a simple blue dress, yet she picked it out herself, and Harry in a blazer minus the tie. They didn't even grumble when I asked them to dress up.

"No pressure but make this a long-run success. I hope to get my money's worth," Stone jokes.

I flash him a sly smile. "Funny. At least you showed up. Nash is still MIA. He may not care, but he still has 10% of this place."

Stone shakes his head. "It doesn't matter. You have 70%."

My head bobs. "True. Besides, I'm not surprised. Happy with the end result of this place?"

His eyes brighten. "It's phenomenal. I'm scared tourists are going to flock here in droves, more than the usual. I don't want to have to wait longer at Jolly Joe's for my coffee."

My brows rise. "Problem solved. The Dizzy Duck has a new coffee machine, and we switched the beans. We now have the best coffee around. Be nice to Stuart at the front desk and he might even grab you a cup whenever you demand."

He smacks me on my shoulder. "Thinking of all the tiny details. Now go give that speech so you can take home that future bride-to-be I saw you making out with."

"Marriage isn't on the radar, but yeah, we're something more than what began," I clarify.

A cheeky grin is glued on his face. "Well, I'll be damned, totally didn't see that coming when you decided to sleep with her." He's completely sarcastic.

I shake my head then decide to let him wallow in his correct prediction.

On my way to the fireplace, in passing I snatch a glass of champagne from the tray a waiter is holding. Arriving at the lit fireplace, I quickly run through the simple fact that despite what everyone may think, I absolutely… did fuck all to prepare for this speech about to happen in three seconds.

An old man who must be a friend of the old owner is sitting on the sofa in my vicinity. "Do you mind, sir, if you clink your glass with the fork on your snack plate? I need everyone's attention."

"Of course, young man." It seems to brighten his day that he gets to do the honors.

The sound of glass being used as a bell begins to cause the noise in the room to subside. Then everyone's eyes are on me.

Clearing my throat, I gather a few thoughts, about to wing this. "Thank you for giving me a moment to say a few words. I just wanted to first of all welcome you to the Dizzy Duck Inn, a staple in Lake Spark for many years. When I heard that the former owner, Mr. Nix, who is here with us tonight, was planning on selling, it caught my attention. After all, what is a pro-hockey player to do once he retires?" It earns me a few chuckles from the room. "Having visited Lake Spark several times due to the sports complex here, and well, the population being overrun by professional athletes, then it seemed fate stepped in."

My eyes catch Lexi's in the back of the room, watching me intently, and it gives me the courage to come up with more words. "The inn was already a little gem, but it was time to freshen it up for a new chapter." I tip my champagne glass up to the bricks above the fireplace. "Which is probably why some of us might be mourning the farewell of Caesar the moose's head that was hanging up there. I promise, he is living a better life somewhere… in a closet… or the bottom of the lake. Not quite sure, but he is happy." More laughs from the room. "Anyhow, I hope you all got a chance to walk around and see for yourself; the inn is ready to welcome guests. It wasn't possible without a few key people. For one, my partner in the inn who prefers to stay anonymous yet reaps the benefits of partly owning an inn." The room enjoys this, more laughter. "Any contractor who came in to use a hammer, because I cannot." I glance to my kids. "My children who are creative in everything they do, whether it gets them grounded or not." Lori and Harry softly smile and the shade of pride on their faces nearly makes a tear form in my eyes.

But then my eyes swing to Lexi whose smile hasn't faded, and it gives me the strength to rid any potential waterworks. "Then there is Lexi, the mastermind behind all of this. It was her doing that you're sitting in a perfectly designed lobby or walking into suites fit for a king." *Or me as her king.* "She walked in here ready to conquer, not afraid and diving right into everything. This is truly what will make the Dizzy Duck the hotel that everyone wants to put their name on the waiting list for."

Summer nearby watches her friend with pride, tipping her glass in her direction as her husband, Zac, has an arm around her waist.

"Lexi tends to blow into your life, ready to change it… Thank you." I don't mean the inn, which is why her lips twitch, because she understands my undertone.

I hold up my glass. "Okay, that's enough speech time. If everyone can hold up your glass and say cheers." The room erupts with the sounds of cheers, clinking a few glasses of people in the vicinity, before the room quiets down as everyone sips from their glass.

With the room revving up again with soft music in the background, I walk to my kids and instantly receive a hug.

"Can we go now?" Harry asks.

"Let me think about that," I pretend. "Uh, no," I flat-out answer, and he grumbles.

My eyes land on Lori who appears content. "This place is kind of cool now."

"I would hope so."

"Does this mean Lexi is leaving since everything is done?"

I'm quick to assure her, "Nah, something tells me that she will be sticking around." Because I love her.

Perfect coincidence, Lexi arrives and plants her hand on my shoulder to rub once. "What's going on, gang?"

I wink at Lori. "Nothing. Just chatting about corn muffins."

"Well, that was a great speech," Lexi praises.

Without thought, I kiss her cheek as a thanks.

"May we have a picture of you two?" one of the photographers asks, who's been working the room all day. We've already had the essential owner and designer photo in front of the inn this morning.

What's one more. "Yeah, sure."

I pull Lexi to my side, and we look at one another. I tuck her even closer and her hands fist my blazer as she looks up at me and I look down. Clearly, we have affection for one another.

"You know, it never crossed my mind that you were my semi-boss. Should that concern me?" she jokes so only I can hear.

"Nah, but I will continue to boss you around anyhow," I reply. She giggles, and it vibrates through my body.

We completely forget that there is someone taking our photo.

23

HOLDEN

"Ouch," Lexi yelps, because I just smacked her ass in passing to grab a water bottle from the fridge. "My hands have a mind of their own," I lie.

It took a few days after the party at the Dizzy Duck to have exhaustion disappear. Not that it stopped Lexi and me from fucking that night after the party. Something about the strong feelings involved and the need to be impeccably silent in the house only heightened the experience. Made it better, and the bar was already high.

But now it's a week later, and Lexi searches the kitchen with my face in her neck. I want to touch her indecently, and she's still trying to get accustomed to my kids catching us, even though I know the clues when to stop. "Harry could walk in at any moment and be grossed out. Let's not do that to him today. He already isn't looking forward to being dragged to the regional skating competition."

My lips quirk out. "You're right. We should probably get going." Lori is already there, as she practiced once more with her coach.

"Sure."

"Harry," I call out and hear a grumbled noise from upstairs.

Lexi is busy checking her purse, but she's a good multi-tasker. "I heard from the mayor, and he actually wants me to change the interior of his house now that he and his wife are heading into a new chapter with grandkids and have more need for guest rooms."

I walk to her to wrap my arms around her body from behind. "That's good. Keeps you around Lake Spark and available to occupy my bed," I tease.

"Funny," she replies.

The reality is that this solves a few of our concerns. There are only so many places to redesign in the area. One project at a time, I guess.

"Give me your credit card." Lexi indicates with her hand to hand it over. "I was going to take Lori for a spa day tomorrow post-competition."

My face screws up. "You do realize I own the place, so a card will not be needed."

She gives me an overdone smile. "I know, but it just sounded more fun to say it." Lexi pats my cheek and walks away to grab her phone. An elated smile hits my own lips.

I glance at the clock on the oven. "Come on," I yell again, and scrambling feet sound a few seconds later, scurrying down the stairs.

"Do I really need to go?" Harry grumbles.

I narrow my eyes at him. "Depends. Do you want me to take away your tablet or…"

"Fine," he groans.

"Good. Because next week when you have the science fair, then Lori will tag along for that."

Harry stomps away to the garage, and Lexi attempts to

keep her smile to herself. Just a usual Saturday morning for us.

The car ride to the ice rink is a breeze. No need to drive slow, as not a duck or deer in sight near the road, and no complaints of hunger since we had donuts and eggs for breakfast. This is our new routine, and it's perfect. The way it should always be.

Today, we've all gathered our energy for a new milestone, Lori's big day.

We got settled in our seats and endured the skate routines of the girls ahead of my daughter on the program, but then my girl shone. Not one little mistake, every jump landed, and her spins stable. I guess I don't get to watch her enough, because in a way, this all surprises me, her talent. I believe in it, just never saw it in live action. She's been working hard for this, and when she skated off the ice after her stellar short program skate, I whistle and clap having watched my little girl amaze the audience.

Lexi squeezes my arm tighter in complete excitement. "She rocked it. I bet she'll get a high score."

"Otherwise, I'll fire her coach," I deadpan but don't mean a word. Lori could get a low score, yet I would still think she's amazing. It's a junior regional competition, but in a few years, she can move into senior, and that's fast approaching. Only if she wants it.

The applause for her performance wears off, and we anxiously wait in our seats behind the boards for her score. Even Harry is invested in this afternoon. Lori sits with her coach, and then again, we find ourselves cheering, because when the numbers appear on the board behind the ice, we have more reason to celebrate.

I can't wait to see her after the competition. We'll have to have a special dinner or something.

The rink grows quiet as the next girl appears on the ice. We're going to have to watch the rest of program until we know who in the end is going on to the next round of competition. Plus, Lori has to sit with the rest of the skaters from her club to show good sportsmanship, which I fully support.

My eyes travel around to observe the crowd, finding it humorous and understandable when I see parents clenching one another with fingers crossed. We're at the age when decisions between parents and daughters need to be made if this will be a hobby or a serious sport to follow.

Harry next to me breaks out his book because that's what he does to pass time when he's bored.

"Hey, maybe show a little more respect to those on the ice and pretend to be interested?" I suggest.

My son looks up with a scowl. "You got me here, I invested full attention to my sister, now let me be."

Lexi's face screws up, and she gives me an understanding pained look. Harry is not in the best of moods, and we shouldn't push.

"Okay then," I give up in defeat.

Lexi reaches over to squeeze my arm. "Not long to go," she reminds me.

I wobble my head gently, internally reminding myself of our schedule today. My eyes scan the rink and the people sitting in the rows before us. A little boy runs from the entrance of the lobby to our section of the stands, and past a woman. I can only see the side profile of the stranger, except she's too familiar, and I squint my eyes to get a better view.

But then something causes me alarm. Or rather someone.

It can't be.

I do a double take because the woman with light hair I notice standing next to the boards is someone unexpected.

This can't be happening.

No fucking way.

Lexi must notice my demeanor change from enjoying this afternoon to utter disbelief and anger. Her fingers touch my elbow from concern, but I barely feel it as my mind is about to combust from the thousands of thoughts running through it.

"Are you okay?" She lowers her voice as she leans in to me and not to scare Harry.

My eyes snap to her. "Just stay with Harry, I need to take care of something. Keep him occupied," my whisper is hoarse.

Even though confusion floods her eyes, she agrees, her head gently nodding. "Of course."

"I'll be right back, buddy. Just going to check on something," I tell my son.

"Sure." He shrugs.

I nearly bolt down the steps to where my dread is confirmed.

My fierce possessiveness for my kids kicks in, which is why I have no qualms about quickly and discreetly grabbing my ex-wife's arm.

"Ouch. What are you doing, Holden?"

With a fast pace, I drag us out of the rink to the lobby which only has a few people, and they're not taking much notice.

I let go of her arm. "Michelle, what the fuck are you doing here?"

She seems taken aback. Even though I know her ability to throw on theatrics and fake any emotion, there is a hint of authenticity shading her face. "I've come to see Lori."

My nostrils flare, and I pinch the bridge of my nose. "Like fuck you are. You happily gave me sole custody and haven't been in Lori *and* Harry's lives for years."

"People change."

I shake my head. "When it involves Lori and Harry, then you're actually going to have to tell the truth, because I won't let you waltz back into their lives only to leave."

Michelle steps closer to me with a sly line on her mouth. This can't be good. "Like I said, I came to see Lori. She's at that age when she needs a mother in her life."

My eyes bug out. "Oh… because all the years before didn't matter? And you keep forgetting that there isn't just Lori but also her brother. How did you know she would be here?"

She shrugs. "A little digging."

I glance over her shoulder to ensure nobody is in earshot. "Cut to the chase, Michelle."

Her eyes dip down, and she seems to be taking a breath for courage. "I saw a photo online of you and your new… girlfriend." She slowly claps her hands together. "Bravo for scoring a younger woman," she seethes, but then her own tone seems to surprise her.

"Don't even get me started. If that's the reason you returned, then that is a shitty reason," I grit out through my anger for this moment.

Michelle holds her palm up. "No." She sighs. "I'm not trying to… What I mean is that I really came for Lori."

I shake my head, still in disbelief that I'm even stuck in this moment. "Suddenly?" My eyes don't blink as I remain suspicious.

"Yes," she shoots back. "She is a beauty on the ice." I'll give her the credit where it's due, and there is a tiny ounce of admiration in her sentence.

Standing taller, a new wave of protectiveness comes over me. "Michelle, you signed that I get full custody and that you wanted zero visitation, even when I offered for the sake of Lori and Harry," I remind her.

"Look, I made a mistake, and I want to rectify it." She sounds sincere to any stranger, but I know her too well, and behind all these words is a flawed logic swirling in her head. "I want to see my kids."

"Not if it's only to abandon them again."

"I won't." She will, I can see it in her eyes.

My entire body tenses. "I need you to leave. They cannot see you until we talk about this further, otherwise you are completely disrupting their lives. If you are serious about everything you just said, then you would know that there is a better way to approach this. But here you are out of nowhere, not being responsible or practical." Her eyes grow anxious. "Now tell me, why the fuck are you here?" I force out.

That ridiculous over-the-top astute leer returns. "Fine. It's simple…" She steps closer, appearing as if she has the upper hand. "Why do you get to have a happy ever after with a woman and my kids? People change, and I also deserve a life fulfilled. And after the shit you pulled—"

I nearly fall back from her twisted perception of history. "You mean, when *you* signed a legal document after *you* abandoned your kids and demanded a shit load of money. It's not just Lori you left but also the son that you never seem to mention." My fists form at my sides, doing my damnedest to keep my rage inside.

"I'm not okay with a woman being in your life since you've held off on that for so long. I have a right to see my kids, and it seems that I need to look into legal options to bring us back to court."

An inferno enlarges my eyes, and I snicker a sound. "Oh boy, blackmail. Should have seen this coming."

Michelle's smile is faintly fake. "I'm concerned for my children, and I'm sure a judge would like to evaluate that."

"What in the world would you even do if you got visitation? Actually try to be a mother? Unsettle their lives?"

"This is me being a good mother." She honestly believes that.

I rub my forehead. "Still delusional, great." I look up to the ceiling to gather an idea of what to do. "Just out to ruin our happiness or is there something else on your agenda?"

"Even though you probably owe me for emotional damage, I'm here because it's time to reconnect with them. Seeing you and your new family just gave me the push to do what has been on my mind for a while now. I have the courage now to do what I've been debating."

"You mean to blackmail me into seeing the kids, or is it money that you want?"

She doesn't answer.

My finger comes up to the air. "Ah, there it is. Money too. You think that I'm just going to fall to your requests?"

She brings her finger to her chin. "Probably. I'm definitely staying to congratulate my daughter."

I'm quick to reply. "No. Do not do that. You will play with her emotions."

"All the more reason she needs me, don't ya think? She's at a sensitive age. The judge will see it that way too. Lori is now old enough to make her opinion known, and the judge will want to hear that."

A groan escapes me. "Leave now and I will meet you tomorrow to discuss this. Can you at least do that?"

Michelle ponders for a second. "Fine. But we better speak tomorrow."

"I'm assuming you're not staying at my inn, as you are on the do-not-allow list." I wish it was sarcasm but sadly not.

"So, my guess is you're staying one town over. If you have the same number, then I will text you tomorrow."

She brightly smiles. "Good." Michelle instantly turns and flicks her hair nearly the way Lori does herself.

My entire body continues to want to break down, unable to fathom what the hell to do. The fear in me is strong about what will happen to Lori and Harry.

A calming hand touches my back. "Everything okay? The results are nearly in."

My eyes lift only for a second to acknowledge Lexi. "It was my ex-wife."

Lexi seems unsure of what to say. "Oh… W-what did she want?"

Sharply, I turn to give her my full attention, even if my face is firmly stoic. How do I say that my ex-wife saw a photo of us and now she is attempting to uproot my life?

A fatherly instinct kicks in that I have two kids in there who need me calm.

"We'll talk later, okay?"

Her look tells me she grasps the seriousness of all this. At the same time, she's innocent but the catalyst to a problem.

24

LEXI

olden is broken.

I see it. He did his best when we drove us home, but I could tell he was about to break into pieces. Holden kept looking back in the rearview mirror to observe his children, and right now, he is spending extra time to get them to sleep. He normally gives them space and says a quick good night as they're old enough.

Standing in the shower, the hot water loosens my muscles as I analyze my concern. We haven't had a chance to discuss what happened yet. I'm trying not to make predictions, but an uneasy feeling fills my body.

With the sound of the shower door opening behind me, there is no need to glance over my shoulder, my sense of him near has been in full force lately. His fingertips fall to my hips and begin to twist my body to face him, and I do, looping my arms around his neck, my eyes fixed on his face with pain flooding his eyes.

"Tell me what's wrong," I softly plead as the steam warms us.

Holden shakes his head gently that he's not ready to talk;

instead, he steps to trap me between the wall and his body in a tight embrace, with his hand sliding up my leg between us. I'm sure he needs comfort.

"I'm on my period," I remind him.

"Shh, I don't care. I need this."

It's a lighter day, and we're in the shower. I'm surprised, and it's new to us, me. But I want to help him grieve whatever the situation is. He desperately needs relief.

I don't answer and reach between us to guide him to my pussy.

The moment he slides into me, senses overload me. It's different both physically and emotionally. Our eyes lock as he begins to move deep within me, our bodies tightly bound together. I let him lead the way because he can take whatever he requests right now. I want to give that to him.

My mouth seals against the shape of his shoulder, burying my whimper and feeling his lips below my ear as his breath and grunt brings more tightness to my nipples. His thrusts turn faster and harder into me. I wrap my leg around his middle to give him more space to rock into me. It won't matter if I come or not, he just needs something to calm down.

The sensual emotions between us build as he moves faster, running toward his release until he reaches his point, and he fills me while he strongly pants, syncing with the pulse of his heart. His head falls to the crook of my neck, and I lower my leg and begin to draw circles on his back.

I've never seen a grown man so fragile. I'm positive we will collapse onto the floor, but instead, we stand for minutes, holding one another with the sound of water in the background. When we do exit the shower, we stay quiet while we dry off. Holden throws on a robe to give me an extra minute to prepare for bed and clean up a bit.

When I enter his room, I see that he must have collapsed onto the edge of the bed to sit, with a lack of energy left in him. I'm quick to crouch down, my eyes drifting up to grab his attention.

"She wants to be back in their lives," he informs me simply.

Maybe that was floating in the back of my mind as a possibility, but for some reason, this doesn't blindside me.

I grab hold of his forearms to ensure our eyes meet. "What are you going to do?"

"I'm not sure. First solve if she is telling the truth. I'm 99% sure she's lying and just wants money. But still, maybe there was a flicker of honesty in what she said too. I think I owe it to Lori and Harry to at least hear Michelle out. Also talk to my lawyer, keep Michelle away from the kids until this is all figured out. They can't have their hearts broken. She already left them years ago," he explains then stands to pace the room with his head hung low. "There is a chance that this will also bring us back to court which is a mess in itself."

I slide onto the mattress and sit patiently to be the sounding board he needs. "I'm sorry. This can't be easy. I wish I could help."

His eyes snap up to observe me, with a snicker escaping his from his mouth. "That might be a problem."

My face puzzles. "Why?"

"She saw a photo of us, and that's one reason why she appeared out of nowhere to blindside me."

My heart sinks because contributing to his current state is the last thing I would want. I want the opposite, to support him.

Words are lost in my throat that now feels strained.

"I'm sure there are other reasons too. She loves money,

after all." He attempts to quell any fears brewing inside me, but it sounds too weak for me.

"I don't know what to say or how to wrap my head around this," I admit.

A long silence hits us again as my face remains blank.

He steps back in my direction. "Let's sleep. Maybe I'll have clearer thoughts in the morning."

I nod once. "Probably the best idea for now."

———

During the night, we barely slept, and even if I tried, I could feel Holden lost in his head. Could it be that when I briefly closed my eyes to capture light sleep, that even while sleeping I still felt him near and knew he was awake?

No amount of holding one another feels like it's leading us to any resolution.

But still, I manage a little shuteye, except I wake to find Holden aimlessly staring out the bay window as he stands with his head against the glass. He's clearly exhausted with no ounce of sleep had.

I sit up and grab my robe at the edge of the bed. Quickly, I walk to him and stand behind him to touch his hanging arms.

"You must be tired," I whisper.

"It doesn't matter. I needed to get my thoughts in order."

I hum a sound of understanding. "I can imagine."

He steps out of my hold and leaves me like an unexpected breeze. When I have the opportunity to study his agitated face, my center point in my stomach begins to twist with fear.

"I should have been wiser," he begins. "I've been careless by letting you into my life, into Lori and Harry's lives."

My attempt to walk to him is stopped when he holds his

hands up indicating not to step closer. But I will say what I need to anyhow. "We can figure this all out together. I won't let you do this alone. I care for Harry and Lori too," I assure him. I'll stand firm on that.

"Lexi, we've been doing everything backwards. Living together, saying feelings that might not be true…" He stalls because my entire body freezes. I want to believe he's just pushing me away and trying to hurt me. "I mean, one day you'll want a husband and a child of your own. You're still young, and we haven't talked about it. I just assumed probably."

My fearlessness and conviction to my beliefs hit me in a flash. I walk to him to grab his arm, as if I can beg. But he only shakes me off. "I know what you're doing, but I'll still be here for you because I love you. You don't have to do this all alone."

He goes even further to the other side of the room, and I keep my feet planted in place. To anyone who might walk in, it would appear as if we are in two separate corners in a boxing match, except no physical pain will happen except in our hearts.

"Lexi, I'm serious. I've made a mistake, and I realize that now." Holden can't even look at me, yet his voice is excruciatingly firm.

I raise my voice. "I'll erase this conversation, because you can't be thinking clearly after being blindsided by your ex-wife and protectiveness for your children because you're a great dad—"

"I need to do this alone." Our eyes meet, and his are a razor to my heart, his eyes dark.

Tears begin to burn, but I won't let them escape. He needs to realize that I will put action behind my words. "I won't let you do it alone. That's how relationships work."

He shakes his head in disagreement, now ignoring my presence, walking to his dresser and fumbling in his drawer. "Not when our relationship is a mistake. We're just two people who have great sex and got lost in lust."

A swoosh of change finally hits me, and his wall is too big and strong. Holden has made up his mind.

Those tears that I've been squeezing tight fall. "If you really feel that way, then I'll pack up my bags now and leave. It seems like I have no choice. You may break my heart now, but I'll still hold on to hope that Lori and Harry will be okay and you'll be at peace with your decision."

He ensures his back is to me, as though he doesn't want me to read his facial expressions. "It is my decision," he reiterates.

I wipe away a tear and take a moment to gather myself. "Well then… goodbye."

Holden storms to the door to leave me to gather myself. But his hand stalls on the knob, and he stands there for a few beats.

"When it comes to you, Lexi, a realization struck me last night…"

"What would that be, since you already made your list of our failures together known," I snipe with bitterness.

Another long pause keeps him stalled as he sighs, but then he opens the door and gives me one last look.

"The moment we kissed is when I should have run."

25

HOLDEN

My fingers tap on the table, as what feels like the devil just arrived. Michelle sits across from me in a restaurant in an old log cabin outside of Lake Spark amongst the woods.

"Here we are." My enthusiasm is non-existent.

She reaches out to touch the back of my hand, and I don't give her a chance by ripping my hand away. Her face falls, and I have no ounce of sympathy. This is a woman who left her kids not because she had an issue that would put Lori and Harry in danger, she didn't need to go away and find herself before returning a better person. It was purely her selfishness to walk away without a backward glance or any hint of remorse. And as a bonus on top, requesting a hefty settlement too. Lori and Harry were young, they barely remember, but it was damage enough.

"I want to see Lori and Harry again. They have a right to see me."

"Nope." My tone is firm. "I make the decisions. That's how sole custody works."

She sighs, and the waitress interrupts us at the wrong moment, but also, I'm thankful.

"Coffee, black," I order without giving any attention to the lady with an apron.

"Same." Michelle presses her lips together and waits for our standoff to continue.

We stare at one another, and I try to remind myself that I owe a chance to Lori and Harry's mother even if it hurts.

"Give me an opportunity. I can see them once even, with you present," she requests with sincerity but not enough for me to be fully convinced, as I was once married to her.

"Then what?"

She shrugs her shoulders. "Maybe I can take them alone somewhere. Pioneer Park is in Lake Spark, they must love that."

I snicker. "Harry has other interests, and Lori is nearly a teenager, she's too old for people in costumes sewing quilts. You yourself argued yesterday that she's at a time in her life when she needs a strong female." My face must appear extremely coldhearted.

Probably because within me, I'm more than aware that Lexi is the strong woman that Lori has become attached to. The type of role model that Lori needs. Nor does Lexi forget about Harry, ever.

Most of all, Lexi is the woman who kindles my heart and made me believe that I could have it all. Now I've broken her heart and severely wounded my own. But my children's mother reappearing must be a sign that this whole situation happened because I'm not allowed to have it all. Fate can play the cruelest of games. As soon as you get something great, then you get knocked by something bad. If I look back in my life, I've never had the balance. I'm not going to drag Lexi deeper into my life if we won't be possible need to protect her not only from my batshit crazy ex's games, but I also need to protect Lexi's heart.

"Holden," Michelle's sharp tone breaks my thought. "You owe me this or I take us to court."

My head juts up, hesitating. "You do realize your time limit to challenge our agreement has passed, right?"

She shakes her head. "But visitation is not impossible, we didn't sign away parental rights. Plus, I can still see them or contact them without you—"

I'm quick to cut her off. "No. If you want to contact them, then we have to discuss that, even if we have to do that in court. You say you care for them, but this approach is a shitty way to show it."

In court, this would be scorching and completely difficult for Lori and Harry too. My hands are completely tied in this impossible situation, and I'm not entirely sure why it never crossed my mind. There was always a chance that this could happen. But I never saw someone so determined to leave their kids in favor of money and a life of jet-setting and boyfriends.

The cracking of my heart is different to last night with Lexi. My children always come first.

"Okay." My eyes glint to examine her words and behavior. "If I agree?"

Hope glazes her eyes. "Then I want to see them tomorrow… without *her*."

I chortle to myself because this predicament really feels like I'm at the gates of Hell. "That won't be a problem, as Lexi's…" Do I admit that I've ruined a strong and loving relationship with so much promise all because of Michelle, who feels like a signal that nobody gets it all? On one hand, it will ease her argument. But on the other, satisfaction gives her power. "It's not an issue."

Michelle seems surprised. "Well then, one less thing to worry about to lead us to a peaceful resolution."

My knuckles form fists, and I'm trying to bite in all my anger that wants to unleash. I need to get this discussion over with before I burst. "Let me talk to the kids. If they don't want to see you, then I don't think we should push this."

"They don't even know me, and they deserve to know me," she defends.

I glance away, trying again to keep my rage in. "Tomorrow, Michelle. That's when you get to prove yourself that *maybe* we can explore this conversation more."

"Fine. But I mean it, Holden. If you don't give me any chance, then I will find a way to ruin you." She stands, her words hostile.

I gently shake my head, not surprised at all. "That's a shocker."

Watching her walk away, a chill hits me. This can't be my life right now. Everything was within my grasp, but it's clear that I'm simply not made for a life with everything that could possibly make a person happy.

———

WALKING through the hall at the Dizzy Duck, my attempt to keep myself busy before school pickup will fail, I know it will. I'm reserving my energy for my call to the lawyer and talking with Lori and Harry.

But this day only sinks me deeper into despair because I feel Lexi's presence. I don't even need to look up. She became a natural magnet to me when it comes to my senses and instinct. But I do look up because her steps have slowed.

At first, we're both silent. Even without sleep, she

appears radiant, in a skirt and heels. She's holding a swatch while her eyes dance side to side.

"Hi." My voice is soft.

"I was just leaving. I forgot I left a few things here for designs." She holds up the swatch ring, clearly wanting to ignore me or be anywhere but here.

When she attempts to walk away, I grab her wrist then the other to keep her in a strong hold. "Wait." I'm not sure what to say, other than I need to touch her one last time.

"What, Holden? You said enough. Your message was clear."

We're both fuming, and she's so close within my grasp. "It's just…" What words do I use?

Her eyes widen, she's growing impatient. "Yes?"

I'm being a coward. Not saying the true reasons behind my need to part ways with her.

When she breaks my hold on her, she catches me off balance when she shoves me. "You are a coward." Ah yes, I forgot she has a talent to read my mind. We both scan the area, and we're all alone, as nobody really comes this way unless they're staff. "What the fuck did you think would happen?"

"Lexi…" Do I argue or attempt to explain?

Her finger darts out to poke my chest. "Even a smart man knows full well that when you bring someone close into your life, interweave them into your circle with the people who you hold dear. When you kiss and whisper 'I love you' or your entire body is aware that when that person says they support you that you know it's true. It's not a surprise that you are heading toward something longstanding. And now you suddenly want to tell me it isn't?"

"Lexi, I…"

"You don't need to say anything because maybe I even

understand. I think you believe this will help your current situation, and I'm the easy answer to soften the blow." Her eyes begin to water, and I hate how she is probably right.

"Lexi, I'm not meant to have everything. That's the reality." I run my tongue along my mouth because I'm nervous around her, wanting so many things with her, but I can't give her any.

She waves her finger in front of her with clear fury apparent and her chest rising and falling from her emotions taking over. "What the fuck did you expect to happen when you light a fire? This flame between us. *We* are what happened. Willingly crossing the line between fucking and having something more. And you…" She tries to gather her words because her lips quiver from the pure destruction that I've caused her.

"Lexi." I want to comfort her, calm her, selfishly make sure she'll be alright to make me feel less of an ass who blew up our bliss.

She steps back with her palm up to indicate that I shouldn't step in her direction. "Don't you dare get close to me," she barks. "You know, I've also never had this connection with someone. At least I didn't get scared and ruin a good thing."

"You don't understand my situation, you don't have kids. You still have life to experience." My tone is weak. I rub my hand across my jaw, trying my best not to look at the image before me.

"Do. Not. Throw that card at me," she grits out.

At this point, I'm waiting for her to slap me because I deserve it. Lexi can be feisty, but right now she's shattered.

Her hand lands on her waist. She looks like she's going to pounce on me, but she has a point to make. I scratch my cheek, waiting for her revelation. "I'm going right now, and the most fucked-up thing about this entire situation is that I'm going to inform you of the obvious. Work out your shit, Holden. Because even though I should be the one to run…" Her strong tone begins to diminish. "I'll still be waiting."

Our eyes can't part, and the air cuts around us. I'm sure I even gasp because I know she's speaking the truth.

Watching her walk away and turn the corner, I slam the wall with my hand and scream to myself.

———

It's not because of my witch of an ex-wife, it's because a stone hit me to slow down. Which means, Lexi will never get what she deserves. Cutting her loose is the only way.

"You look like shit."

My eyes snap up to my daughter due to her brazen tone, as she just slid into the front seat after I picked her up from skating. "Aren't we honest," I say, my tone flippant.

"Well, you do," she justifies. "It's like one day without Lexi and you've turned into a grumpy old man." My kids haven't heard the news about Lexi and me yet, only noticed that she wasn't at breakfast.

I don't bother turning the engine back on; instead, I decide it's time to bite the bullet. Harry is at a friend's house, and Lori will probably comprehend the news of her mother in a different way.

Swallowing, I nibble on my bottom lip, wanting to be tactful. "There is something I kind of want to talk to you about."

"No," Lori exclaims, with her face falling. "You and Lexi? Did something happen? She's really cool, Dad."

My head falls back to the seat while I curse to myself internally. Which bombshell do I deliver first? I slant my body to face Lori better. I'm dreading every second of this conversation.

"It's your mom." I wait for Lori to react, but she just stares blankly, blinking a few times. "I wanted to talk to you first before Harry. You're more of an adult than I would like right now."

"What about her?" I almost can't hear because she speaks so softly. Suddenly my child with a strong personality looks like a ghost.

I sigh. "Hypothetically, what would you do if she showed up wanting to see you and Harry?"

Lori takes a moment to digest my sentence, but then something snaps in her mind, and she immediately shakes her head repeatedly. "I wouldn't want to see her. And I don't think this is hypothetical at all."

Closing my eyes, I gather my strength yet again. "I understand your feeling, but she's also your mother, and maybe it matters to Harry. She says she wants to be serious."

"Do you really believe what you just said?"

My head drops low. "I don't think I have much of a choice." Legal action is not something my daughter needs to know. "Maybe one day you will look back and wish you saw her."

Lori crosses her arms. "Well, I don't want to see her. I barely remember her, and I've forgotten her." She's adamant, and as much as a parent sometimes needs to guide their child on the future, I'm not going to push this. Right now, Lori and Harry are carefree children who deserve to stay that way.

I bite the corner of my lip while I sit as fragile as Lori right now. "And what do you think Harry would want?"

She sneers. "She's probably as good as dead to him. He never even knew her."

Sighing, I pause for a few seconds. "Do you think I should ask him? You two have a strong bond."

Lori shakes her head no, just as she did before. "I don't think you should ask because I don't even call her Mom, and Harry barely mentions her… ever. I want her to go away."

Oh how I want that too.

Her face is heartbreaking because I can see that she truly means every word leaving her mouth. "I… I will try." Is it a lie? Or am I not trying hard enough?

She slouches into the seat and turns away from me to gaze out the window. "Promise me, she'll go away."

I squeeze my eyes closed with my entire body tense. "Maybe I shouldn't have had this conversation with you, but if there was any ounce that you would want to see her then I owed it to you to ask."

"Well, now you know, and we can forget this conversation," she snipes, and I'm not sure if it's me or her mom that she's angry at.

At this moment, I don't dare mention about Lexi and me. One step at a time.

"Okay, Lori," I promise.

Starting up the car, I drive us away in silence, wondering how many more mistakes I can make in the span of 48 hours.

Because I'm walking through a maze and failing miserably at discovering the end.

26

LEXI

Opening my suitcase that I threw onto the edge of the bed in Summer's spare room, I sigh. Zac is away at a medical conference, so we're all alone for a few days. Still, I debate if I should even unpack anything.

"Here. Have some water," Summer offers when she strolls into the room. She hands me a bottle while she too observes my predicament. "You're just going to live out of a suitcase?"

I take a sip of the drink then flop onto the mattress next to the bag. "I'm not sure. I feel like Holden will come to his senses, but then again, he trampled on my heart, so that's my sign to leave Lake Spark. *Except…*" I sigh. "I already accepted my next project, and I think my new addiction to Jolly Joe's coffee can't simply be ignored." I must sound miserable.

Summer stares at me with a glint of amusement as she crosses her arms. "Do you truly believe he is going to beg for you to come back?"

I bite my inner cheek and ignore the dullness in my belly.

"Maybe I want to imagine it far too much that I'm blinded by the obvious."

She grabs a nightgown from the top of the pile in my luggage and holds the lace up by her finger as she inspects it. "Does this even cover anything?" Her face screws up.

My brows rise because this is the last thing we should be discussing, yet it's still a nice memory with Holden. "I think that's the point."

She stutters a laugh and drops it back onto the clothes. "I want to root for you two. I'm sure you're right, that he's pushing you away due to his current situation, although…" She bobs her head side to side. "It's a shitty way to do it. *But* sometimes in life we need to let go because it isn't meant to be." Her eyes fill with sorrow, and I wonder if she's speaking of herself in her current marriage.

I throw my closed bottle of water behind me. "This hurts too much. You could be right. No more chance for us." A cry bursts up through my body to hit the back of my throat and sting my eyes. A wound he caused that makes my lips quiver. "I'm sure as hell not going to chase him or try and speak to him again any time soon. He has to figure everything out, and if he didn't mean what he said, then he must make the next move. But that's the problem…"

Summer walks to lean against the dresser. "Go on."

"It could very well be that Holden meant every word." I scoff a sound and fall back onto the mattress. "What a naïve woman I've been."

Summer sighs. "It will be okay, either way."

I wipe a tear away. "Why does it have to hurt this much?"

"Sometimes love hurts us."

My attention causes me to shoot up onto my elbows. "I guess I've never looked at it from that angle. Still doesn't make it any less painful. When he first broke it off, his conviction was strong, but yesterday at the hotel it was less. Still, I'm hopeful, even if he doesn't deserve it."

"Maybe space will help. But why are you so adamant to wait for him? He ran away when things got tough." It keeps sounding as though she is speaking to herself.

A faint wry smile brings a line to my mouth. "I've always treated life with such ease. But now, I see what I've been missing, and Holden surges into my life and I see everything through a different lens. I didn't know I was waiting for that. Now? My instincts scream that I shouldn't let go. That's what you do when you love someone."

"Don't confuse attachment with love," she highlights.

I swing my legs off the bed and stand. "I hear you. But I feel it in my bones that we are the real thing. It's so twisted, but I will wait a long time if it means he comes around." I search for my sweater that I tossed somewhere in my anguish.

Summer slants her shoulders up. "As long as he can fix the wound that he caused, then maybe you have the outlook that more of us should have." There's that sorrow again underlying in her voice. I really need to make sense of what's going on with her, but right now, I'm selfish and need to deal with my situation.

I find my sweater on the floor and bundle up. "I can't think of it any other way, otherwise the pain will only grow and be hard to fade away. Actually, our relationship moved fast, but the pain might last longer if this is our end."

Her eyes widen. "You really are optimistic."

I lick my lips and puff out my chest, attempting to gather strength to ensure I don't mope around. "Don't worry, I'm raging with anger, but this fucked-up sympathy inside of me has me unable to run. I can only imagine what he's going through.

And saying he doesn't love me or that we were a mistake stings like hell." She looks at me, unsure, while I point my finger to the door. "I cried all night. But right now, I need a break from the waterworks and to go get a damn coffee at Jolly Joe's."

A renewed energy hits me, and Summer grins. "Well, before you go, I wanted to tell you some happy news." I smile and patiently wait. "Zac and I are having a baby." She appears happy.

I squeal in delight. "Finally, some great news in this shitty day. This is wonderful." I jump up to give her a hug.

"I think so. It feels like life is happening quick, but this is a gift." She glances down at her flat belly.

"It is." And maybe one day, I'll have a baby, too. With Holden's eyes and his humor and his nose…

Lexi, stop.

"Well, I just wanted to let you know in case I throw up at some point. But I'm nearly at the end of my first trimester, and it hasn't been bad."

"Well, I'll be there to clean up any puke if you do."

She nods in appreciation. "Okay, I'll let you be so I can focus on some work. Just don't wait forever, Lexi. Nobody deserves that heartache."

I nod that I understand, but I can't go down the rabbit hole of rehashing all of my feelings. I gently touch her shoulder in passing as I leave. Maybe she understands more than I could imagine, and she is wiser than me.

———

OKAY, my confidence that everything will resolve was a fucking lie. Or that's what I feel as that swirling sadness and anger hits me again somewhere between parking my car and walking down Main Street. My head hangs low, and my misery returns, as if my rant earlier didn't happen.

"Lexi?" a young faint voice says, and my eyes snap up to see a beautiful 12-year-old with sass walking my way. She's missing a smile, though.

"Hey, Lori." I search the area, concerned that I will run into Holden again. But there's only a group of her friends from school heading into Jolly Joe's.

She quirks her mouth and tucks her hands into her jeans pockets. "Won't you come back?"

My nose rises because I'm not entirely sure what their dad told them. "Uh, I'm not…"

"He didn't say anything, probably because, well, someone showed up. But you haven't been around, and I'm smarter than my little brother."

Ah, Holden has spoken with Lori about her mother. "It's kind of complicated."

"He's being an ass."

Her blunt statement causes my head to perk up from surprise. "You're not afraid to be bold, huh."

Lori rolls a shoulder back, and her eyes peer down. "I don't want to see her and still my dad is walking around moody."

Indicating with my head, I suggest we sit down on the bench nearby, and she follows me. "If only it was that easy." I'm sure he didn't get into the specifics with her. "Sometimes adulting really sucks." I sigh and try to level with her age.

"Yeah, I can clearly see that." Her flippant tone brings a half-smirk to my face. "Just, please, can't you talk to him? You're just having a disagreement, and someone has to say sorry, right? You'll be there when we order pizza this weekend."

I glance away. "Lori, it's… I want to be honest, and time will tell."

A long silence floats in the air. "Please, Lexi, can't you talk to him? Maybe he'll listen. He can deal with my mom and fix whatever it is with you."

My eyes snap in her direction and see her hope. I touch her arm. "I-I... My only answer is to give him space. There is nothing else."

"Okay, but you'll be back tomorrow? Surely, that's all it will take for you both to be happy together again. I've never seen him this happy, well, until he lost it a few days ago."

My heart breaks more, and I do my best to keep my tears at bay in front of her. "Lori, I do appreciate that you felt the need to talk to me." I spot one of her friends at the door of Jolly Joe's, and she calls Lori's name. "You should go to your friends, okay?"

She nods in agreement and stands. "Just…" Lori can't finish her sentence.

But still, I give her a knowing look.

I should have seen that Holden making my heart crack would affect more than just me. If only he could see that mistakes can be rectified.

27

HOLDEN

I rub my hands together before I groan into my palms. I'm sitting on the bench swing outside the Dizzy Duck near the dock, looking at the serene lake that doesn't reflect my current mood. I have a headache of my own doing. It's also risky sitting here because everything here reminds me of Lexi.

Stone is sitting next to me, also staring out at the lake. "This is kind of weird, right? Sitting on a swing together?"

"Then leave," I snipe.

"Whoa there, don't take your aggression out on me due to your current life turmoil," he volleys back. I've brushed him up on everything that's happened, but now I feel like he's about to lecture me with that the wise logic that he believes he has.

"Look, Lori doesn't want to see Michelle, Michelle forgets she even has a son, and I sure as hell don't want to see my ex-wife again. My lawyer better hurry up with this call back. He was looking into options," I explain.

"Did you forget the other matter?"

I sideline my eyes and meet his neutral look. "No, that's

on my mind non-stop. Breaking up with Lexi wasn't the high-light of my week—or life, for that matter." It's fucking incin-erating.

"Yet you did it. I'm not sure why since she would only help you," he reminds me.

I run the back of my finger along my jaw, and my eyes whirl side to side as I try to push my theory out of my head. "I don't think I can think clearly, and why sink her down into this situation with me. A perfect life isn't for me, and she deserves one. This week was just a sign of that. Why put Lexi through misery by sticking around if eventually my content-ment breaks because I'm unable to balance amazing kids, great work, and Lexi, who gets her own category."

Stone sputters a sound. "That is the most fucked-up thought. Get it together and realize that it doesn't have to be that way."

I rub the back of my neck in pure agony due to the days past. Time to admit the truth to my friend. "I'm scared shit-less, okay?"

He smirks. "We kind of all figured that out, but kudos for saying it out loud and avoiding an expensive therapist."

I glare at him, not entertained. "It is what it is."

He tips his head to the side and makes a sound of doubt. "I don't exactly agree. There must be a reason you feel that way. You sure as hell were fearless back in your pro days."

"I had a very busy life until Michelle kind of ruined that with months of mediation with lawyers and unreasonable demands, but I was willing to do anything for Lori and Harry."

Stone snaps his fingers. "Bingo. You do everything for them but never yourself, and because of that, you're letting a difficult divorce stop you from actually getting what you deserve."

Just like dominoes toppling, every brick that quickly falls in my head leads me to another realization, another connection of thoughts now becoming clearer. A sort of epiphany that begins to fuel one thought: I need to turn around this future.

I inhale a sharp breath, nearly ashamed that I let this happen. "I can't go back in time," I say softly.

He smiles to himself and leans back with pride. "But you can change the future, and that, my friend, is my amazing advice that you're going to follow."

Stone is so sure of himself, and that cockiness causes me to smirk weakly. "Not sure the damage with Lexi can be fixed. I was beyond what she deserves. Not at all showing the love that I have for her."

It's a few seconds before he slaps a hand on my shoulder. "You don't know until you try."

I slant a shoulder up to my ear, trying to comprehend this conversation and form a plan of action. "You're right. I just wish I didn't first have to conquer the ex-wife who is intent on breaking my kids' hearts yet again. I can't even manage to say *our* kids. Hell, in that short time, Lexi has been more of a mother than they've ever had."

Stone stands. He mentioned earlier that he needed to meet Harlow so they could babysit his niece. "Then beat Michelle at her tricks then calm the hell down, before you find Lexi to fix both of your broken hearts. Every heart can be mended." He brings a hand to his chest. "Damn, I'm on fire today with this sappy advice. Owe that to my soon-to-be wife."

A soft smile spreads on my mouth at the happiness in his life that I'm desperately intent on getting back.

———

Am I really standing in a parking lot about to do this? After a long call with my lawyer and documents sent by courier, here I am. Maybe it's the worst mistake of my life or one day Harry or Lori might hate me. But this is me protecting their interests. I'm the adult here, and this is what feels to be the best solution for us all.

Michelle stands by her car with her arms crossed, waiting for me to speak.

"Lori doesn't want to see you, and I'm not going to force it," I begin.

Her face is blank, but I see the glaze of her eyes that she doesn't seem surprised.

"Harry doesn't remember you, and you haven't actually mentioned his name once, as though you've forgotten about him."

She stands tall. "That's because a daughter needs her mother more."

I shake my head gently. "Not true. But we've managed just fine since you left."

"Did you even ask him?"

"He's ten years old and doesn't remember you at all. Not once has he mentioned you, since you were never in his life. Harry only knows that you weren't around, and he never asked again because he's been a kid with a strong head on his shoulders from the moment he could walk. It's in his best interest that he doesn't know about your unexpected appearance unless you provide proof that you want to make an effort. I'm making the choice to see you for him."

Irritation is seeping through her deep exhale. "He has you, and Lori has me."

I rub the back of my neck in utter disbelief. "As in separate them when you would visit?"

She shrugs. "Maybe. I don't know how to approach this."

I pinch the bridge of my nose, feeling the rage forming. "Fuck this illogical thought of yours. Be honest and tell me that you truly want. You're really going to tell me that you will make an effort with them, and if I were to offer you money beyond our settlement from years ago that you wouldn't blink an eye and would refuse it because the kids are more important?"

She seems to be prolonging her answer because I know it's not good. "Fine. You're right, I can't."

A sound escapes me because my instincts are unfortunately true. "Let me guess. You did reappear to cause chaos and try to get money in return?"

Her body relaxes from her charade no longer needed. "I did think about seeing them again." Her voice is delicate, and this I do believe. "But you can also make this go away."

"Thought so. Especially since you recently went through divorce number three." I glance down at the papers in my hand. "So, let's solve this right away." I hand her the documents. "You never showed interest in the kids, and I'm not going to chance you returning, as they still have quite a few years until they are legal adults."

She examines the papers, but she doesn't seem to have any feeling. "Voluntarily relinquish parental rights." She holds the sheets up, unimpressed.

"Yeah. You can sign the form, or if you're not sure, go to counseling before you sign the form to ensure you've thought this through, or we could have a judge approve, if you want someone to hear why I'm doing this. I know it's a big decision." I do have sympathy for that.

"Even though it would be voluntary, I will still pay you one last sum. If you ever had any ounce of love for them then I think you know this is the way."

Her arm drops low as the papers hang from her hand, and

we stand here for a long few seconds. "Does this mean… that one day someone can adopt them to be their mother?" I don't think she's being vindictive in this moment. She may have a few narcissistic bones too many but right now she's trying to understand, truly understand, what this all means.

My shoulders slant up as my face remains serious. "Hasn't crossed my mind. If you mean Lexi… we're going at our own pace, and I haven't thought about it, but she cares for them as her own." And I need to get us back on the road. "But would it be so bad that one day Lori and Harry might have an even stronger family unit?"

Michelle thinks to herself, with her eyes reeling side to side before she sighs. "Maybe I'm just a horrible person and you're right." She's actually seriously reflecting on herself.

I rub my eyebrow, remembering that sometimes people need a little compassion, and our marriage may have gone wrong, but she was part of my life and gave me Lori and Harry. "Even horrible people can turn their life around. But after nearly ten years away with no contact with the kids, then I think when you look deep within yourself, you can make a decision that maybe you aren't as horrible as you might imagine... It's okay to say that you never wanted to be a mother."

She nods gently in agreement and appears thankful that I've calmed and am attempting to show understanding. "Okay." Her shoulders slump. "If I do this then…"

My lips curl because why am I not surprised. "Last page." I look away from this because I knew deep down that getting something in return would be the only way to seal the deal, even if in the bottom of her heart she feels it's the truth.

"Fine."

My head whips up now, astonished how fast she answered. "Wow. Proof for your presence in Lake Spark."

She tosses the papers on the hood of her car. "I'll sign."

"Okay. But you can think about it, too. I know it's a big decision. Probably a good idea that we don't stretch this out. I'm giving you a deadline to make the choice. Won't keep any of us in a limbo."

"Agreed. I'll be in touch soon," she responds and stalls for a second before swiveling away to avoid prolonging this discussion any longer.

It's heartbreaking for Lori and Harry. They just don't know it because I'm carrying the brunt for them.

But the heartbreak I'm carrying inside for Lexi, both her heart and my own, is shared with her, and I need to gather my plan of action to rectify that.

———

SPREADING the cream cheese mixture into the cake pan, I hate to admit that I'm not making my signature peanut butter and jelly cheesecake for my kids. It's because I need a distraction, as tomorrow, after an attempted night of sleep and going through all the reasons that life could actually be full on all fronts, I need to find Lexi.

Holding up the spatula, I debate licking it. Normally, I don't do that, but I guess trying new things and views begins now. But I laugh to myself, because before the spatula can hit my lips, my son comes racing to the counter.

"Hey, you're making the cheesecake. I bet it's for Lexi and not me."

My brows furrow because I haven't yet spoken to them about Lexi, only kept it vague, and thank the heavens, because now I don't have to explain what I'm doing. Well, first I need to win back Lexi, but I won't relent.

"What do you mean, buddy?"

"She was busy with her friend, that's why she hasn't been around lately."

I attempt to hide my relief at his theory. "Yeah… this might be for her." If I can convince her of my true feelings. I hand my son the spatula to lick as a peace offering for baking his favorite cake and not having notified him.

"Dad, I finished my homework, now can I please have my phone back?" Lori yells as she walks down the stairs.

Life is feeling back to normal, except with one giant piece missing.

Lori has a bounce in her step. "Oh hey, it's cake baking. What's the special occasion?"

My eyes travel between my children. "Just wanted to…"

Lori gives me a peculiar smile. "I saw her today in town." Instantly, I know she means Lexi, but I like it a lot that Lexi still seems to give Lori attention, even if I may have ruined a good thing. "I think she'll… like it." The corner of her mouth hitches to give me a sort of secret assurance before she grabs an apple and takes a big bite.

And that gives me promise.

28

LEXI

hy oh why does Lake Spark do this to me? I think as I stare at the general store. There's a sign on the door that says they've closed early due to a staff meeting. It throws a wrench in the works for me to buy a bottle of wine and drown in it. I know drinking alcohol is not the best way to cure the misery that I'm mired in, but I've cried enough today, the numbness overbearing.

There's Catch 22, but right now that feels like too far of a walk. Jolly Joe's doesn't serve alcohol, and I'm not sure whose home wine supply I can steal without them asking how I am and then I'd break down in tears.

"Damn it," I growl to myself. My only option right now is the Dizzy Duck, and I should avoid that place like the plague… except… it's late, and a school night which means Holden won't be there, since that's the time he's with Lori and Harry who I already miss.

Ugh, I'll take the risk and go for it. Maybe Stuart will be at the front desk or Jonathan behind the bar. They're good company, and they don't really talk to me as they seem to lose their words if I'm around. Talking to a wall could be good. Okay, the Dizzy Duck it is.

It's a ten-minute walk to the Dizzy Duck, and when I walk in, there is only Jill tonight working in reception, but she's friendly and smiles at me. The line of my mouth snags in an attempt to return her sentiment. I spot the plate of chocolate chip cookies that are always available for guests in the lobby. Walking by, I grab one then stuff it into my mouth as if I'm a savage, because I don't care that my mouth is full or that I'm leaving crumbs. Straight to the bar I go and greet Jonathan.

"Hey, Lexi, I'm surprised to see you. It's been a while since the re-open." He places a clean wine glass back on the rack. "What can I get you?"

Sliding onto the stool, I cut to the chase. "White wine. Wait, no… go straight for something stronger. A vodka tonic, please." I slump over to rest my head on my hands. "Don't forget to add a slice of lemon," I order.

I am *not* the best version of myself right now.

In my peripheral view, I see that there's a hockey game on the television. A line on my mouth twitches. Hockey. It's my dad's team, and I always forget to tune in, but after years, it's impossible to watch every game. Hockey; it's also the reason I first met Holden. A flicker inside me hits, and that only causes me to sigh.

"I'll be right back, need to get more ice from the back," Jonathan informs me.

My eyes bug out. "Hurry. Can't you see I'm a woman who is desperate?"

He tries to suppress his humored look, and I just snarl to myself. My nails begin to tap the wood of the bar as I contemplate what to do going forward. I'm supposed to stay in Lake Spark for my next project, and I only want to stay at Summer's place for so long. Plus, my chances of running into Holden are too statistically high.

Tonight, though, I will just drown in my sorrows while I try to take my mind to a happy place of thinking about refurbished wood and hanging lights.

Jonathan returns with a small bucket of ice. "Back. Okay, let's get you that drink."

"Let's." My tone is flippant.

His brows furrow as he gets to work on my drink. I stare aimlessly at the floor while I wait.

"Here you are."

I turn my head, and he sets my napkin down, and I do a double take because something catches my eye. There is black writing on the napkin. From a dark pen, and my eyes focus to read the writing.

I owe you an apology and a future.

"An IOU on a napkin. Just like all those years ago." My head whizzes to search the bar area, and I spot Holden as he slowly saunters to me. I hate to say it, but his swagger is already weakening me. My jaw drops, but I'm speechless as my eyes follow his every step until he slides onto the stool next to me.

"I don't believe this seat is taken," he conveys to me. There is satisfaction shading his gentle smirk that he's stunned me a little.

Once again, my eyes circle the nearly empty bar area. "It would seem so," I whisper.

"I'm sorry," he begins. I give him my full attention. "I've made a lot of mistakes lately, and you're one that I want to fix, because you're right, we could be everything."

The speed of my heart picks up.

My eyes stay locked on Holden. "Will you hold off on that drink, Jonathan?" I don't bother turning my head, as I'm still in disbelief.

Holden's mouth snatches up slightly. "He already left us alone about thirty seconds ago."

"Guess I didn't notice. I wasn't expecting you here, which is why I came to bless this place with my presence," I explain.

"Lori and Harry are at sleepovers with friends. I kind of needed some space to figure out my shit, and it just so happens I was here, ready to find you, but it seems fate gave me a break and here you are."

I wet my lips, gathering my emotions, then finding words. "You hurt me," I state blankly.

He scoops my hands up in his. "I'm aware. I just believed complete happiness wasn't meant for me."

I chortle bitterly. "That belief is the biggest lie of the century. Everyone is allowed to have it all if they want."

Holden squeezes my hands and his head tips slightly to the side. "I needed to discover that myself, it seems."

"Shitty way of communicating that." I do make my disappointment apparent, yet I will listen for as long as I need to.

He exhales a deep breath. "I didn't mean what I said, any of it. I'll keep apologizing even if it takes eternity."

"Eternity is a long time." My neutral tone doesn't change as I study his eyes, soaking in his honesty.

"Well, that's kind of what I want, and since you mentioned that you would still be waiting even though I don't deserve it, then I'm hoping you would be along for the ride." A line draws across his mouth.

Lightness begins to flow through me. "I think…" I bob my head side to side. "You might have to grovel a bit more.

Probably for a while, but my heart won't tear away from that future that I desperately want with you."

He lifts my hand to kiss the back of it, with his eyes raking up to ensure our connection doesn't break. It makes me smirk because it's such a classic gesture, a saccharine move, yet it breaks another piece of sadness from the last few days away.

"Is the issue with your ex-wife solved?" I wonder.

Holden glances away for a few seconds before swinging back with an impartial face that I can't read. "Very much so. I got closure too. She signed away her parental rights."

My jaw drops, as that's such a big milestone for any parent. "That's… a lot."

"It's sad but the right move. No potential return that could hurt Lori and Harry," he explains.

A long breath draws out from my body. "I'm relieved for you." I press my lips tightly together, as I owe it to myself to confront any doubt I may have. "But you can't be sitting before me just because the issue with your ex-wife is solved. If that was the reason you pushed me away, then… it was a weak reason. I refuse to be reunited with someone just because they let something like that get in the way."

His finger instantly lands on my mouth to hush me. "I shouldn't have let it all affect me, even though it was scary to have any potential harm to my kids. However, the reason that I pushed you away is because I felt maybe the situation was a warning that it was all too good to be true. Because, Lexi, *you* are too good to be true. But lucky for me, you entered my life. Life feels complete when you're with me, with my kids, in our house. Finally, I have it all, and it's scary as hell because does anybody get that lucky? For a few days, I thought it wasn't what I was allowed."

Tears build in my eyes. Everything he says helps me

understand his mind frame lately, and it's full of promise. "I've been miserable without you. I'm missing you and everything in your life, it's as though I'm not complete. It makes no sense because our speed is fast but so right."

Holden brings his hands to cradle my face. "It is right, and I just need you back, desperately. Because I fucking love you so much."

A smile stretches on my lips. "Me too."

"We're a team, like you said. You didn't give up on me and stayed feisty the way I like. I want us to move forward, and I promise never to doubt our life again."

I nod up and down. Maybe I'll be hesitant to trust the coming days or weeks, but it's only because I need to shake off the fear of losing him and the pain of the last few days. "Forward it is."

He crashes his lips down onto mine but kisses me slowly, gentle yet sensual and completely loving. I accept all of it because with him is where I belong, and I promised to be waiting because I believed he would find his way back to me.

Our lips part, and we both have giddy looks on our faces, ready for our next step.

"Move back in?"

My mouth slides side to side. "Yeah." I smirk to myself. "I mean, I did accidentally leave behind a bra in a drawer, and that was going to be awkward trying to get it back anyhow."

He feigns doubt. "Did you now?" His voice rises an octave. "That is the oldest trick in the book."

"Completely."

That repartee I love returns to us, and I'm relieved and curious if I will fall in love with him all over again, because the first time was already amazing.

"Lori and Harry let me bake a peanut butter and jelly

cheesecake last night that wasn't for them. Harry thought it would convince you to come back."

My face completely brightens. "I love that. What do they know?"

Holden's shoulder lifts. "That we were taking some time apart, and they both instantly told me they didn't agree with my choice. Lori even told me that I suck at emotions."

A giggle escapes me. "Was that before she flipped her hair and stormed upstairs?"

"Obviously."

"Harry and I have some catching up to do, too. He needs to update me on my stock choices." My smile is pure contentment.

"He did mention something about that."

I stand between the seat and Holden, bringing my arms up to drape off his shoulders. "Don't ever run away again."

He pulls me close, a jolt that sends fire through me. "Can't. You've locked me down."

Kissing him, goosebumps bubble on my skin and an uncontrollable need to take more of him, away from here.

"Want to get out of here? I might have checked that our favorite room is free," he murmurs against my lips with pure trouble in his tone.

"Someone is presumptuous." I grin.

Holden stands too, and our bodies glue together for another kiss that's a warning for the night ahead. I love it.

"Does it fucking matter? Even if you didn't want to take me back, I would have found a way to get you to the room and convince you that we're meant to be."

"Hmm, that might have been a better experience," I tease him. He yanks me in the direction of the exit, but I resist. "Wait, I need something." I reach behind me and sweep the napkin off the bar top. Holding it up, I show Holden. "A memento that we need to keep."

He smiles in agreement.

————

CLOTHES SCATTER to the floor within seconds of closing the door. But we don't even manage to make it to the bed because we fall to the rug, laughing when one of us trips on his belt that fell somewhere in our frenzy. We explore one another with our hands as our lips stay melded to one another as we kneel. We're in this crazy frenzy of wanting it all at once.

The moment his fingers sneak between us to circle my clit, I'm already shuddering from an orgasm that will hit me soon. Holden always knows how to touch me, the map of my body he long ago discovered and imprinted in his head.

His skims down my neck, nipping a few times as he strokes my pussy. "So fucking ready for me," he mutters against my collarbone. He brings his soaking fingers up to twist my nipple, and he latches his mouth onto the other.

"Please," I croon. "Inside of me now."

He answers by guiding me back onto the floor and parting my thighs with my knees up. "I need to come inside you." He slips inside of me, taking me deep on the first thrust, my entire body buzzing with anticipation and desire. Surrendering to Holden leads us on this session of clinging to one another, his cock hitting that spot and his tip going as deep as possible. I'm snug around him, squeezing a little extra, with my arousal covering his length.

"You're mine," he whispers in my ear.

"I'm yours," I rasp back.

We move together in sync, and I don't even care that our bodies are roughly mounting against the rug.

It only takes a few minutes until we both collapse, seeing stars. Holden stays in me, his ear resting against my chest where my heart feels like it might explode.

A droll smile ghosts my lips. "I'm positive I might have bruises tomorrow." I laugh. We have every reason to be happy right now.

He kisses the top of my breast. "Sorry."

"I'm not. It's kind of funny."

Holden looks up at me with skeptical eyes, only to notice my overjoyed face. "We didn't even make it to our favorite bed."

I rake his hair with my fingers. "Meh, we now know the rug I chose is perfect for all activities."

He chuckles. "Let me get you something." The moment he pulls out, I feel a loss and want him back. But the logistics of sex on a rug that isn't ours is crucial right now. Holden returns with a towel and cleans me up. "On the bed."

My eyes turn into saucers. "I know you used to be an athlete but surely your recovery time after what just transpired can't be that quick."

He shakes his head ruefully then offers me his hand to yank me up. "To actually enjoy the bed. We can even sleep here tonight. That's a first and a cause for celebration."

I snort a laugh. "Oh, because our making up is not at all important," I say sarcastically as I find my way under the duvet with Holden.

"We can go back and forth like this for eternity." His smile is something new to me; he's truly happy and at peace. My head finds the center of his chest to rest on, and he kisses the top of my hair. "Speaking of eternity, do you ever want to get married?"

My eyes turn bold because he said that so easily. "Oh." I bite my bottom lip. "I guess, yet again, we might have missed a tiny detail or two in terms of discussions we probably should have had." A sound of humor rumbles in the back of his throat. "But yes."

He squeezes me close. "Okay. I'm on board. Kids?"

Something inside me twists. He already has two kids, so maybe he doesn't want to relive having a baby around, but honesty is essential. "Yes, one baby."

"I can do that. Or rather, I would love it. To see you pregnant with my child." God, I love the certainty in his voice.

"All the checkmarks complete… Oh, wait."

Holden gives me a peculiar look. "Yes," he draws out.

"I want a dog too. That would be fun."

He rolls his eyes. "Have you been talking to Harry?"

"Hmm. Would you still say no if I did?"

"For now, yes. I can barely keep them in order. Adding a dog would just bring more disarray."

I shift my position to straddle him, and I bop the tip of his nose with my finger. "You know that I will still come home with a dog without your approval."

He grips my hips to yank me down. "And that's why I love you."

"Thought so." Then we kiss because we have all night to be tangled in the sheets while the moon shines in.

———

HARRY AND LORI stare at me as I slide my suitcase down the hall from the garage.

"Can't my dad be a gentleman and do that?" Lori questions as she observes the scene.

I continue to kick my suitcase as it moves a few inches since it's on wheels. "He can, but he's busy grabbing another bag from my car."

"Duh, leave it there and he'll carry it later. He's supposed to be strong. Otherwise, why does he bother with his protein shakes?" I love the wit and attitude of this almost teenager.

"Come on, Lexi. I've been waiting for you to come back. Now I can eat my cake." Harry turns to nearly stomp to the kitchen.

I'm slightly taken aback but not surprised, he's a kid. "Thanks for showing your true excitement that I'm back and that it's more fun than cake," I call out. "Never mind that we have my stock profile to talk about and you're holding my financial future in the palm of your hand," I add.

Lori grows quiet, and that just means she's about to share some of her wisdom that is far too clever for a girl her age. "Finally, my dad can be happy… it loosens him up." That's sweet, and I give her a soft smile. "It's perfect, really." My heart melts more. "Now he won't freak out when he finds out that there are boys meeting our group when I go to the movies on Friday." My own smile drops while hers just rises. "Thanks, Lexi." She nearly skips away.

I blow out a breath, already trying to think of a way to calm this blow to Holden; better yet that Lori just charmed me and now I need to form a team with Holden. To think that I got him to agree to buy her concert tickets for her birthday. Chaperone duty here I come.

But a few minutes later, I enter the kitchen with Holden, and Lori comes to hug me, then Harry, before they hop onto their stools. As if it was an everyday occurrence, and my heart is completely soft for them.

We all assess the peanut butter and jelly cheesecake that's waiting for us to cause some serious carnage on the snacking front. I interlace Holden's arm with mine and lean my head against his shoulder.

"I love you," I whisper.

Holden continues to look forward. "That's good to know since I just carried all your stuff upstairs and will never ever carry that stuff down again since it's dead weight. But yeah, I love you too," he teases me.

My eyes follow the line from Holden to the kids already using their fingers to grab crumbs.

And this scene is perfect.

It feels like home.

EPILOGUE: HOLDEN

"This is the worst idea in the entire history of civilization," Lexi chastises me.

I continue to look intently at the movie screen with my jaw tight while everyone rustles into their seats in the cinema, waiting for the movie to start.

"Lexi," I grind out a warning, letting her know that I'm not impressed by her words. She throws a piece of popcorn at me, and I reluctantly drag my eyes away to ten rows up ahead.

"Holden, everyone knows when the parents of a group of thirteen-year-olds discuss having a chaperone to the movie theater that you absolutely, 100%, under no circumstances *ever* volunteer to be that parent. Yet, here we are. Every. Single. Time."

My attention completely snaps in her direction. "First off, Mrs. Overthrew the Parent Committee President—"

She waves her finger in front of me. "Don't you dare. Kate McClearly had it coming, and I'm the best damn parent-board president there is. Everyone loves me." Her loud whisper squeaks. "I started the moms-who-wine club. Thank. You. Very. Much."

I want to smirk with pride, but I need to focus on what the actual fuck is going on right now. "Don't you remember what you were like when you were thirteen?" She winces because I'm completely right. "Besides, that little punk sitting next to her doesn't seem to care that I can watch his every finger. He's unaffected."

Lexi gives me that sexy eye roll and is well aware there is no taming this tiger.

"They are a group of like eight teenagers. All the other parents just carpool, drop off their kids, and go have dinner somewhere, then pick them up again. But *no,* here we are eating popcorn that tastes kind of weird." She studies the box of popcorn.

I lean back in my seat and sigh a breath. "Maybe you're right. We need to nail this down because Harry will be here in a year or two. It's just… the lights? They go off. Then maybe it's a scary movie where hand squeezing needs to happen or it contains scenes that I sure as hell don't need my daughter watching with a guy that seems intent on kissing her."

Lexi shakes her head at me. "Chill out, seriously. She already hates us for this. So good luck dealing with that when she comes home tonight. We're not stalking them when they all go for after-movie hot chocolate, are we?" Her concern is apparent.

"Well… I mean, I kind of—"

She grips my arm to stop me. "I'm putting my foot down. If you do that to her, then you are not getting sex tonight. In fact, I'll even go to bed in lingerie and nope, no action."

The older man behind us clears his throat where he's

sitting next to his wife, clearly having heard. I give him a curt nod before focusing on my target again.

Licking my lips, I interlace my fingers with my wife's as we sit there. I know I should calm down, but my daughter is beautiful, witty, smart, and from what I hear, boys even in the eighth grade are lining up. No way am I going to sit at home and wait for her to return.

"How about you promise to fuck me just so I can relax?" I attempt to ask seriously.

Lexi's face floods with disbelief, and I vaguely hear the old man clear his throat again. "How do you suggest we do that here?" She loops her arm with mine to pull me close as the lights dim. "Will I be able to leave you alone for like two minutes later? I've been dying to pee for what feels like forever but needed to rein you in a bit upon arrival."

I kiss the top of her head and regain some fucking composure, let Lori be, and focus on my wife cuddling into my arm. It's been years since I've been in a movie theater.

After cooling off after five minutes and being convinced that the group of teenagers with hormones raging are actually watching the movie, Lexi risked a run to the ladies' room and then came back with chocolate with mint filling.

"Of all the options, you pick that? What a bad choice," I berate her.

She gets comfortable back on her chair again. "Sorry if I'm making bad choices today. My husband must have rubbed off on me," she loudly whispers her sarcasm.

"Don't throw me attitude now. I had to deal with that for fifteen minutes from our daughter before we left the house." Because my kids have Lexi locked into that role, even if it's not official.

In the corner of my eye, I can see that Lexi is smirking. Those facial expressions of hers always calm me, which is why we do enjoy the rest of the action movie, and I only spy on our daughter a few times.

I even give them space when the group heads to Jolly Joe's for a November hot chocolate with whipped cream. We stay seated on the bench down the street, bundled in coats and scarfs.

"Aren't you proud of me?" I smile brightly at Lexi.

She swoops her hand under my chin to guide my eyes to hers. "Very." Lexi kisses me, a soft warm kind that still feels sensual.

"Are you sure I can't convince you to shower with me before bed? I've been a good boy," I murmur into her hair as she nuzzles me.

Her fingers crawl on my thigh. "Maybe… if you can get me a hot chocolate with marshmallows and a candy cane." Her tone rhapsodizes but underneath she's serious.

"Oh, come on," I raise my voice. Now I'm annoyed and sit up straight. "All night, I get the third degree, and *now* you want me to actually go invade their space?"

She shakes her hands as though she's flustered. "I'm sorry, but that popcorn sucked."

"It tasted fine," I counter.

"But I'm kind of hungry and those chocolate things didn't cut it."

I stare at her blankly. "Because you pulled a rookie move and got chocolate with mint."

Lexi shrugs. "So? I would go myself, but truthfully, my legs feel like I can't walk after that Pilates class this morning nearly killed me."

I stand and take a few paces. Walking to Jolly Joe's right now will be similar to a man getting eaten alive by sharks, except it's purely through glares of disdain from our daughter and her friends.

Dragging a hand across my face, I gather some strength. "Fine." I sound completely unenthused.

She tries to give me an innocent happy smile, but she knows that I'll make her pay later, which in retrospect just thrills her more.

I begin to walk away. "Whipped cream on top?" I call out over my shoulder as I begin my journey to hell.

"No. By the way, I'm pregnant." Her monotone statement doesn't faze me for a second.

My feet freeze instantly, and I blink a few times. Did I hear her right? Turning on my heel, I face Lexi casually sitting on the bench with her arms stretched out along the back, her smirk completely honest.

"What did you say?" I don't blink.

"I'm pregnant," she repeats, with her smile warming as she waits for it all to sink in for me.

She caught me off guard, which was probably her intention.

A smile spreads on my mouth, and I stride straight back to her and kneel down, sliding her hands into mine. "We're pregnant?"

Lexi's lips quirk out. "That we are, Husband."

We haven't been trying with intention or thinking about it non-stop, but we did decide to see where things go when Lexi went off birth control. The baby will have quite an age gap with his or her brother and sister, but it makes it all the more fun.

My lips meet hers for a kiss that is mixed with love and happiness. "This is so much better than getting that puppy that drives me insane," I whisper against her lips.

"I hope so." She laughs, and her smile must hurt from how happy she seems.

Pulling away, I narrow my eyes. "Wait, do you really want hot chocolate?"

Lexi pretends to debate. "Nah. But the popcorn was disgusting, the chocolate mint was a bad choice, and along with the need for the bathroom, they were probably the hints I was wondering if you would pick up on."

I flex my jaw side to side. "Ah, maybe they were."

"This morning, you were occupied with tonight, so I didn't tell you. But I don't know, I didn't want to hold out until tomorrow's breakfast at the Dizzy Duck." Sunday brunch is our family tradition, dog included, as he just chills by the fireplace in the lobby and guests love it.

Blowing out a long breath, I am so ecstatic with this news. Maybe it was never on my mind to have more kids, but with Lexi, it was clear as day that we should have a baby. She'll be so relaxed and still keep us all in line.

I kiss her again and again, her cheek, jaw, neck, everywhere that would be appropriate for a bench on Main Street.

"I love you so much," she tells me, the streetlight causing her eyes to glint with a twinkle.

"Me too." I kiss our intertwined hands.

She peers over my shoulder. "You're happy?"

I nod. "Of course, what kind of question is that?"

"Good, because Harry isn't at his friend's house. They seem to be over there where they are about to light firecrackers on the street, and the old lady walking with her hot drink looks pissed." Her face looks strained and cautious.

My head draws a line from her eyes to where she's pointing to see my son is messing around with a friend from math club.

Because our family has a difficult time enjoying a calming day, and that's kind of the way we like it. Or I keep telling myself that every breakfast when chaos exists and my wife just calmly sits there while reassuring me with a wink, because later she'll swing by the Dizzy Duck like old times to get sassy with me as she sneaks her hands up my shirt.

I don't dare say life is perfect, but it's pretty damn close.

It's true, and I repeat it to myself right before I puff out my chest, gather a breath, and prepare to face my son.

But I don't get far.

The sound of a couple arguing causes me to pause.

Lexi squeezes my arm as we both dart our sight to the other corner of Main Street where we see Summer.

She's been through hell in recent months. Her husband passed, and she's used working at the Dizzy Duck as a distraction and appears strong. That was until her late husband's brother, and the Dizzy Duck's 10% owner, Nash, showed up.

Summer yanks her arm away from Nash's hold. "This shouldn't be happening," Summer protests, and she looks fired up.

Nash steps closer to her. "You know that's a lie."

Lexi and I glance at one another, very well aware that nobody should be witnessing this…